W9-CCN-933

THREE HARE-RAISING TALES IN ONE VOLUME

Books by James Howe

Bunnicula Books

Bunnicula
(with Deborah Howe)
Howliday Inn
The Celery Stalks at Midnight
Nighty-Nightmare
Return to Howliday Inn
Bunnicula Strikes Again!
Bunnicula Meets Edgar Allan Crow

Bunnicula and Friends

The Vampire Bunny
Hot Fudge
Scared Silly
Rabbit-cadabra!
The Fright Before Christmas
Creepy-Crawly Birthday

Picture Books

There's a Monster Under My Bed
There's a Dragon in My Sleeping Bag
Teddy Bear's Scrapbook
(with Deborah Howe)
Horace and Morris but Mostly Dolores
Horace and Morris Join the Chorus (but what about Dolores?)
Kaddish for Grandpa in Jesus' name amen

Tales from the House of Bunnicula

It Came from Beneath the Bed!
Invasion of the Mind Swappers from Asteroid 6!
Howie Monroe and the Doghouse of Doom
Screaming Mummies of the Pharaoh's Tomb II
Bud Barkin, Private Eye
The ~~Amazing~~ Odorous Adventures of Stinky Dog

Sebastian Barth Mysteries

What Eric Knew
Stage Fright
Eat Your Poison, Dear
Dew Drop Dead

Pinky and Rex Series

Pinky and Rex
Pinky and Rex Get Married
Pinky and Rex and the Mean Old Witch
Pinky and Rex and the Spelling Bee
Pinky and Rex Go to Camp
Pinky and Rex and the New Baby
Pinky and Rex and the Double-Dad Weekend
Pinky and Rex and the Bully
Pinky and Rex and the New Neighbors
Pinky and Rex and the Perfect Pumpkin
Pinky and Rex and the School Play
Pinky and Rex and the Just-Right Pet

Novels

A Night Without Stars
Morgan's Zoo
The Watcher
The Misfits
Totally Joe

Edited by James Howe

The Color of Absence: Twelve Stories about Loss and Hope
13: Thirteen Stories That Capture the Agony and Ecstasy of Being Thirteen

The Bunnicula Collection

Three Hare-Raising Tales in One Volume

Bunnicula

Howliday Inn

Bunnicula Strikes Again!

James Howe

Atheneum Books for Young Readers
New York London Toronto Sydney

Atheneum Books for Young Readers
An imprint of Simon & Schuster Children's Publishing Division
1230 Avenue of the Americas, New York, New York 10020

Printed in the United States of America
Library of Congress Control Number: 2003110804
ISBN-13: 978-1-4169-7949-4
ISBN-10: 1-4169-7949-2
These titles were originally published by Atheneum Books for Young Readers.

THREE HARE-RAISING TALES IN ONE VOLUME

Bunnicula

Bunnicula

A Rabbit-Tale of Mystery

by DEBORAH and
JAMES HOWE

ILLUSTRATED BY ALAN DANIEL

Atheneum Books for Young Readers

Atheneum Books for Young Readers
An imprint of Simon & Schuster Children's Publishing Division
1230 Avenue of the Americas
New York, New York 10020

Designed by Mary M. Ahern

Library of Congress Catalog Card Number: LC 7811472

To

MILDRED AND LESTER SMITH

—with love

Contents

We wish to thank
Lucy Kroll, Bernice Chardiet
and our editor, Jean Karl,
for their guidance and encouragement,
and to acknowledge
the love and support of our family
and friends.

[EDITOR'S NOTE]

THE BOOK you are about to read was brought to my attention in a most unusual way. One Friday afternoon, just before closing time, I heard a scratching sound at the front door of my office. When I opened the door, there before me stood a sad-eyed, droopy-eared dog carrying a large, plain envelope in his mouth. He dropped it at my feet, gave me a soulful glance and with great, quiet dignity sauntered away.

Inside the envelope was the manuscript of the book you now hold in your hands, together with this letter:

Gentlemen:

The enclosed story is true. It happened in this very town, to me and the family with whom I reside. I have changed the names of the family in order to protect them, but in all other respects, everything you will read here is factual.

Allow me to introduce myself. My name is

Harold. I come to writing purely by chance. My full-time occupation is dog. I live with Mr. and Mrs. X (called here the "Monroes") and their two sons: Toby, aged eight and Pete, aged ten. Also sharing our home is a cat named Chester, whom I am pleased to call my friend. We were a typical American family—and still are, though the events related in my story have, of course, had their effect on our lives.

I hope you will find this tale of sufficient interest to yourself and your readers to warrant its publication.

Sincerely,
Harold X.

Bunnicula

[ONE]

The Arrival

I SHALL never forget the first time I laid these now tired old eyes on our visitor. I had been left home by the family with the admonition to take care of the house until they returned. That's something they always say to me when they go out: "Take care of the house, Harold. You're the watchdog." I think it's their way of making up for not taking me with them. As if I *wanted* to go anyway. You can't lie down at the movies and still see the screen. And people think you're being impolite if you fall asleep and start to snore, or scratch yourself in public. No thank you, I'd rather be stretched out on my favorite rug in front of a nice, whistling radiator.

But I digress. I was talking about that first night. Well, it was cold, the rain was pelting the windows, the wind was howling, and it felt pretty good to be indoors. I was lying on the rug with my head on my paws just staring absently at the front door. My friend Chester was curled up on the brown velvet armchair, which years ago he'd staked out as his own. I saw that once again he'd covered the whole seat with his cat hair, and I chuckled to myself, picturing the scene tomorrow. (Next to grasshoppers, there is nothing that frightens Chester more than the vacuum cleaner.)

In the midst of this reverie, I heard a car pull into the driveway. I didn't even bother to get up and see who it was. I knew it had to be my family —the Monroes—since it was just about time for the movie to be over. After a moment, the front door flew open. There they stood in the doorway: Toby and Pete and Mom and Dad Monroe. There was a flash of lightning, and in its glare I noticed that Mr. Monroe was carrying a little bundle—a bundle with tiny glistening eyes.

Pete and Toby bounded into the room, both

talking at the top of their lungs. Toby shouted, "Put him over here, Dad."

"Take your boots off. You're soaking wet," replied his mother, somewhat calmly I thought, under the circumstances.

"But Mom, what about the—"

"First, stop dripping on the carpet."

"Would somebody like to take this?" asked Mr. Monroe, indicating the bundle with the eyes. "I'd like to remove my coat."

"I will," Pete yelled.

"No, I will," said Toby "I found him."

"You'll drop him."

"I will not."

"You will too."

"Mom, Pete punched me!"

"*I'll* take him," said Mrs. Monroe. "Take off your coats this minute!" But she became so involved in helping the boys out of their coats that she didn't take him at all.

My tranquil evening had been destroyed and no one had even said hello to me. I whimpered to remind them that I was there.

"Harold!" cried Toby, "guess what happened

to me." And then, all over again, everyone started talking at once.

At this point, I feel I must explain something. In our family, everyone treats everyone else with great respect for his or her intelligence. That goes for the animals as well as the people. Everything that happens to them is explained to us. It's never been just "Good boy, Harold," or "Use the litter box, Chester" at our house. Oh no, with us it's "Hey Harold, Dad got a raise and now we're in a higher tax bracket," or "Come sit on the bed, Chester, and watch this *Wild Kingdom* show. Maybe you'll see a relative." Which shows just how thoughtful they are. But after all, Mr. Monroe *is* a college professor and Mrs. Monroe *is* a lawyer, so we think of it as a rather special household. And we are, therefore, rather special pets. So it wasn't at all surprising to me that they took the time to explain the strange circumstances surrounding the arrival of the little bundle with the glistening eyes now among us.

It seems that they had arrived at the theater late, and rather than trip over the feet of the audience already seated, they decided to sit in the last row, which was empty. They tiptoed in and sat down very quietly, so they wouldn't disturb anyone. Suddenly, Toby, who's the little one, sprang up from his chair and squealed that he had sat on something. Mr. Monroe told him to stop making a fuss and move to another seat, but in an unusual display of independence, Toby said he wanted to see just what it was he had sat on. An usher came over to their row to shush them, and Mr. Monroe borrowed his flashlight. What they found on Toby's chair was the little blanketed bundle that was now sitting on Mr. Monroe's lap.

They now unwrapped the blanket, and there in the center was a tiny black and white rabbit, sitting in a shoebox filled with dirt. A piece of paper had been tied to his neck with a ribbon. There were words on the paper, but the Monroes were unable to decipher them because they were in a totally unfamiliar language. I moved closer for a better look.

Now, most people might call me a mongrel, but I have some pretty fancy bloodlines running through these veins and Russian wolfhound happens to be one of them. Because my family got around a lot, I was able to recognize the language as an obscure dialect of the Carpathian Mountain region. Roughly translated, it read, "Take good care of my baby." But I couldn't tell if it was a note from a bereaved mother or a piece of Roumanian sheet music.

The little guy was shivering from fear and cold. It was decided that Mr. Monroe and the boys would make a house for him out of an old crate and some heavy-duty wire mesh from the garage. For the night, the boys would make a bed for him in the shoebox. Toby and Pete ran outside to find the crate, and Mrs. Monroe went to the kitchen to get him some milk and lettuce. Mr. Monroe sat down, a dazed expression in his eyes, as if he were wondering how he came to be sitting in his own living room in a wet raincoat with a strange bunny on his lap.

I signaled to Chester and the two of us casually moseyed over to a corner of the room. We looked at each other.

"Well, what do you think?" I asked.

"I don't think rabbits like milk," he answered.

CHESTER and I were unable to continue our conversation because a deafening crash commanded our attention.

Pete yelled from the hallway: "Maaa! Toby broke the rabbit's house!"

"I didn't, I just dropped it. Pete won't let me carry it."

"It's too big. Toby's too little."

"I am not!"

"You are too!"

"Okay, fellas," Mrs. Monroe called out as she entered with the milk and lettuce. "Let's try to get it in here with as little hysteria as possible, please."

Chester turned to me and said under his breath, "That lettuce looks repulsive, but if there's any milk left, *I* get it." I certainly wasn't going to argue with him. I'm a water man myself.

At that moment, the crate arrived, barely standing the strain of being pulled in two directions at once.

"Ma, Toby says he's going to keep the rabbit in his room. That's not fair. Harold sleeps in his room."

Only sometimes, I thought, when I know he's got a leftover ham sandwich in his drawer. Toby's a nice kid, don't get me wrong, but it doesn't hurt that he shares his stash with me. It was, after all, at one of those late night parties in Toby's room that I first developed my taste for chocolate cake. And Toby, noting my preference, has kept me in chocolate cake ever since. Pete, on the other hand, doesn't believe in sharing. And the only time I tried to sleep on his bed, he rolled over on me and pinned me by my ears so that I couldn't move for the rest of the night. I had a crick in my neck for days.

"But he's mine," Toby said. "I found him."

"You sat on him, you mean!"

"I found him, and he's sleeping in my room."

"You can keep smelly ol' Harold in your room, and Chester too, if you want to, but I'm going to keep the rabbit in mine."

Smelly ol' Harold! I would have bitten his ankle, but I knew he hadn't changed his socks for a week. Smelly, indeed!

Mr. Monroe spoke up. "I think the best place for the rabbit is right here in the living room on that table by the window. It's light there, and he'll get lots of fresh air."

"Pete's taller than I am," Toby cried. "He'll be able to see the rabbit better."

"Too bad, squirt."

"Okay," said Mrs. Monroe through clenched teeth, "let's put him to bed and make him comfortable, and then we can all get some sleep."

"Why?" Pete asked. "I don't want to go to sleep."

Mrs. Monroe smiled a little too sweetly at Pete.

"Look, Ma," said Toby, "he's not drinking his milk."

Chester nudged me in the ribs. "Didn't I tell you?" he asked. "Excuse me while I make myself available."

"Hey," said Toby, "we gotta name him."

"Can't that wait until tomorrow?" asked Mr. Monroe.

The boys shouted in unison: "No! He has to have a name right now." I have to say I agreed with them. It took them three days to name me, and those were the three most anxious days of my life. I couldn't sleep at all, worrying that they were really going to call me Fluffy as Mrs. Monroe had suggested.

"Well, all right," sighed Mrs. Monroe, "what about . . . oh, say . . . Bun-Bun?"

Oh, oh. There she goes again, I thought. Where *does* she get them?

"Yech!" we all said.

"Well, then, how about Fluffy?" she offered hopefully.

Pete looked at his mother and smiled. "You never give up, do you, Ma?"

Meanwhile, Chester (who had also been named Fluffy for a short time) was rubbing against Mrs. Monroe's ankles and purring loudly.

"No, Chester, not now," she said, pushing him aside.

"He wants to help us name him, don't you Chester?" Toby asked, as he scooped him up into his arms. Chester shot me a look. I could tell this was not what he had in mind.

"Come on, Harold," Toby called, "you've got

to help with the name, too."

I joined the family and serious thinking began. We all peered into the box. It was the first time I had really seen him. So, this is a rabbit, I thought. He sort of looks like Chester, only he's got longer ears and a shorter tail. And a motor in his nose.

"Well," said Pete, after a moment, "since we found him at the movies, why don't we call him Mr. Johnson?"

There was a moment of silence.

"Who's Mr. Johnson?" asked Toby.

"The guy who owns the movie theater," Pete answered.

No one seemed to like the idea.

"How about Prince?" said Mr. Monroe.

"Dad," said Toby, "are you kidding?"

"Well, I had a dog named Prince once," he replied lamely.

Prince, I thought, that's a silly name for a dog.

"We found him at a Dracula movie. Let's call him Dracula," Toby said.

"That's a stupid name," said Pete.

"No, it's not! And anyway, I found him, so I should get to name him."

"Mom, you're not going to let him name him, are you? That's favoritism, and I'll be traumatized if you do."

Mrs. Monroe looked in wonder at Pete.

"Please Mom, please Dad, let's name him Dracula," cried Toby, "please, please, please." And with each *please,* he squeezed Chester a little harder.

Mrs. Monroe picked up the bowl of milk and moved toward the kitchen. Chester followed her every movement with his eyes, which now seemed to be popping out of his head. When she reached the kitchen door, she turned back and said, "Let's not have any more arguments. We'll compromise. He's a bunny and we found him at a Dracula movie, so we'll call him Bunny-cula. Bun*nic*ula! That should make everybody happy, including me."

"What about me?" muttered Chester. "I won't be happy until she puts down that milk."

"Well, guys, is that okay with you?" she asked.

Toby and Pete looked at one another. And then at the rabbit. A smile grew on Toby's face.

"Yeah, Ma, I think that name is just right."

Pete shrugged. "It's okay. But I get to feed him."

"Okay, I'm going to put the milk back in the fridge. Maybe he'll drink it tomorrow."

"What about Chester?" Toby said, dropping the frantic cat to the floor. "Maybe he would like it." Chester made a beeline for Mrs. Monroe and looked up at her plaintively.

"Oh, Chester doesn't want any more milk, do you, Chester? You've already had your milk today." She reached down, patted Chester on his head and walked into the kitchen. Chester didn't move.

"Okay, bedtime," said Mr. Monroe.

"Good night, Bunnicula," Toby said.

"Good night, Count Bunnicula," Pete said sarcastically, in what I took to be his attempt at a Transylvanian accent. I may be wrong but I thought I saw a flicker of movement from the cage.

"Good night, Harold. Good night, Chester." I licked Toby good night.

"Good night, smelly Harold. Good night, dumb Chester." I drooled on Pete's foot. "Mom,

Harold drooled on my foot!"

"GOODNIGHT, PETE!" Mrs. Monroe said with great finality as she came back into the living room, and then more calmly, "Good night, Harold. Good night, Chester."

Mr. and Mrs. Monroe went up the stairs together.

"You know, dear," Mr. Monroe said, "that was very clever. Bunnicula. I could never have thought of a name like that."

"Oh, I don't know, Robert." She smiled, as she put her arm through his. "I think Prince is a lovely name, too."

The room was quiet. Chester was still sitting by the closed kitchen door in a state of shock. Slowly, he turned to me.

"I wish they *had* named him Fluffy," was all he said.

[TWO]

Music in the Night

I FEEL at this time there are a few things you should know about Chester. He is not your ordinary cat. (But then, I'm not your ordinary dog, since an ordinary dog wouldn't be writing this book, would he?)

Chester came into the house several years ago as a birthday gift for Mr. Monroe, along with two volumes of G. K. Chesterton (hence the name, Chester) and a first edition of Dickens' *A Tale of Two Cities*. As a result of this introduction to literature, and given the fact that Mr. Monroe is an English professor, Chester developed a taste for reading early in life. (I, on the other hand, have developed a taste for books. I found *Jonathan Livingston Seagull* particularly delicious.) From Chester's kittenhood on, Mr. Monroe has used him as a sounding board for all his student lectures. If Chester doesn't fall asleep when Mr. Monroe is talking, the lecture can be counted a success.

Every night when the family is sleeping, Chester goes to the bookshelf, selects his midnight reading and curls up on his favorite chair. He especially likes mystery stories and tales of horror and the supernatural. As a result, he has developed a very vivid imagination.

I'm telling you this, because I think it's important for you to know something of Chester's background before I relate to you the story of the events following the arrival of Bunnicula into our home. Let me begin with that first night.

It seems that after I went to sleep, Chester, still stewing over the lost milk, settled down with his latest book and attempted to ignore the rumbling in his stomach. The room was dark and quiet. This did not prevent his reading, of course, since as you know, cats can see in the dark. A shaft of moonlight fell across the rabbit's cage and spilled onto the floor below. The wind and rain had stopped and, as Chester read Edgar Allan Poe's "The Fall of the House of Usher," he became increasingly aware of the eerie stillness that had taken their place. As Chester tells it, he suddenly felt compelled to look at the rabbit.

"I don't know what came over me," he said to me the next morning, "but a cold chill ran down my spine."

The little bunny had begun to move for the first time since he had been put in his cage. He lifted his tiny nose and inhaled deeply, as if gathering sustenance from the moonlight.

"He slicked his ears back close to his body, and for the first time," Chester said, "I noticed the peculiar marking on his forehead. What had seemed an ordinary black spot between his ears took on a strange v-shape, which connected with the big black patch that covered his back and each side of his neck. It looked as if he was wearing a coat . . . no, more like a *cape* than a coat."

Through the silence had drifted the strains of

a remote and exotic music.

"I could have sworn it was a gypsy violin," Chester told me. "I thought perhaps a caravan was passing by, so I ran to the window."

I remembered my mother telling me something about caravans when I was a puppy. But for the life of me, I couldn't remember what.

"What's a caravan?" I asked, feeling a little stupid.

"A caravan is a band of gypsies traveling through the forest in their wagons," Chester answered.

"Ah, yes." It was coming back to me now. "Station wagons?"

"No, covered wagons! The gypsies travel all through the land, setting up camps around great bonfires, doing magical tricks, and sometimes, if you cross their palms with a piece of silver, they'll tell your fortune."

"You mean if I gave them a fork, they'd tell my fortune?" I asked, breathlessly.

Chester looked at me with disdain. "Save your silverware," he said, "it wasn't a caravan after all."

I was disappointed. "What was it?" I asked.

Chester explained that when he looked out the window, he saw Professor Mickelwhite, our next door neighbor, playing the violin in his living room. He listened for a few moments to the haunting melody and sighed with relief. I've really got to stop reading these horror stories late at night, he thought, it's beginning to affect my mind. He yawned and turned to go back to his chair and get some sleep. As he turned, however, he was startled by what he saw.

There in the moonlight, as the music filtered through the air, sat the bunny, his eyes intense and staring, an unearthly aura about them.

"Now, this is the part you won't believe," Chester said to me, "but as I watched, his lips parted in a hideous smile, and where a rabbit's buck teeth should have been, two little pointed fangs glistened."

I wasn't sure what to make of Chester's story, but the way he told it, it set my hair on end.

[THREE]

Some Unusual Goings-On

THE next few days passed uneventfully. I was very bored. Our new arrival slept all day, and Chester, whose curiosity had been aroused by the strange behavior of the rabbit that first night, had decided to stay awake every night to observe him. Therefore, he too spent most of his days sleeping. So *I* had no one to talk to.

The evenings weren't much better. Toby and Pete, who used to play with me as soon as they got home from school, now ran immediately to that silly rabbit's cage to play with him. Or at least they'd try to. Bunnicula did not make the most energetic playmate. It took him quite a while to wake up each night and then when he did awaken, he didn't do much except hop around the living room. He didn't play catch, he didn't fetch, he didn't roll over to get his tummy rubbed. I couldn't understand why they played with him at all. I expect it was because he was new and different. But I was confident that they would soon tire of him and come back to trusty ol' Harold.

Finally, on the morning of the fourth day, I caught Chester bleary-eyed over the water dish. He grumbled at me in a most unpleasant manner.

"You know, Chester, you were never exactly charming in the morning, but lately you've become downright grumpy."

Chester growled in response.

"What are you doing this for anyway? What are you looking for? He's just a cute little bunny."

"Cute little bunny!" Chester was amazed at my character analysis. "That's what you think. He's a danger to this household and everyone in it."

"Oh, Chester," I said, with an indulgent smile, "I think your reading has gone to your head."

"It's just because I do read that I know what I'm talking about."

"Well, what are you talking about? I still don't understand."

"I'm not sure yet, but I know there's something funny about that rabbit. That's why I have to keep alert."

"But look at you—you're exhausted. You sleep all the time. How can you call that alert?"

"I'm awake when it's important. He sleeps all day, so I sleep all day."

"So just what have you seen since that first night that makes you uneasy?"

"Well . . ." said Chester, "I, uh . . . that is . . ." At this point, Chester started to bathe his tail, which is a cat's way of changing a subject he finds uncomfortable. He then stumbled sleepily into the living room.

"So?" I asked again, following him, "what have you seen?"

"Nothing!" he snapped, and proceeded to curl up on his chair to go to sleep. After a moment, he opened one eye. "But that doesn't mean there's nothing *to* see."

For the next few mornings, it was the same routine. I'd be ready for a good romp around the living room, and Chester would go to sleep. Pete and Toby were at school. Mr. Monroe was at the university (he never did too much romping around, anyway). And Mrs. Monroe was at her office.

No one to play with poor, neglected Harold. At first, I thought I could strike up a friendship with Bunnicula and maybe teach him a few tricks. But I could never wake him up. He was always waking up just about sunset, when I wanted to take a snooze. A rabbit, I concluded, is cute to look at, but is generally useless, especially as a companion to dogs. So, I would retire each day with my favorite shoe to the rug and chew.

Now, some people (especially Mr. and Mrs. Monroe) can't understand my taste for shoes and yell at me for snacking on them. But I always say there's no accounting for taste. For instance, I remember one evening when Mr. Monroe picked some of his sour balls out of the bowl by his chair and dropped a green one on the floor. He didn't notice as it rolled across the room and landed near my nose. I decided this was a perfect opportunity to try one for myself. I placed it in my mouth . . . and wished immediately that I hadn't. As the tears started running out of my eyes, I thought, What's wrong with my mouth?! It's turning inside out!

Mr. Monroe immediately noticed that something had happened. "What's the matter, Harold? Are you looking for someone to kiss?"

"Help! Help!" I wanted to cry, but all that came out was an *"ooooo"* sound. I *"ooooo"*-ed for days.

So how can anyone who likes green sourballs criticize me for preferring a nice penny loafer or a bedroom slipper?

But back to the matter at hand:

One morning, Chester had news.

"That bunny," he whispered to me across our food bowls, "got out of his cage last night."

"Don't be ridiculous," I said. "How could he break through that wire? Look how little he is."

"That's just it! He didn't break through any wire. He got out of his cage without breaking anything, or opening any doors!"

I looked puzzled. So Chester told me the following story.

"Now, Harold," he said, "I don't want you thinking I'm not a good watchcat, but after a few hours last night, I grew curious about the time. I went into the hallway and . . . you know that new clock they've got? The big one? That goes all the way to the ceiling? Well, see, it has this thing in the middle called a pendulum. At first, I figured I would just leave it alone. It looked like that spool they tied on a string and hung from the doorknob for me to play with when I was a kitten. Everytime I hit that silly spool with my paw, it would swing back and hit me on the nose. I hated that toy. So naturally, when I saw this one, I decided not to have anything to do with it. I checked the time. It was midnight. I was all set to go back to the living room when something stopped me."

"Curiosity?" I ventured.

"I suppose you could call it that. I prefer to think of it as the challenge of the unknown. I put one paw over my nose and reached out with the other one and gave it one good smack. I darn near broke my arm. It's still tender; see how swollen it is."

He showed me his little paw. I couldn't see anything wrong. But I knew better than to argue with him. "Oh yes," I said, "that looks terrible. You must be suffering awfully. You'd better go easy today." He limped dramatically, just far enough to display his new handicap, and continued.

"I couldn't even get to the pendulum. Somebody had put glass in front of it, and I was pretty mad. I was all set to go back, but at the same time, I couldn't help watching the thing move back and forth, back and forth. Back and forth . . . It was so easy to watch, and before I knew what had happened, I was waking up."

"You fell asleep?" I asked incredulously.

"I couldn't help it. I didn't even know it had happened. But I looked up at the face of the clock and it was twelve forty-five! I'd been gone forty-five minutes. I ran back into the living room, looked at Bunnicula's cage, and it was empty. I couldn't imagine where he was. Then I noticed a light coming from under the kitchen door. I went into a crouch, stalking the light, when . . . *click* . . . I heard the refrigerator door close, and the light went out."

"It must have been Mr. Monroe having his midnight snack," I suggested.

"No, that's what I thought. I jumped on my chair, curled up real quick and kept one eye open, pretending to be asleep. Slowly, the door to the kitchen squeaked open. This little head poked out from around the corner and looked to either side to see if the coast was clear. Then . . . guess who came bouncing out all by himself, and with that idiotic grin of his plastered all over his face?"

"Well . . . I guess it wasn't Mr. Monroe," I said.

"Not unless he wears bunny pajamas and gets very tiny at night."

"Bunnicula, huh?"

"You got it. Unfortunately, I hadn't positioned myself so that I could see him get back into the cage. And I didn't want to let him know that I had seen anything, so I had to stay put. I still don't know how he got out, or back in."

At this point, Mr. Monroe came downstairs to make breakfast.

I wondered if Chester hadn't dreamed the whole thing. He did admit he'd fallen asleep and, as I've said, he has quite an imagination. But I was game. After all, there hadn't been any excitement in this place for days. Chester and I took our positions under the kitchen table. We didn't have long to wait.

"Holy cow!" Mr. Monroe yelped as he opened the refrigerator door. He took this funny-looking white thing out of the fridge and held it at arm's length.

"Peter, come down here!"

"What is that?" I whispered.

"Beats me," Chester answered. "It looks like a white tomato."

"Very funny," I said, as Pete came into the kitchen.

"Peter, have you been playing with your chemistry set in here?"

"No, Dad, why?"

"I thought this might be one of your experiments. Do you know what it is?"

"Gee, Dad, it looks like a white tomato."

Just then, Mrs. Monroe and Toby came in the door.

"What's all the fuss about?" Mrs. Monroe asked.

"We were just trying to figure out what this is."

Toby pulled it down so he could get a better look.

"Well," he said, "it looks to me like a white tomato."

Mr. Monroe took a good long look. "You know," he said to his wife, "it really does look like a white tomato."

"There's one way to find out," said Mrs. Monroe, who always was the practical one. "Let's cut it open and see what's inside."

Everybody gathered around the table. I jumped up on a chair, and in all the excitement, no one noticed that I had my paws on the table (which under normal circumstances was discouraged, to say the least). Chester wasn't so lucky.

"Chester, get off the table," Mrs. Monroe said. Chester jumped onto Toby's shoulders, where he stayed to view the proceedings.

Mrs. Monroe took her sharpest knife and cut cleanly through the thing. It fell into two halves.

"It's a tomato, all right," said Mrs. Monroe. "Here are the seeds."

"But it's all white," Toby observed.

"And look," said Pete, "it's dry."

"So it is," Mr. Monroe said, as he picked up one of the halves. "There is no juice at all. Well, Ann, what do you think?"

"It's gone bad, I guess, though I've never heard of a tomato turning white before. Come on," she said, clearing the table, "let's throw it out and have breakfast. And Harold, get your paws off the table."

Rats.

Chester jumped down from Toby's shoulders and motioned for me to follow him into the living room.

"This had better be important," I said. "They're cooking bacon."

"A white tomato. Very significant," Chester murmured.

"So it's a white tomato," I said, edging my way back to the kitchen door. "What does that have to do with Bunnicula?"

"I can tell you one thing," Chester said. "I got a good look at the tomato. There were very suspicious marks on the skin."

"So?"

"I believe they're teeth marks."

"So?"

"So tonight I'm going to reread a book I read last year."

"How fascinating," I said, as the aroma of frying bacon wafted across my nostrils. "And what book might that be?"

"The Mark of the Vampire!"

"What!" I stopped dead in my tracks.

"Meet me tonight after the others have gone to sleep. You'd better take a nap today so you can stay awake."

Chester closed his eyes. I shifted my look to Bunnicula, who seemed to be asleep in his cage. A tiny smile sat upon his lips. A happy dream? I wondered, or something else?

My reverie was broken by the sound of crunching bacon. I was in the kitchen in a flash.

[FOUR]

A Cat Prepares

I ALMOST didn't make it to my meeting with Chester that night. Toby had a feast in his room. It was Friday night, and on Friday nights, Toby gets to stay up and read as late as he wants to. So, of course, he needs lots of food to keep up his strength. Good food like cheese crackers, chocolate cupcakes (my very favorite, the kind with cream in the middle, *mmmm!*), pretzels and peanut butter sandwiches. The last I cannot abide because my mouth always gets stuck. Chocolate cupcakes with cream in the center, however, are another story.

This particular evening, I stationed myself on Toby's stomach. Usually, I'm a little more subtle but, having missed out on the bacon at breakfast, I was not about to take any chances on the chocolate cupcakes (with cream in the center).

Toby knew what I was after. But sometimes he thinks he's funny, and he plays little games with me.

"Hi, Harold, I'll bet you'd like a peanut butter sandwich, wouldn't you? Here, you have this one that's leftover from yesterday, while I eat this boring old chocolate cupcake—which is nice and fresh and has cream in the middle. Okay, Harold?"

Ha ha. My sides are splitting.

"What's the matter? Don't you want the peanut butter sandwich? All right, I'll put it away for another night. Oh, here's something you might like. It's a green sourball from Dad's candy dish that was stuck to my sock. Would you like that, huh, pal?"

Oh boy, the kid is really hot tonight.

"No, huh? Well, I'd give you one of my cupcakes, but I know how much you hate chocolate."

Would a little drooling on your stomach help convince you otherwise?

"Oh, you like chocolate! Okay then, you can have both of them!"

One thing I have to say about Toby: Although he's got a rotten sense of humor, he's a nice kid. Naturally, once I'd eaten both cupcakes (which took approximately four seconds), I felt obliged to hang around and let Toby know I was grateful. What better way than to share a few of his cheese crackers?

"Well, Harold," Toby said some time later, "we've had quite a party, but I have to go to sleep now. I can't keep my eyes open, so I'll have to wait until tomorrow to find out what happens in the next chapter. This is a good book, Harold. It's called *Treasure Island,* and it's by a man named Robert Louis Stevenson. It's kind of hard reading, though. I have to keep looking the big words up in the dictionary, so it's taking me a long time to get through it."

I've always had trouble with words myself. Half the time they don't mean what I think they're going to, and then, even when I do find out what they mean, I forget the next day anyway. You might say that I'm smart—but just not the scholarly type.

"But it's a really good story," Toby continued. "It's all about pirates and this little boy just like me."

No dogs?

"And a parrot, Harold."

A parrot? What's a parrot? Is there anything about chocolate cake? That's my idea of a treasure.

"Well, good night, Harold. If you're going to sleep here, you'll have to get off my stomach because it's a little full right now."

Good night, Toby.

I curled up at the foot of the bed, but I couldn't sleep trying to figure out what a parrot was. I thought it might be a lady pirate, since the words sounded something alike, but then again, I thought it might be an umbrella. Chester would know, I thought, so I went downstairs to ask him.

"WELL, you certainly took your time," Chester snapped as I sauntered casually into the room. "I finished my book half an hour ago. Where were you?"

"It so happens I was discussing great works of

literature with Toby."

"Since when is a Twinkies wrapper considered a great work of literature?"

I decided to ignore that. Unfortunately, several chocolate crumbs fell from my mouth to the floor at precisely that moment.

"As a matter of fact," I said, trying valiantly to regain my dignity, "we were talking about *Treasure Island.* Ever hear of it?"

"Ever hear of it?" he sneered. "I read *that* when I was a kitten."

"Oh. Then, tell me, Chester, what is a parrot?"

Chester looked at me scornfully. "A parrot," he said, "is a tropical zygodactyl bird (order psittaciformes) that has a stout curved hooked bill, is often crested, brightly variegated and an excellent mimic. In other words, Harold, a parrot is a little bird with a big mouth."

"Oh," I said after a moment. "I thought maybe it was an umbrella."

"Did you get so busy discussing parrots with Toby that you forgot you were going to meet me here? This is important, Harold."

I still wasn't sure what a parrot was, but I

decided this was not the time to pursue it.

"Come over here," Chester commanded, indicating his chair, "and let me show you this book."

I looked at the chair. Chester was already sitting in it, with a very large book open in front of him.

"I don't think there's going to be room for both of us, Chester," I said.

"Come on, come on, you're wasting time. Just jump up here."

I surveyed the scene carefully. I knew I would have to get a running start since there was just a tiny spot left for me and I would never be able to fit into it if I pulled myself up slowly. Apparently, I was taking too long for Chester's liking.

"Will you get up here?" he hissed.

Okay, if that's what you want. I ran and jumped onto the chair, landing with a great kerplop.

"Chester, where are you?" I cried. I couldn't see anything but the back of the chair. I'd forgotten to turn myself around.

"I'm here, you great oaf!"

I turned my head. "What are you doing on the floor?" I asked.

"You knocked me off the chair. Now just stay put. I'm coming back up."

I moved to the back of the chair, and Chester landed on the front.

"Now, let's see," he said, "we both have to see the book. You come over here, and I'll move this way."

I don't know if you've ever watched a cat try to decide where to sit, but it involves a lot of circling around, sitting, getting up again, circling some more, thinking about it, lying down, standing up, bathing a paw or tail and . . . circling! A dog, on the other hand, sits. "This looks like a good spot," a dog will say to himself. He will then lower his body to the spot in question and is usually so secure in his decision that he will fall asleep immediately.

Chester took what felt like twenty minutes to settle himself in, and just as I was drifting off, the kicks started. "Come on, Harold, quit hogging the seat. And wake up. What were you trying to do? Take a little cat nap? Ha ha ha."

I yawned.

"Now," said Chester, turning to the book, "let's get down to brass tacks."

"What exactly is on your mind?" I asked.

"This book and that rabbit," Chester replied. "Now tell me, Harold, have you noticed anything funny about that rabbit?"

"No," I said, "but I've certainly noticed a lot of funny things about you recently."

"Think about it. That rabbit sleeps all day."

"So do I. So do you."

"Furthermore, he's got funny little sharp teeth."

"So do I. So do you."

"Furthermore, he gets in and out of his cage by himself. What kind of rabbit can do that?"

"A smart one," I said. "I could do it."

"We're not talking about you, Harold. We're talking about the rabbit. Now, where did they find him?"

"At the movies."

"Yes, but *what* movie?"

"Dracula," I said, "so?"

"So," he said quickly, "remember the note around his neck? What language was it in?"

"An obscure dialect of the Carpathian mountain region," I answered smugly. He didn't know everything.

"Ah ha!" Chester said, "but what *area* of the Carpathian mountain region?"

Area? What's an area? I looked at him blankly.

"Transylvania!" he cried triumphantly. "And that proves my point."

"What point? What are we talking about?"

"And don't forget the white tomato! That's most important of all!"

"But, what . . ."

"This book," said Chester, disregarding me, "tells us just what we need to know."

"What?" I practically screamed. "What does it tell us? What does this book have to do with Bunnicula? What are you talking about? What's going on here? I can't stand it anymore!"

Chester regarded me coolly. "You're really very excitable, Harold. That's not good for your blood pressure."

I put my paws around his throat. "Tell me," I said in a low, threatening voice, "or I'll squeeze you till you pop."

"Okay, okay, don't get upset. Now this book tells you everything you've always wanted to know about vampires but were afraid to ask."

Personally, I had never wanted to know anything about vampires, but at the moment, I was afraid to tell that to Chester.

"I still don't understand what vampires have to do with our little furry friend."

"One," Chester said, "vampires do not sleep at night. They sleep only during the day. The same holds true for this rabbit. Two, vampires can get in and out of locked rooms. Bunnicula gets in and out of his locked cage."

This was beginning to interest me. "Didn't you say something about the refrigerator?"

"That's right. He got the refrigerator open . . . all by himself. Three, vampires have long pointed teeth. They're called fangs."

"Well, don't we have fangs?"

"No, we have canines. That's different."

"What's different about it?"

"Fangs are more pointed, and vampires use fangs to bite people on the neck."

"Yech! Who'd want to do that?"

"Vampires would, that's who."

"Wait a minute. I saw Mrs. Monroe bite Mr.

Monroe on the neck once. Does that mean she's a vampire?"

"Boy, are you dumb. She's not a vampire. She's a lawyer."

"She bites necks."

"I don't think that's quite the same thing. Now, Bunnicula does not bite people on the neck. At least, not so far. But he does bite vegetables . . ."

"On the neck?" I asked.

"Vegetables don't have necks, Harold. Vegetables are like that. It's like dogs. Dogs don't have brains. Dogs are like that."

"Oh yeah?" I said. "Of course he bites vegetables. All rabbits bite vegetables."

"He *bites* them, Harold, but he does not eat them. That tomato was all white. What does that mean?"

"It means . . . that he paints vegetables?" I ventured.

"It means he bites vegetables to make a hole in them, and then he sucks out all the juices."

"But what about all the lettuce and carrots that Toby has been feeding him in his cage?"

"Ah ha, what indeed!" Chester said. "Look at

this!" Whereupon, he stuck his paw under the chair cushion and brought out with a flourish an assortment of strange white objects. Some of them looked like unironed handkerchiefs, and the others . . . well, the others didn't look like anything I'd ever seen before.

"What are they?" I asked.

Chester smiled. "Lettuce and carrots," he said. "*White* lettuce and carrots. I found them hidden behind his cage."

I was aghast. What did it all mean? Could Chester be right? Was this harmless looking little ball of fluff really a vampire? Just then, Chester let out a yelp.

"Look," he said, "the cage is empty again. Oh, we're fools, we're fools! We've let him get out of our sight. It's your fault."

"My fault! You're the one who took twenty minutes to sit down."

"Well, if you hadn't knocked me off in the first place—"

"Wait a minute, why are we arguing? Let's find Bunnicula."

Just then, we heard a click in the kitchen.

"Refrigerator," I whispered. Chester nodded. We jumped down and moved cautiously to the kitchen door.

"Sshhh," Chester warned unnecessarily as we crept along, "don't make any noise. We don't want him to hear us coming."

"Obviously," I retorted.

The light went out under the door.

"He must have closed the refrigerator," Chester said. "Easy now." We pushed the door open. The kitchen was dark. There was not a sound.

"Pssst, Chester . . ."

"What?"

"I can't see."

"I can. But I can't see *him.*"

"He's not here."

There was a soft scamper across the linoleum, and we turned just in time to see a little white tail bounce out the door into the living room.

"Drat! We've missed him. Come on, Harold, let's see if we can catch up with him." Chester started toward the door.

"Wait, Chester, what's that on the floor by the refrigerator?"

He turned. This new object interested him more than following Bunnicula. "Watch out," he said, "I'll take care of this." He slunk across the room slowly, muscles taut, eyes alert. When he was about six inches away, he stuck out his paw, closed his eyes and batted at the object tentatively. I don't think he made any contact.

"Get closer," I said.

Chester's eyes popped open. "Who's the cat here?" he asked. "I know what I'm doing." And he proceeded to bat the air three more times.

"What is it?" I squealed, as my throat contracted in fear.

"I don't know yet, but whatever it is, it's not alive."

"Oh boy, if I wait for you, we'll be here all night." I walked bravely to the object and sniffed it.

"Well?" asked Chester.

"Beats me."

Chester came closer. After a moment of close examination, he gasped.

I jumped. I could feel my heart pounding in my chest.

"Harold . . ." Chester blurted.

"What? What?"

"It's . . ."

"Yes?"

"It's . . ."

"What is it, Chester?!"

"It's a white zucchini!"

[FIVE]

Chester Goes into His Act

THE next morning, I was awakened by a scream.

"Robert! Robert, come down here right away. There's something wrong in the kitchen!"

For a moment, panic seized me. I thought she'd run out of dog food. But then I remembered the events of the previous evening.

Mr. Monroe came bounding down the stairs. "Chester! Chester!" I cried. "Did you see Mr. Monroe? His face has turned white! It's Bunnicula, isn't it?"

"No," he said calmly, "it's shaving cream, you idiot."

By now, the excitement in the kitchen was at full throttle. The table was covered with Bunnicula's handiwork. There were white beans and white peas and white squash and white tomatoes and white lettuce and white zucchini.

"What can it mean, Robert?" Mrs. Monroe was saying. "I'm getting worried. One tomato is a curiosity, but this is unheard of."

"There must be something wrong with our refrigerator. That's it. It's turning all the vegetables white."

"But look," she said, "I left these tomatoes on the windowsill, and they're white too. And this squash I left in the bowl on the table."

At that moment, Pete and Toby came into the kitchen.

"Holy cow! What's going on?"

"Hey! Maybe it's a vegetable blight, Mom."

"Could that be, Robert? Did you ever hear of anything like that?"

"Well . . . uh . . . no, actually . . . that is, I've heard of blight, but nothing like this."

Chester leaned my way. "This will take forever if we leave it up to them. Sometimes, human beings can be so slow." I started to answer him, but he was heading for the table.

"What about that friend of yours in the Agriculture Department?"

"Oh, Tom Cragin?"

"Could we call him and ask him if we're doing something wrong?"

"It's DDT, Mom," Peter interjected, "I know about this stuff. It's because you buy vegetables that aren't organic."

"All vegetables are organic, Peter," Mrs. Monroe replied.

"That's not what my teacher says. See, Toby, I told you this would happen. They're using chemicals on our food, and if you're not careful, you'll turn white, too."

"Like Dad?"

"Robert, couldn't you take that shaving cream off your face?"

"Oh yes, of course. Where's my towel? I know I brought it down with me."

For that matter, where was Chester? I'd seen

him going toward the table, but I'd lost track of him listening to all that talk about DDT. I just hoped they didn't use any of that stuff where they grew chocolate cupcakes.

"Pete, did you take my towel?"

"Why would I take your towel, Dad? I don't shave."

Just then, the door swung open. I could not believe my eyes. There was Chester, with Mr. Monroe's towel draped across his back and tied under his neck like a cape. That was strange enough, but on his face was an expression that sent chills down my spine. His eyes were wide and staring. The corners of his mouth were pulled back in an evil grimace. His teeth were bared and gleaming in the morning light. He cackled menacingly and threw back his head as if he were laughing at all of us. I thought he'd completely lost his mind.

"There's my towel. What's the matter, Chester, were you cold?" Mr. Monroe bent down to take the towel from Chester. Before he could lay his hands on it, Chester flipped over onto his back, closed his eyes and folded his paws over his chest.

It was a hideous sight. He opened his eyes wide. With paws outstretched, he . . . slowly . . . lifted . . . his . . . head . . . his eyes glazed and vacant. Soon the upper half of his body followed, all in one smooth flow, until he was in a sitting position.

"Hey, Dad, did you leave your brandy glass out last night? Chester is acting a little weird."

"Well, son, cats are funny creatures . . ."

I glanced at Chester. He wasn't laughing.

"Psst, Chester. What are you up to?"

"I'm a vampire, you dolt. Can't you tell? I'm trying to warn them."

"Well, it's not working. You'd better think of something else." Chester frowned, apparently deep in thought.

". . . so you see, Toby," Mr. Monroe was explaining, "all cats are as individual as all people. Maybe he just wants to get our attention. Isn't that right, kitty-cat?" Ordinarily, Chester would have left the room upon being called "kitty-cat," but he was lost in thought.

"Come on, Chester, give me back my towel." Mr. Monroe moved toward Chester. Chester's

eyes lit up. He looked at me and smiled. I sensed I was not going to like what he had in mind. I was toying with the notion of slinking under the table when Chester fixed me with his eyes. How deep they were, like black pools. I felt myself floating, lost in them, my will no longer my own. I felt an inexplicable urge to murmur "Yes, Master," when he walked slowly, steadily toward me. As he drew nearer, I found myself unable to move. He stopped before me, never taking his gaze from me, and lunged.

"YEOW!!!"

"Mom, Chester bit Harold on the neck!"

"Aw, that wasn't a real bite, was it Chester? That was a love bite. Isn't that cute?"

Love bite, my foot. That hurt!

"Chester, what's the matter with you?" I sputtered. "Do I look like a tomato?"

"Oh, it doesn't matter anyway, Harold. They don't understand. How can human beings read the same books I do and still be so thick?"

Our conversation was interrupted. Mrs. Monroe picked Chester up and cuddled him. I was praying she would not add insult to injury by kissing his nose, which he hates more than anything.

"Poor Chester, do you need a little love? Do you know what I'm going to do, you big ball of fuzz, you?" Oh, oh. I could tell what was coming. "I'm going to kiss you on your little nose." Yep, I could tell that was coming, all right. Chester knew better than to resist. He went limp in Mrs. Monroe's arms. Mr. Monroe took his towel off Chester.

"I still don't know why he's wearing my towel," he said.

"I think he must be cold, dear. Here's your towel. Why don't you get his kitty sweater . . ." Chester looked ill. ". . . and he can wear that all day."

As Chester was being buttoned into his bright yellow sweater (with little purple mice in cowboy hats all over it), Mr. Monroe said, "What about those vegetables? Shall I speak to Tom Cragin?"

"Yes, dear," Mrs. Monroe said, "why don't you? I'm sure there's some explanation. In the meantime, I'll change markets. To tell you the truth, I'm really much more worried about Chester. We'd better keep our eye on him."

CHESTER and I did not speak until late afternoon. I was busy nursing my neck, and Chester was busy hiding under the sofa, too embarrassed to be seen. When we did speak at last, it was a brief exchange.

"Hey, Chester," I called when he finally crawled out from under, "we don't have to worry about any vampire bunnies anymore. All you have to do is stand outside his cage in that sweater, and he'll laugh himself to death."

Chester was not amused. "That's right, make fun. All of you. No one understands. I tried to warn them, and they wouldn't heed. Now, I'm going to take matters into my own hands."

Whereupon, Chester and his sixteen purple mice went into the kitchen for dinner.

[SIX]

Harold Helps Out

THAT night, I had an uneasy sleep. Strange noises emanated from downstairs. It sounded like toenails clicking back and forth on the floor. It must be Bunnicula making his midnight run, I thought, although I'd never known him to make a sound. And I smelled the funniest odor in the air—something familiar, though I couldn't place it. As the night progressed, it grew stronger and stronger until finally it tickled my nose and I sneezed myself awake. I jumped off Toby's bed, still sniffling, and headed down the stairs for the living room to find Chester, to see if he could smell it, too.

The odor grew even stronger as I approached

the living room. Standing in the doorway was Chester, a strange pendant hanging from his neck.

"Phew, Chester," I said, "what are you wearing that awful thing for? It smells!"

"Of course it smells," he replied. "Here, I made one for you, too. Put it on."

"Are you kidding? That thing smells like garlic."

"It is garlic," Chester stated matter-of-factly.

"Why are you wearing garlic?" I asked, thinking that by this time Chester was capable of anything. As we walked into the living room, I tripped on another piece of garlic lying in the doorway.

"Careful," said Chester, "watch your step."

I surveyed the room and saw that it was strewn with garlic. On the doorways . . . over the windows . . . and around Bunnicula's cage. The poor little fellow had buried his nose as far as possible under his blanket.

I was about to follow his example and return to Toby's bed to bury my nose under the blankets when Chester grabbed my tail with his teeth.

"You're not leaving this room until you put

this on," he grumbled at me. I think that's what he said. I wasn't sure because he had my tail in his mouth.

"It's not polite to talk with your mouth full,

Chester. Drop that tail." Meanwhile, my eyes were beginning to water.

"Listen," Chester snapped at me (fortunately letting go of my tail first), "the book said to use garlic."

"What book?" I asked. "*The Joy of Cooking?*"

Chester continued, "*The Mark of the Vampire* says garlic renders vampires immobile."

"What does that mean?"

"It means they can't go anywhere if there's garlic around."

"Well, I've got news for you, Chester. I can't go anywhere either. The smell is killing me—"

"But you've got to put it on; it says so in the book. If you don't put it on, I'll put it on for you."

"Doe, Chester," I said as my nose suddenly and involuntarily closed, "I'be leaving dis roob right dow." And I did.

I was so sick to my stomach from the aroma that I decided to spend the early morning hours outdoors. As dawn approached, it seemed that it would be a peaceful day. The sky was clear, the birds were singing, and I felt contented after my difficult night just to be lying in the grass, feeling the ladybugs crawl up my ears. Suddenly, the calm was broken. Strange piercing screams came from the area of the kitchen. Not again, I thought. What's turned white now?

As it happened, it was Chester. There in the sink, lathered with soap, was the feline detective, yelling his head off. Mrs. Monroe was scrubbing him vigorously and, from the sound of her voice, was in the middle of a long lecture.

"I don't know what's gotten into you, Chester. You never played with garlic before. I thought you hated the smell of it, and here you've gotten it all over yourself. Stop wriggling, you'll get soap in your eyes. If you want to chew on something, I'll get you some catnip. But stay out of my herbs!" Then she rinsed him off, rubbed him with a towel, and plunked him down in front of the stove to finish drying.

"Shut the door," he hissed at me. "I'm freezing. That silly woman, doesn't she know *cats don't get baths?"*

"What do you mean? I get baths all the time," I said, closing the door with my back foot.

"That's because you're too dumb to bathe yourself. Cats always bathe themselves, it's a rule. Everyone knows that."

"Well, at least it smells nice in here again." I sniffed as I settled down next to Chester by the stove. "And it's all toasty warm here in the kitchen."

"Sure it smells nice again," he said, "but now the house isn't safe anymore."

"What do you mean?" I asked, getting closer.

"I mean, it worked last night. The garlic worked. No more vegetables turned white, did they?"

"No, but . . ."

"That means Bunnicula didn't get out of his cage last night."

"Maybe he was just tired," I said, "or maybe he was full."

"Don't be ridiculous," he replied. "It was the garlic. He *couldn't* leave his cage. But tonight he'll be free to roam again, and I've got to find a way to stop him that isn't smelly."

Mr. and Mrs. Monroe were hurrying in and out of the room, stepping over us, late for work. Mrs. Monroe yelled up to Toby, "Don't forget to take the steak out of the freezer when you get home today, Toby, and leave it on the table to defrost. And this time, remember to put a plate under it."

Chester's ears perked up. "Of course!" he said, "that's what I'll do." And he strolled past me with a knowing smile. Mrs. Monroe turned off the stove and left the room. It was too much for me to figure out, so I went to sleep on the nice, warm kitchen floor.

I was awakened by a bite on the ear. Chester was sitting by me, looking very impatient.

"Boy, nothing wakes you up," he said. "I've been yelling and poking at you for ten minutes."

"I was dreaming," I answered defensively, "about a place where there weren't any cats around to bother nice dogs and wake them up when they needed their rest."

"You can finish sleeping later," he said crisply. "Right now, you have to help me."

"Do what?" I asked.

"Get Bunnicula out of the cage."

I sprang back. "Get him out of the cage?! I thought that was what you didn't want. I thought you said he was dangerous. What if he attacks me?"

"Aren't you ashamed?" Chester replied. "Afraid of a harmless little bunny?"

"Harmless? I thought you said he was a threat to this house and everyone in it. Isn't that what you said? Isn't that what we've been talking about all this time?"

"He is a threat, but only at night. During the day he's just a very sleepy rabbit, and that's why we have to do it now, while the sun is still up. Follow me," he said. "There isn't much time. Toby stayed down here forever, and the others will be home soon. Boy, you must have been tired, Harold. You slept through lunch."

I followed Chester into the living room. My heart was pounding as he unlocked the cage door with his paw. (It looked as if he'd had years of experience opening locks.)

The door swung open; Bunnicula was sleeping peacefully. He did, however, look a little green around the gills, probably from the garlic. I was just wondering how a rabbit could have gills when Chester said, "Okay, Harold, do your stuff while I get what I need from the kitchen."

"Well, what do you want me to do? I can't read your mind."

"Get him out of the cage and onto the floor, and I'll be right back," Chester said.

What? What?

"What?" I verbalized. "How am I supposed to do that?"

"Use your head," he answered. And he was gone. Looking at the cage, I realized that was precisely what I would have to do.

Until this moment, I had never had to face the possibility of actual physical contact with a real, live rabbit. I looked upon my chore reluctantly. I seemed to recall my grandfather telling me that one picked a rabbit up by its neck with one's teeth. This I attempted, though the very idea set my stomach churning. I squeezed my head through the tiny door and gently placed my teeth around the skin of the bunny's neck. To avoid any suggestion of violence (I've never been one for the sport of hunting), I preferred to think of myself as the creature's mother, carrying it off to safety.

Unfortunately, I couldn't carry it anywhere, for once my head was in the cage, it wouldn't come out again. I could go neither forward nor backward.

At that moment, Chester appeared at the door, carrying in his mouth what looked every bit like a nice, big, juicy raw steak. My eyes popped, my teeth dropped Bunnicula, my mouth opened, and I began to drool. After all, I *had* missed lunch.

"Chester, what are you doing with that steak?"

"Haven't you gotten him out of there yet?"

"I can't get either of us out of here. My head's stuck."

"Oh, Harold, sometimes I despair. Here, I'll get you both out. I should have done everything myself."

He came over, dropped the steak just a few feet away from me, and climbed up on my shoulders. "You pull your head out while I push against the cage."

"Who gets the steak?" I asked.

"Don't worry about the steak, Harold. Just pull."

"I would have more motivation if I knew who

is to get the steak."

Chester ignored me. I pulled. He pushed. I felt something go POP! We all fell in a jumble: Chester, the cage, Bunnicula, and me. When I looked around, Bunnicula was lying next to me, still sound asleep.

"There you are," I said. "We got him out. Now, let's eat."

"No dice," Chester said. "Just read this to me so I'll be sure I'm doing it right." And he handed me a book. *That* book, *again.*

"Start at the top of the page," Chester said, as he picked up the steak.

"Why don't *you* read, and I'll hold the steak?"

"Mmphph," Chester replied. I took it to mean that I was to start reading.

" 'To destroy the vampire and end his reign of terror, it is necessary to pound a sharp stake . . .' "

Chester interrupted. "A sharp steak?" he asked. "What does that mean?"

"I'll taste it and tell you if it's sharp," I offered.

"Oh, never mind. This will do. It's sirloin. Keep reading."

" '. . . to pound a sharp stake into the vampire's heart. This must be done during the daylight hours, when the vampire has no powers.' "

"Okay," he said, "this is it. I'm sorry I had to go this far, but if they'd listened, this wouldn't have been necessary." He dragged the steak across the floor and laid it across the inert bunny. Then with his paws, he began to hit the steak.

"Are you sure this is what they mean, Chester?"

"Am I anywhere near his heart?" he asked.

"It's hard to tell," I said. "All I can really see are his nose and his ears. You know, he's really sort of cute."

Chester was getting that glint in his eyes again. He was pounding away at the steak, harder and harder.

"Be careful," I cried, "you'll hurt him."

Chester increased his attack. I was really getting worried when the door opened and Mr. and Mrs. Monroe were suddenly with us in the room.

"Chester!" Mrs. Monroe screamed. "What are you doing with my dinner? Robert, get that steak away from Chester. And what's the matter with Bunnicula? Why is he on the floor?"

Mr. Monroe took the beautiful steak away. I

wished it a fond farewell with tears in my eyes. As the kitchen door swung open, Chester whispered with cold determination, "All right, the last resort!" and dashed into the kitchen. Seconds later, he was back, carrying his water dish between his teeth. He ran toward Bunnicula and with a mad yowl threw the dish of water at the rabbit. Unfortunately, he was so hysterical that his aim was not the best. With water dripping from my ears, I watched Mrs. Monroe pick Chester up by the scruff of his neck and toss him unceremoniously out the front door.

"Robert, we are going to have to do something about that cat. Look at this mess. Dinner's ruined, the poor bunny is out of his cage, and Harold is sopping wet." I tried to look as pathetic as I knew how.

"Aw, poor Harold," Mrs. Monroe cooed as she dried me off. "You've had a rough day . . . you and Bunnicula. I don't know what's the matter with your friend. But unless he learns how to behave, he'll just have to spend the night outside."

Mr. Monroe meanwhile had restored Bunnicula

to his cage and the cage to the windowsill. I couldn't believe it when I saw that Bunnicula was still asleep.

"Ann," Mr. Monroe said, "the steak is ruined. Why don't we let Harold have it? He deserves a treat anyway, don't you, ol' boy?"

I panted appropriately.

AFTER my delicious dinner, I turned my attention to the book still lying open on the floor.

" 'Another method of destroying the vampire is to immerse the body in water. The body will then shrivel and disappear, as the vampire emits one last scream of terror.' "

Whew, I thought, so that's what he was trying to do. Thank goodness he missed. I had no regrets about missing a scene like that. Poor Bunnicula.

I looked over toward the cage, and there on the other side of the window was a pathetic tabby face looking in. His little nose was pressed against the window. I couldn't hear him, but from the movement of his lips, I could see he was very unhappy. Poor Chester.

As for me, Mrs. Monroe spent the evening

petting me and the family chatted with me all night long. And of course, I'd had my yummy steak dinner. So . . . it wasn't such a bad day after all.

Except that now my steak was all gone. Poor Harold.

[SEVEN]

A (New) Friend in Need

IN the days that followed, Chester's behavior was exemplary. He purred and he cooed and he cleaned his paws. And he rubbed up against everyone's legs to show what a good boy he was. I was getting worried. Chester acts that way only when he has something devious in the back of his mind. But I didn't know what it was. He had tried everything in the book to get rid of vampires, and all his efforts had failed. But I knew from the expression on his face that something was definitely up. Of course, I didn't know for certain because he had not spoken to me since the steak incident. I guess he realized that my heart just wasn't in the destruction of the bunny vampire.

In fact, I was beginning to like the little fellow.

The Monroes were relieved by Chester's improved behavior. They didn't know how to account for his strange doings but, to their credit, they were willing to let bygones be bygones. The only disturbing factor in all our lives was the reappearance of the white vegetables each morning in the kitchen. And yet, after a few days, even that stopped and life seemed to return to normal.

One evening, I dropped by Bunnicula's cage to chat. I'd found myself doing that more and more since Chester had stopped talking to me. Of course, Bunnicula didn't talk back, but he *was* a good listener. I'd begun to think of him as a friend—a strange one, granted—but one can't always choose one's friends. I was distressed this particular evening to see that he was dragging his ears, as it were. He looked tired and listless. I felt his nose and it seemed a little warmer than it should have been. I became alarmed.

I ran over to Toby who was doing a picture puzzle on the floor and began to bark—something

I do only in cases of extreme emergency, since even I do not care for the sound.

"What's the matter, Harold?" Toby asked without moving. "Are there burglers?"

I ran to the cage and looked at Bunnicula. I looked back at Toby and whimpered. Toby just looked confused.

"Do you want to play with Bunnicula? Shall I take him out of the cage?"

"Woof," I responded, indicating, I hoped, that that was indeed what he should do.

"I'll ask Mom and Dad, Harold. You wait here." He was back in a minute, shaking his head. "I'm sorry, Harold, but Mom says you can't play with the rabbit. It causes too much commotion."

I looked down at the floor and whimpered again.

"Sorry, Harold, maybe later when we're all in here together."

I regarded Bunnicula whose eyes met mine. He gave a little shudder, and I felt like crying. My friend was sick, and I didn't know what to do. I wished I could tell Chester, but I knew it was no use. He was just too mad at me. I would have

to sort this one out on my own.

That night, I couldn't sleep worrying about Bunnicula. I decided to go downstairs and check on his condition. What I saw when I entered the living room horrified me. Bunnicula was out of his cage on the floor, while Chester stood in front of him, a piece of garlic around his neck and his arms outstretched, blocking the kitchen door. Suddenly, it all fell into place. Chester was starving Bunnicula! Of course, *that's* why he seemed so listless, and that's why the vegetables had stopped turning white. Chester had made it impossible for Bunnicula to eat.

"Chester!" I cried.

Chester jumped a very high jump.

"What are you doing down here?" he spat at me, as he landed.

"I know what you're doing, Chester, and the jig is up. That little bunny never hurt anybody. All he's doing is eating his own way. What do you care if he drains a few vegetables?"

"He's a vampire!" Chester snarled. "Today, vegetables. Tomorrow . . . the world!"

"I think perhaps you're overstating your case," I suggested cautiously.

"Go back to bed, Harold. This is larger than the two of us. It may seem harsh, but I'm only being cruel to be kind."

Who's he being kind to? I wondered, as I went back upstairs. The tomatoes and zucchinis of the world? Maybe a few cabbages? It just didn't make sense. But I could see I wasn't going to get anywhere with Chester tonight. Tomorrow, however, would be another story, and I was determined that, by hook or by crook, my friend Bunnicula would eat by sundown the next day.

[EIGHT]

Disaster in the Dining Room

I REALIZED that there was nothing I could do for Bunnicula during the day, since he was sleeping. But that gave me time to plan my strategy. At first, I thought I would bring food to his cage, but then it occurred to me that Chester must be taking everything away that was given to him. Pete and Toby usually left lettuce for Bunnicula during the day while he was sleeping, and Chester, ever watchful, probably nabbed it each evening just before the rabbit woke. No, there would have to be another way.

I thought and thought all afternoon, and I

could see that Chester had done a good job of isolating Bunnicula from his food. There was no way I could think of to overcome Chester's game plan. As evening drew closer and I grew more and more frantic, I stumbled into the dining room . . . and saw the answer to my problems sitting before me on the table. It was a big bowl of salad! All I had to do was get Bunnicula to the salad and let him get his fill before the family came in to eat. With that funny white dressing on it, they would never notice if a few vegetables were white.

I ran to the hallway to check the clock. Six fifteen. It would be fifteen minutes before the sun went down and Bunnicula woke up. I would then need at least five minutes to get him from his cage to the table and feed him. All I had to do was make sure no one came into the room until he had finished. I needed a good twenty minutes, at least.

I went back into the living room. Chester was asleep on his brown velvet chair, shedding in his sleep, still worn out from the previous night's activities. I checked upstairs. Toby was reading in his room, the last chapter of *Treasure Island,* I noted. Pete, who should have been doing his homework, was listening to records in his room.

I ran down to the kitchen.

"Hello, Harold," Mrs. Monroe said as I came through the door. "What's new?"

Other than a rabbit starving in the next room and an imminent attack on your salad bowl, nothing, I thought. I stood at her feet and panted. She scratched my head. This gave me a moment to check out how far she was in her cooking.

"Sorry, Harold," she said. "I have to baste this chicken." I noticed the oven timer still had thirty-five minutes to go. It'll be tight, I thought, but I can make it. Now, where is Mr. Monroe?

I went to the front door and whimpered loudly. Mrs. Monroe followed me.

"Are you waiting for Daddy, Harold? He'll be home soon."

Soon isn't good enough. *How* soon? I whimpered again.

"Patience, boy. He's late at a school meeting. He should be here any time."

She went back into the kitchen and I checked the clock. Six twenty-five. It was getting dark and

Chester was still asleep. Time to swing into action.

Having watched Chester undo the lock on Bunnicula's cage and having participated in that unfortunate steak episode some days earlier, I knew I would have no problem getting Bunnicula out. I just had to be a little more careful where I positioned my head so that I wouldn't find myself in the humiliating predicament of getting stuck a second time. My timing was perfect. With Bunnicula swinging peacefully from my teeth, I made my way stealthily toward the dining room as the last rays of sunlight gave way to the dark of night. Once inside the dining room door, Bunnicula awakened in great bewilderment. It is not everyday, after all, that one finds oneself, upon awakening, hanging from the jaws of a fellow creature—even so caring and gentle a creature as myself.

Bunnicula opened his eyes wide and turned his face, as best he could, to me. I jumped up onto the nearest chair and placed the rabbit safely on the table's edge.

"Okay," I whispered, "there's your dinner. Go to it! Get your fill as fast as you can, poor bunny.

I'll stand guard." I don't know that Bunnicula fully understood what was going on, but the sight of the vegetables piled high in the center of the table sent him scurrying in their direction. He was *very* hungry!

As luck would have it (and as I should have anticipated), Chester's sense of timing was as astute as my own. No sooner had Bunnicula reached the edge of the salad bowl than the door swung open and Chester bounded into the room. He surveyed the scene frantically. I was unable to act fast enough. Upon seeing Bunnicula about to enjoy his first bit of nourishment in days, Chester leaped across the table, seemingly without touching floor, chairs, or anything else between himself and our furry friend and landed directly on top of the bunny.

"Oh no, you don't!" he shrieked. Bunnicula, not sure what to do, jumped high in the air and landed, with a great scattering of greens, smack in the center of the salad bowl. Lettuce and tomatoes and carrots and cucumbers went flying all over the table and onto the floor. Chester flattened his ears, wiggled his rear end and smiled

in anticipation. To cat observers, this is known as the "attack position."

"Run, Bunnicula!" I shouted. Bunnicula turned in my direction, as if to ask where.

"Anywhere!" I cried. "Just get out of his way!"

Chester sprang.

Bunnicula jumped.

And in the flash of a second, they had changed positions. Chester now found himself flat on his back (owing to the slipperiness of the salad dressing) in the bowl. And Bunnicula, too dazed to even think about food now, hovered quivering on the table.

Chester was having a great deal of difficulty getting back on his feet, but I knew it was only a matter of seconds before he'd attack again. And I knew also that Bunnicula was too petrified to do anything to save himself. So I did the only thing I could: I barked. Very loudly and very rapidly.

The whole family rushed through the doors. Mr. Monroe must have just come home because his coat was still on.

"Oh, no!" cried Mrs. Monroe. "That's it, Chester. This is Chester's last stand!"

Chester rolled his eyes heavenward and didn't even try to move.

"Mom," said Toby, tugging at his mother's arm, "look at Bunnicula. How did he get out of his cage? He looks scared."

"Of course, he's scared," Mrs. Monroe said. "We probably forgot to latch his cage and he got out. And I think Chester has been chasing him."

Toby put his face close to the rabbit. "Mom, doesn't Bunnicula look kinda sick?"

"We'd better take them all to the vet to see if any damage was done," she answered.

I started to whimper. No need for *me* to go to the vet.

Mr. Monroe patted my head. "We may as well take Harold along," he said. "He's probably due for his shots."

Mrs. Monroe carefully picked Chester out of the salad bowl and carried him by the scruff of the neck to the kitchen. "I'm going to give Chester a quick bath," she said to Mr. Monroe. "Why don't you put together a fresh salad? Toby, you and Peter put Bunnicula back in his cage and then clean up the table."

I didn't stick around for an assignment. This was not the time to be in the way.

And besides, I now had a whole evening and night ruined worrying about the next morning's visit to the vet. This little effort of mine, I thought, has been a disaster in more ways than one.

[NINE]

All's Well that Ends Well . . . Almost

LOOKING back on that night, I remember thinking that this whole mess could never be resolved happily. What would become of Bunnicula, my new friend, who was suffering from starvation? And what of Chester, my old friend, who seemed to have flipped his lid and, if you'll pardon the expression, was in the doghouse with the Monroes? Of far greater concern at that time, of course, was my own future, for on that night all that consumed my thoughts was the fear of the next day's injections! It all seemed hopeless indeed.

But looking back on the next *day,* I can tell you that happy endings are possible, even in situations as fraught with complications as this one was.

Early the next morning, we all piled into the car, some of us with greater reluctance than others, and trundled off to the vet. And by afternoon, we were on our way to solving our problems.

The vet worked everything out very nicely. He discovered that Bunnicula was suffering from extreme hunger. (*I* could have told him that.) Rather than jar his fragile stomach with solid foods, the doctor decided he should be put on a liquid diet until he got better. So Bunnicula was immediately given some carrot juice, which he drank eagerly. After he finished, he looked over at me with a great grin on his face and winked.

Chester was diagnosed as being emotionally overwrought. It was suggested that he start sessions with a cat psychiatrist to work out what the doctor called a case of sibling rivalry with Bunnicula. I asked Chester later what a sibling was, but he wasn't speaking to me. So I looked it up. It's like a brother or sister. And sibling rivalry means you are competing with your brother or sister for attention. I wasn't sure this was Chester's problem, but it sure explained a lot about Toby and Pete.

As for me . . . well, I came out the best. Dr. Wasserman was all set to give me my shots when the nurse came in with my card.

"Wait, doctor, this dog doesn't need his shots yet. It's too soon."

So I got a pat on the head and a doggie-pop instead.

THESE days, everything is back to normal in the Monroe household—almost. Bunnicula liked his liquid diet so much that the Monroes have kept him on it. And oddly enough, there have been no problems with vegetables mysteriously turning white since. Chester, of course, insists that this proves his theory.

"Obviously, Harold, the liquified vegetables take the place of the vegetable juices, so Bunnicula has no need to go roaming anymore."

"Then he's not a vampire," I said.

"Nonsense. He's a vampire all right. But he's a modern vampire. He gets his juices from a blender."

"Case closed, Sherlock?" I queried.

"Case closed."

"Oh, Chester . . ."

"Yes, Harold?"

"What are those two funny marks on your neck?"

Chester jumped and I laughed. "Very funny," he said as he began to bathe his tail, "very funny."

The Monroes never knew anything of Chester's theory. They changed markets and to this day believe they were the victims of a curious vegetable blight.

Bunnicula and I have become good friends. He still doesn't say anything, but he snuggles up next to me by the fireplace and we take long cozy snoozes together. One night, I sang him a lullaby in the obscure dialect of his homeland, and he slept very peacefully. It was that night that cemented our friendship.

Now—about Chester. I said that everything

was back to normal—almost. Naturally, Chester is the "almost." He has been seeing his psychiatrist, Dr. Verrückt Katz, twice a week for some time now. He takes his therapy *very* seriously.

The other morning, I was trying to get a little sleep, when Chester came over and nudged me in the ribs.

"Harold, do you realize we've never really communicated? I mean *really* communicated?"

I opened one eye cautiously.

"And in order to communicate, Harold, you have to really be in touch with yourself. Are you in touch with yourself, Harold? Can you look yourself in the mirror and say, 'I know who I am. I am in touch with the me-ness that is me, and I can reach out to the you-ness that is you'?"

I closed my eye. I'm used to it by now. He talks like that all the time. He no longer reads Edgar Allan Poe at night. And once he concluded that he had been right about Bunnicula, there has been no more talk about vampires. *The Mark of the Vampire* sits, its usefulness obsolete, on its shelf. Right now, he's reading *Finding Yourself*

by Screaming a Lot, and the other night, when I heard the most awful noise coming from the basement, I didn't even bat an eyelid. I knew it was just Chester "finding himself," as he calls it. He explains to me that he's getting in touch with his kittenhood. And I've told him that's fine—just to let me know when he's going to do it, so I can be elsewhere. I've had enough trouble from Chester's adventures.

SO that's my story. And the story of a mysterious stranger who no longer seems quite so mysterious and who is definitely no longer a stranger. I've presented the facts as clearly as I could, and I leave it to you, dear reader, to draw your own conclusions.

I must now bring this narrative to a close, since it is Friday night—Toby's night to stay up late and read—and I can hear the crinkling of cellophane. I can only hope it covers two chocolate cupcakes with cream filling.

Howliday Inn

Howliday Inn

by JAMES HOWE

ILLUSTRATED BY LYNN MUNSINGER

Atheneum Books for Young Readers

Atheneum Books for Young Readers
An imprint of Simon & Schuster Children's Publishing Division
1230 Avenue of the Americas
New York, New York 10020

Composition by American Book—Stratford Graphics,
Brattleboro, Vermont
Printed and bound by Fairfield Graphics,
Fairfield, Pennsylvania
Designed by Mary M. Ahern

LIBRARY OF CONGRESS CATALOGING IN PUBLICATION DATA

Howe, James. Howliday Inn.

SUMMARY: While their family is away, Harold
and Chester, a dog and a cat, are boarded
at Chateau Bow-Wow where Chester becomes
increasingly alarmed by the strange behavior
of his fellow guests and
the sudden disappearance of one of them.
[1. Cats-Fiction. 2. Dogs-Fiction. 3. Mystery
and detective stories] I. Munsinger, Lynn. II. Title.
PZ7.H8372Ho [Fic] 81-10886
AACR2

In memory of

DEBBIE

EDITOR'S NOTE

I HAD THOUGHT I'd heard the last of Harold, the writing dog, when he delivered his book, *Bunnicula,* to my office some time ago. Much to my surprise, he suddenly appeared again one recent rainy Wednesday afternoon. The dreary weather had made the day useless for anything more than catching up on all those boring little chores one puts off for just such days and drinking a lot of reheated coffee to cut the constant chill that sneaks in through the cracks in the windows. When I heard scratching at my door, I thought it was probably a stray cat looking for a warm radiator and a saucer of milk. That alone, I reasoned, would provide some relief from the monotony of the day's non-events.

You can well imagine my delight when I opened the door and saw Harold standing on the other side of the portal, his hair drenched and hanging from him like an unwrung mop. From his teeth dangled a plastic bag. I asked him in and examined the contents of the bag that he'd dropped at my feet. What I found was the manuscript of Harold's new book, together with this note:

My dear colleague,
I had not planned to write again. Indeed, after my friend Chester read my first book, he accused me of writing without a literary license. I had settled into my comfortable life as a nice American middle-class dog with my nice American middle-class family when strange events once again engulfed me. Naturally, after all the fur had flown and the dust had settled, I felt compelled to write the story down.

What resulted is the manuscript you now see before you. I do hope you will enjoy it and, as before, find it worthy of your readers' attentions.

Your humble servant,
Harold X.

I convinced Harold to stay long enough for a doughnut and a bowl of hot chocolate. Then, as suddenly as he'd appeared, he was gone, leaving behind him the pages of his story, which he has chosen to call *Howliday Inn.*

Contents

Howliday Inn

[ONE]

The Departure

LOOKING back on it now, I doubt that there was any way I could have imagined what lay ahead. After all, I'm not as well read as Chester, and except for the time I'd run away from home as a puppy and spent a fitful night under a neighbor's Porsche, I really had had very little experience of my own in the outside world. How could I have begun to imagine then what would befall me that fateful week in August?

If the memories of that week no longer make my blood run cold, they still have enough of a chilling effect to give me pause. Why, you may wonder, do I wish to stir them up now when I could so easily curl up in front of a nice warm radiator and think of happier times instead? The answer, a simple one really, is just this: whatever else may be said of that week, it was an adventure. And adventures, no matter how dark or disturbing to recall, are meant to be shared.

IT BEGAN innocently enough on a beautiful summer's day, the kind of day, I remember thinking, when the universe seems in perfect order and nothing can go wrong. A soft breeze ruffled the hairs along my neck. Birds chirped happily in the trees. A butterfly landed on my nose and would have stayed for a while, I think, if I hadn't sneezed him off. The sky was blue, the sun was gold, the grass was green. Such riches cannot be bought for any price, I thought, as I lay stretched out on the front lawn chewing contentedly on one of Mr. Monroe's new running shoes.

Without warning, my blissful mood was shattered by the sound of Toby's voice coming from within the house.

"Why?" he kept repeating, a bit unpleasantly.

His mother answered him in that ever-patient

way of hers. "You've asked me several times, Toby, and I keep telling you the same thing. I know you're not happy about it, but we can't take them with us."

"But why? Why?" Toby insisted loudly. I noticed several butterflies flutter away from our yard defensively. "We've taken Harold and Chester on vacation with us before," he whined. My ears perked up. *I* was the topic of discussion.

"Just to the lake house, Toby, never on a car trip," Mrs. Monroe answered. "There won't be room. Besides, you know Harold gets carsick. You wouldn't want him to be miserable, would you?"

"No," Toby agreed sensibly, "I guess you're right."

Darn right she is, I thought.

"But I'm going to miss them, Mom," Toby added.

Mrs. Monroe's voice softened. "I know you are, Toby. We'll all miss them. But we'll be gone only a week, and then we'll see them again. Think of everything you'll have to tell Harold when you get home."

"Yeah, I guess so," Toby said, his voice trailing off in defeat. Poor kid, I thought, he's really broken up. Well, I couldn't blame him. I *was* a lot of fun, after all, and it was natural he'd want to take me along. I mean, who would he play fetch-the-stick with? Whose tummy would he rub?

Suddenly, panic seized me. Who was going to feed us? I dropped my Adidas, moved quickly to the front door and began scratching on the screen.

"Hi, Harold," Toby said as he let me in. He looked at me sadly and put his arms around my neck. "I'm sorry, boy. Mom says we can't take you on vacation this time. I'll bet you feel real disappointed, huh?"

Who's going to feed me? I asked with my eyes.

"But don't worry. We'll be back in a week. It won't be so long. Still, you feel bad you're not going, don't you? I know."

Who's going to feed me? I pleaded, with a hint of a whimper.

"Oh, and if you're wondering what's going to happen to you while we're away . . ."

Yes? I asked, my eyes growing wider.

". . . don't worry. Mom and Dad have that all figured out. See, Bunnicula is going to stay next door at Professor Mickelwhite's house . . ." I glanced over at the windowsill where the rabbit's cage was kept and saw that it had already been removed. I felt myself breaking into a cold sweat. What was going to happen to *me?* ". . . and you and Chester are going to be boarded."

Oh, I thought, feeling relieved immediately, that's all right then. Just one little detail troubled me: I didn't have the slightest idea what being boarded meant. I decided to find Chester and ask him about it, since Chester knows, or thinks he knows, something about almost everything.

When I found him, he was sitting in the back yard staring off into space. Chester, being a cat, is very good at staring off into space. He once explained to me that this was his way of meditating or, as he liked to put it, "getting mellow." At the moment I found him, he looked so mellow I thought there was a good chance of his ripening and rotting right there before my eyes if I didn't shake him out of it quickly.

"The Monroes are leaving, and they're going to do something to us with boards," I told him.

"Don't say hello or anything," Chester replied, without moving a muscle.

"Oh, sorry. Hello, Chester. How's it going?"

Chester just nodded his head slowly as if that were supposed to be telling me something. "Now what was that about boards?" he asked at last.

"I'm not sure. They're leaving, and they're going to tie us to boards or something, that's all I know."

"I'm sure that's not *all* you know, Harold," he said smoothly. "It may be all your brain can handle right now, but I'm sure you know at least one or two things more. Now, let's try again. What exactly did you hear?"

"Well," I explained, "Toby told me that while the family goes on vacation, you and I are going to be boarded."

"Boarded?!!" Chester exclaimed, his mellowness suddenly gone with the passing breeze. "We're going to be boarded? I can't believe they'd do this to us. It figures! That's all I can say. It just figures!"

"What figures?" I asked. "What are they going to do to us?"

"Oh, just lock us up and throw away the key, that's all. Prison, Harold, that's what it boils down to. We're in their way now that they want to go off and have some fun. So out the door we go and into some dank, dark pit where we'll be fed moldy bread and rainwater—*if* we're lucky! You don't know what these places are like, Harold. But I do!"

"How?" I asked. "Were you ever boarded?"

"Was I ever *boarded?* Was *I* ever boarded?"

"That's what I asked, Chester. Were you ever boarded?"

"*I*'ve read Charles Dickens, sport," was his only reply, and he turned his attention to his tail, which he suddenly felt compelled to bathe. A scowl grew on his face, and I thought that if it were possible, dark rain clouds would have formed around his eyebrows.

"I'll tell you something else, Harold," he muttered. His hysteria had subsided, and he spoke now in a low, serious tone.

"What's that?"

"You have to keep your eyes open all the time in places like those. You never know what will happen next."

"What do you mean?" I asked.

"Think about it," he went on. "A group of strangers are thrown together by circumstance. Who knows who they are? Where they've come from? What they're doing there? The one smiling at you across the food dish in the morning could murder you in your sleep at night."

"Chester," I said, interrupting, "I think perhaps your imagination is running away with you."

"Hah!" Chester snorted. "Mark my words, Harold. Keep your eyes open and your door shut. Just remember: they aren't called strangers for nothing!" And he walked away, leaving me alone with my thoughts.

With everything Chester had said about strangers, it was hard for me at that moment to picture anyone stranger than Chester. But time would certainly bear out his warning. And I have to admit that even then there was something in the conviction with which he spoke that made me uneasy. So much so that when I saw Mr. Monroe coming in my direction, I was immediately distrustful. And this of a man whose home I had lived in for years and whose running shoes I had been eating but moments before!

"Hey there, Harold, guess what? You're going away on a little vacation. Aren't you lucky?" I smelled a con job and kept my distance. "You and Chester are going to stay in a nice animal hotel for a few days. You'll meet some new friends and have a lot of fun. Doesn't that sound terrific?" Interesting he doesn't mention the food, I thought. Having no intention of being conned into living on mold and rainwater, I decided to try a tactic I save for only the most dire of circumstances. As pitifully as I knew how, I started to whimper.

"Aw, poor Harold," Mr. Monroe said quietly, reaching down to pat me on the top of my head (I was sure I had him hooked), "I wish we could take you with us, fella, but we can't." Rats. "Besides, you'll have a good time at Chateau Bow-Wow. Doesn't that sound like a nice place to stay? Now, come on, boy," he said, moving back toward the driveway, "jump up here into the back of the station wagon."

Hmm, Chateau Bow-Wow, I thought as I followed him, it doesn't sound so bad. Not the Waldorf-Astoria maybe, but not bad. Still, I wasn't sure I wanted to go anywhere, particularly after everything Chester had just told me. I lifted my head and let out a soft, muted moan. When I dropped my head again, I noticed Chester lying under the car in the shade by the rear tire. He looked at me and shook his head slowly.

"What a disgusting display," he said, sighing heavily. "But what can one expect from a dog, after all?"

"Well," I replied, "I'm glad to see that you're so resigned to being dragged off to prison."

"I'm not resigned," he said calmly, licking a paw. "I'm not going."

"Oh really?" I asked. "And just how do you intend to manage that?"

Before he could answer, Mrs. Monroe came out of the front door with Chester's carrier, a large square box with a little window in one end. I always tell Chester that it looks like he's on television when he's inside. He doesn't find that very amusing. In fact, just the sight of his carrier is usually enough to send him into a panic, hissing and hyperventilating up a storm. This time, however, he seemed determined to remain cool.

"Toby," Mrs. Monroe instructed her youngest son, "see if you and Pete can find Chester, will you?" Pete appeared at the door behind Toby.

"Excuse me," Chester said to me, "it's time for my exit." And so saying, he made a mad dash for the nearest lilac bush.

Unfortunately for him, Toby and Pete were on to his favorite hiding places. And Pete, who had taken up jogging with his dad, was fast on Chester's heels. Grabbing him by the tail (not the best place to grab anyone, let alone a cat), Pete yanked him back and into his arms before Chester could do much more than let out a yelp of disapproval. Pete then attempted to force

Chester into the waiting carrier, but Chester spread out all four of his legs so that his paws tightly clamped the edges of the box. With his legs held rigidly in place, he screamed and he hissed and he generally let it be known in no uncertain terms that he had no intention of going anywhere. All, however, was to no avail, for he was quickly surrounded by the entire Monroe family, and before he knew what had happened, he was squashed into the carrier and plopped into the car.

I, on the other hand, went with quiet dignity, allowing myself to be lured into the back of the station wagon by a chocolate cupcake and Mr. Monroe's calm affirmation that adventure was good for the soul.

Chester and I had a few moments alone before the rest of the family joined us. Licking the last traces of chocolate frosting from the tip of my nose, I turned to the beast growling inside the cat carrier. I was intrigued by Mr. Monroe's statement about the effect of adventure on the soul and thought perhaps I could pass the time engaging Chester in a deep philosophical conversation.

"Well, Chester," I began, "what do *you* think?"

"I think you made a fool of yourself over that cupcake," he said.

Then again, I thought, perhaps not. I decided to try another tack.

"You know, Chester," I said, trying to sound cheerful, "maybe there's nothing for us to worry about. The way Mr. Monroe tells it, Chateau Bow-Wow sounds like a really nice place."

Chester, who had been grumbling under his breath all this time, was suddenly silent.

"What did you say?" he asked after a moment.

"I said, 'Chateau Bow-Wow sounds like a really nice place.' "

"Chateau Bow-Wow?"

"Chateau Bow-Wow."

Chester's face appeared in the window. His eyes were gleaming.

"What's the problem?" I asked.

"Oh, there's no problem, Harold. No problem at all. Just because I'm being forced to spend a week of my life in a place obviously run by dog chauvinists who are totally insensitive to my feline feelings! Why should that bother me? No, I don't have a problem, Harold. It's the rest of the world who have the problems!"

"Gee, you know, Chester," I said to him, "you look just like a guest on a talk show."

"Harold, have you heard one word I've said?"

"Chester, could you pretend you're on a talk show? You know—just say, 'Gee, it's swell to be here today, Merv,' or 'Well, you know, Mike, it's funny you should ask about that. . . .' Okay, Chester? Huh? Sing 'Feelings,' okay? Chester? Chester?"

Chester glared at me and dropped out of sight. I heard him muttering something about dogs, but I couldn't understand what he was saying. I stopped trying after the Monroes had gotten into the car and I noticed we were pulling out of the driveway.

There was a rumble of thunder in the distance as the car went over a bump and my stomach lurched. Why, I asked myself, had I eaten that chocolate cupcake? I closed my eyes and gritted my teeth.

Toby and Pete were fighting about who had the best window. Mrs. Monroe was trying to quiet them down, at the same time pointing out to Mr. Monroe that he had just taken a wrong turn. Chester, meanwhile, was grumbling and hissing inside his carrier. "Mark my words, Harold," I heard him say at one point, "there's trouble ahead. Don't say I didn't warn you."

As I was thinking back on the feelings of peace and contentment with which I'd started the day, Mr. Monroe turned up the volume on the radio. ". . . so the outlook for the rest of the week," the announcer was saying, "is heavy rain and thunderstorms."

Everyone groaned. The car hit another bump, and my stomach began to feel like a washing machine on the spin cycle. This adventure, I thought, may be terrific for my soul, but it's going to wreak havoc on my digestive system.

[TWO]

Welcome to Howliday Inn

THERE was something about Chateau Bow-Wow that made me uncomfortable from the moment I saw it. Sitting alone on the top of a hill, it inspired a feeling of desolation. Of course, the bumpy ride up the long, winding country road that led to it inspired a feeling of upset tummy, but that's another story.

"Where are we?" I asked in a hushed whisper. I had never seen this part of town before.

"No man's land," Chester growled reassuringly from the bottom of his box.

A second low rumble of thunder resounded in

the distance, and then as we pulled into the driveway, I became aware of another sound.

"Do you hear all that barking?" I asked Chester. A chill went through me.

Together, we listened for a moment. Then Chester spoke. "No doubt the victims of some fiendish laboratory experiment," he said.

I gulped.

"Well, this is the place," Mr. Monroe called back cheerily from the front seat as he brought the car to a halt. "You two stay put. We'll be right back." And all the Monroes went off through a door marked "Office" to do whatever it is people do in offices.

Not to mince words, I was petrified. Where were the Monroes leaving us, anyway? Boy, I thought, you trust some people, you give them the best years of your life, and what does it get you? Abandonment and despair. A fine kettle of fish, that's what I had to say.

I looked around after a moment. The place didn't seem quite so bad close up. I suppose it was the sign that helped most. It was on the gate of a wall behind the house, and when I saw it, I began to feel better. It read:

CHATEAU BOW-WOW
A Special Boarding House
For Special Cats and Dogs

"Look, Chester," I said to the box sitting beside me, "there's a sign on the gate over there. You know what it says?"

"I give up," Chester replied. " 'Abandon All Hope Ye Who Enter Here'?"

I squinted my eyes to see if I could make out any fine print. "No," I answered after looking carefully, "but it says we're special."

"Hmmph," Chester grunted.

"And here's something you'll appreciate," I added, hoping this might cheer him up a little, "it also says 'cats and dogs.' You see, this place is for cats, too. And the sign even puts cats first. Isn't that nice, Chester?"

Chester raised his head to window-level and looked out at the sign. He didn't change his grumpy expression a bit as he said to me, "They probably did it alphabetically." And he dropped out of sight again.

Just then the front door of the office opened and Toby came running out. "Here they are," he called to the strange-looking chap who loped along slowly behind him. This fellow, whoever he was, was older than Toby and Pete but not as old as Mr. and Mrs. Monroe. Having seen some of Mr. Monroe's college students when they'd come to the house to beg for mercy, I estimated that this new chap was roughly their age. He had a shag of brown hair that kept falling into his eyes and a T-shirt that spilled out over the top of his pants. His sneakers were untied, and as he was coming toward us, he stepped on one of the laces and almost fell on his face.

Toby opened Chester's carrier and pulled the reluctant cat out. Chester hung from Toby's arms like Spanish moss and wore an expression that would have soured milk chocolate.

"This is Chester," Toby said, by way of introduction. "Chester, this is Harrison."

Chester turned to me with a smirk. "What am I supposed to do now?" he asked. "Curtsy?"

Harrison, I thought. What a weird name for a person.

"Hey there, kitty," Harrison said, instantly not endearing himself to Chester.

"And this," Toby went on, "is Harold."

"Wow," Harrison said. "What a weird name for a dog."

I looked at Harrison. Harrison looked at me. I thought to myself, this Harrison fellow really has a knack for putting the wrong foot forward.

"Well," Harrison said, "you guys are the last of the arrivals for this week. Now we've got a full house."

The door to the office popped open, and a girl with red hair and a lot of freckles stuck her head out. She seemed to be about the same age as Harrison, but she looked more tucked in.

"Harrison," she called, "do you know where Chester's file is? Dr. Greenbriar wants to look at it while the Monroes are here, and I can't find it anywhere."

"But you were looking at it this morning, Jill," Harrison answered.

"I know, I know," the girl named Jill said, shaking her head. "I just can't remember where I put it. I was hoping you'd seen it."

Harrison shrugged his shoulders and smiled at Jill. "Wish I could help you out," he said, "but I don't pay much attention to the files. That's your territory."

Jill sighed. "I don't know what's the matter with me lately. I'm so tired from all this work I can't remember where I put anything anymore."

"I guess old age is setting in," Harrison said with a laugh.

"Ha ha," Jill answered without one. And she went back inside, letting the door slam behind her.

Chester gave me a look that said he was clearly unimpressed with the staff.

The door opened a third time, and Dr. Greenbriar stepped outside with the rest of the Monroes. I became nervous at once. There's nothing like the sight of a white jacket with creepy little stains all over the front of it to get the old heart pumping.

Dr. Greenbriar walked in our direction, his movements steady and unwavering. The light reflected strangely off his glasses so that it was hard to see what was going on under his thick, bushy eyebrows. When he spoke, his words came as slowly and evenly as his steps.

"Hello, Chester. Hello, Harold," he said to us both as if he were not sure which of us was which.

Chester was apparently as delighted to see Dr. Greenbriar as I was, since his response to the doctor's hello was to begin hissing and shedding hair frantically all over Toby. Dr. Greenbriar just smiled.

"Now, now, Chester, what's the matter, hmmm? You're not afraid, are you?" I suppose his words should have been comforting, but I could feel myself beginning to shake. "You're both going to have a *won*derful time here at Chateau Bow-Wow while your family is away. Aren't they, Harrison?" Harrison looked at Dr. Greenbriar as if he were crazy. The doctor turned back to us. "Harrison and Jill are going to take good care of you. There's nothing to worry about."

Mrs. Monroe seemed a little uneasy. "Are you sure everything will be all right, doctor?" she asked. "I don't mean to question you, but—"

"Everything will be just *fine,* Mrs. Monroe," he answered her sharply. "Surely you don't question my staff?"

Mrs. Monroe's eyes grew wide. "N . . . no, of course not," she answered, taken aback.

"Harrison has worked for me for three summers now, and Jill is studying to be a veterinarian. I trust them both completely. As should you."

"But we thought you'd—" Mr. Monroe started to speak, but was cut off by the doctor.

"Yes, yes, I know. But I simply must take some time off. No one appreciates just how hard I work." His face took on a pained expression as he continued. "This has been a difficult summer. I'll work myself into a collapse if I don't get away." With furrowed brow, he looked into Mrs. Monroe's eyes. Then his features relaxed. "Anyway," he went on, "it isn't as if I were going to the other side of the world. I'll be right here in town, just a phone call away, should any problems come up. I know you have two very special pets here, and believe me, nothing is going to happen to them."

Harrison snorted. "*This* is a special pet?" he asked, pointing to Chester. Chester, who had calmed down a bit, began hissing at Harrison.

"Oh yes," Dr. Greenbriar replied seriously, "Chester is a very special cat. Most . . . *unusual.* Isn't that so, Mr. and Mrs. Monroe?"

"Unusual, hmmm," Mr. Monroe said, reflecting, "I'd say that's *just* the word for Chester. Wouldn't you, dear?"

"That's the word all right," Mrs. Monroe agreed.

At that moment, Jill came through the gate marked "Chateau Bow-Bow." She tripped on a tree stump as she moved toward us. Chester dropped his head sadly. I heard him sigh, I assumed in resignation to his fate.

"Okay, their bungalows are all ready," she said as she approached. She took Chester from Toby and carried him off. He didn't even resist as they disappeared into the world beyond the gate.

"Bungalows are what we call cages here at Chateau Bow-Wow," Dr. Greenbriar was saying to the Monroes. "We think it has more class."

"Oh yes," Mrs. Monroe answered. "Class. Yes." She and Mr. Monroe exchanged a look.

"Well, we should be going," Mr. Monroe said then. "Come on, boys, let's leave Harold to his new home."

Suddenly, Toby threw himself around my neck.

"Goodbye, Harold," he cried. "I'm going to miss you. Be a good dog, okay?" I felt a tear come to my eye.

Pete snickered. "Yeah, Harold," he said sarcastically, "try not to stink up the joint." I felt a bite coming to my teeth.

"Bye, Harold," Mr. Monroe said, leaning down to pat me on the head. "Remember," he added in a whisper, "it's good for the soul."

"Harold," Mrs. Monroe said firmly, "be of good cheer. And keep your eye on Chester, will you? Try to keep him out of trouble." Mrs. Monroe often left me with instructions, but rarely so impossible a task as this. Still, I vowed inside myself to do my best.

Chateau
Bow Wow
a special boarding
house for special
cats and dogs

Toby was holding me tightly. His tears flowed freely now. "I don't want to leave Harold, Mom," he was saying between sniffs. A lump formed in my throat.

Gently, Mrs. Monroe separated Toby from my neck. As she led him by the hand to the car, Harrison took me by the collar to the waiting gate. Just as I was about to enter, I looked back at Toby who was waving to me sadly. A tear at last escaped my eye, and I turned to step through the gate.

Harrison pulled the door shut, and Chester's words popped into my head. "Abandon all hope," he had said, "ye who enter here."

ONCE inside the gate, I got my first real look at my new home, as Mr. Monroe had called it. Chateau Bow-Wow consisted of nine bungalows. (Whatever they were called, they looked like cages to me.) These stood on three sides of a big grassy play area, which Harrison referred to as the compound. The fourth side of the compound was the back wall of the house. A door in this wall led directly into Dr. Greenbriar's office. This door and the main gate seemed to be the only ways to get in or out of the place. A high wooden fence stood behind all the bungalows. It was impossible to see over it, and the only relief from the drabness within was the presence of a few trees here and there.

Oh well, I thought, I had been right about one thing. The Waldorf-Astoria it wasn't.

Harrison led me to the first bungalow we came to after entering the compound. I was relieved to see that Chester was being housed next door. After Harrison left me, I whispered to Chester through the wall.

"What's it like where you are?" I asked. "This isn't so bad. I've got a nice carpet on the floor and a couple of rubber bones for chewing. It's not home, but at least they've tried to give it a personal touch."

"Oh really?" Chester snapped back. "Like what? Aside from a disgusting looking lump of cloth hanging from a string in here, there isn't much in the way of interior decoration."

"Oh, I'm sorry to hear that, Chester."

"It looks as if it's been hanging here since they built the place," he went on. "Probably supposed to be some sort of cat plaything. To tell you the truth, it looks like a mouse with a serious medical condition."

"I'm sorry," I said again.

"Probably got that way from eating the food here," he muttered.

"Oh, this is nice," I said, noticing my food dish for the first time. "It says 'Doggie's Din-Din' on the side. Does your dinner bowl say anything?"

There was a long silence from the other side of the wall.

"Chester? Chester?"

"I hear you, Harold."

"Does your food dish say anything?"

"Yes, Harold. It says, 'Tuna Tonite! Kitty's Delite!' "

"Oh, that's cute, Chester. Don't you think so?"

"I may throw up."

"Pardon?"

"Never mind, Harold."

After a pause, Chester spoke again.

"Harold?"

"Yes, Chester?"

"This place is a loony bin, Harold. Any place that has a dead mouse hanging on a string as guest room decor is a loony bin."

"Oh, Chester, I think you're exaggerating—" I started to say, but I was cut off by a sudden burst of barking from the two dogs in the bungalows directly across from ours. Straight ahead of me was a bulldog in a white turtleneck sweater. Next to him was a French poodle. They seemed to be in the middle of an argument, and it was the poodle who spoke first.

"Oh, yes, yes!" she was saying. "Over and over you say the same thing. But don't think I am so easily fooled, Monsieur Max. You cannot pull the —how you say—wool over these eyes so easily."

"Louise, lower your voice," the bulldog replied. "Everyone can hear you."

"Let them! I do not care! Why should I? After what you've done to me? Humph!"

Even at a distance, I could see that Max was embarrassed. He tried to pull his head further back into the turtleneck sweater, which already threatened to engulf him. He kept pacing back and forth as they spoke.

"So?" Louise pressed on relentlessly. "What do you have to say for yourself, Monsieur Fancy-Pants?"

"I think you're making a mountain out of a molehill, that's what I have to say," Max responded. "You're making a little hello into—"

"A little hello?!?" Louise shot back. "This kind of little hello, as you call it, I will make into a big *au revoir*—that's what I will do with this little hello."

"Louise," a soft breathy voice interjected. I strained my head to see where it was coming from. The speaker was in a bungalow off to my right, but I couldn't see inside.

"Oh no!" Louise exploded. "This is too—oh, what is that word!? Oh yes—much. Now *she* wants to speak!"

"Now, Louise," Max said, his anger building, "she has just as much right to speak as you do."

"Yes, yes, defend her, why don't you?"

"Louise, I don't need defendin'," said the feathery voice. I noticed the speaker had a slight Southern accent. "I've done nothin' wrong."

"Max is mine! Do you hear me, Scarlett?" Louise fairly ranted across the empty space.

"Georgette," the voice responded gently.

"What?" Louise shrieked.

"My name is Georgette," Georgette repeated.

"Scarlett, Georgette—it's all the same to me. You may want him, but he's mine, do you hear? Mine!"

"Louise!" Max bellowed in a full, rich voice. "Enough! I've had enough of your wild accusations! Now, let it be!"

There was the sound of a crash, and Louise vanished to the back of her bungalow. Max looked sullenly out into the distance.

"Oh dear," Chester said drily next door, "I do believe Louise has thrown her din-din dish against the wall." And then he let out a screech.

"What is it, Chester?" I cried. "What's wrong?"

"Something—something—landed on my door. I don't know . . . what . . . what . . ."

"You've got to help me!" a new voice hissed eerily. There was the sound of wire rattling. "I can't take it anymore."

"Chester, is that you?" I whispered. "Is this some kind of joke?" Suddenly, a head appeared upside-down over the edge of my bungalow. I jumped and hit my own head on the ceiling. That must have jarred my visitor, for he flopped to the ground before my door.

"You're new here, aren't you, buster?" he snarled.

"Uh, yes, yes, I am," I replied, trying to size up the vision before me. He was a cat, that much was clear, but a cat unlike any I'd ever seen. He looked like a walking, talking, patchwork quilt.

He glanced furtively over his shoulder before he spoke again, and then it was in a low, intense whisper. "Tuesday," he uttered. "Over the wall. Don't tell the others. Just you and me."

"Just you and me," I repeated. I didn't have a clue as to what he was talking about.

"Sshh," he said quickly, "not so loud. We'll get out of here, pal, don't worry about it."

"Oh, I'm not," I answered. "At least, I think I'm not."

"Okay, just keep cool." Again, he looked around him. "Watch out!" he snapped all at once. "It's them!" And he was gone.

I cast my eyes in the direction he'd just been looking and saw Harrison and Jill coming with our dinners.

"Oh no," Jill was saying, "will you look at that? Lyle's gotten out again. He's a regular terror. Come on, Lyle, let's go now. Come on, be a nice kitty."

Lyle swept by my bungalow, flattening himself against it as if trying to escape a searchlight. I could see he was the very same cat who had just been talking with me. Harrison swooped down on him suddenly and had him back in his bungalow a few seconds later. I heard Lyle muttering under his breath all the way.

"You know," Jill said to Harrison as he returned to passing out our dinners, "we're going to have to do something about that cat. He gets out of his cage all the—"

"Bungalow," Harrison mumbled irritably.

"Right," she said, "I stand corrected. Oh, by the way, I found Chester's file. It was under your stack of comic books."

"Oh?" Harrison looked up from Max's bungalow, a puzzled look on his face. "I wonder how it got there."

"That's what I wondered," Jill said. "Why do you read those things anyway?"

"Comic books?" Harrison shrugged. "It's something to do," he said simply.

Jill stopped where she was and regarded Harrison. Shaking her head, she said. "What are you going to do, Harrison? Read comic books all your life? Don't you want to *be* something?"

"You mean, go to college like you?" he asked. "No thanks. I don't have the time. I want to retire at twenty-one. All I have to do first is make a million bucks."

"Oh, is that all?" Jill replied. "And how will you do that, if I may ask?"

"*That* is what I haven't figured out yet. But don't worry. I will. I'm thinking all the time."

"I'll bet you are," Jill said. "I'll just bet you are."

"Oh, I am." There was a growl of thunder. "We'd better hurry," Harrison said. "It may start raining."

Quickly, they finished dishing out our food and started toward the door. Jill turned back. "Okay, everyone," she called out, "enjoy your dinners! I'll check in on you later."

I stared down at the fare that had been set before me and wondered what Chester had been so worried about. After all, any place that would put a sprig of parsley on top of a bowl of dog food couldn't be all bad. Mold and rainwater, indeed! I dug in.

IT WAS much later that night when we first heard it. Jill had already checked in on us as promised, and now the sounds of snoring and deep breathing convinced me that most of the guests at Chateau Bow-Wow were already fast asleep.

I was thinking what a strange bunch they were: Max, Louise, Georgette, Lyle—Dr. Greenbriar and Harrison and Jill. Who would I meet tomorrow? I wondered. I was just about to ask Chester what he thought, when—

"Aaah-ooooooooooooooo!"

I sat bolt upright, a violent chill racing down my spine.

"Chester!" I cried. "Did you hear—"

"Aaah-ooooooooooooooo!" it went again.

It was a howl, of that I was sure. But a howl so terrible, it was unlike the howl of any dog I'd ever heard. Apparently, Chester felt the same way.

"Werewolves!" I heard him utter from his bungalow next door.

"Oh come on, Chester," I said, "you're letting your imagination run wild."

"Werewolves!" he exclaimed again, as the howls reverberated through the night air, alternating with the thunder, which was growing in loudness and intensity.

"Beware!" Chester hissed at me. "Beware!"

"Aaaaah-oooooooooooooooooooooo!" went the cry in the night.

There was a sudden silence. Exhausted, but unable to sleep, we sat, side by side, staring into the blackness before us. I held my breath in anticipation of the next sound I would hear. As it turned out, it was Chester.

"Chateau Bow-Wow, my foot," he uttered in a deep, throaty voice. "Welcome to Howliday Inn."

[THREE]

An Uneasy Calm

I AWAKENED to the sound of rain pelting the roof above me. As my eyes began to focus, I found myself staring at the words, "A Bow-*Wow* Breakfast." After a moment of confusion, I realized I was reading the side of my new food dish. What I saw when I raised my head a little was not what I personally would have described as a bow-wow anything. My dish was heaped with some sort of grayish gruel that was rivaled in dreariness only by the day outside. Perhaps Chester had been right, after all.

"Chester," I called out over the patter of the falling rain. "Chester, are you there?"

"Of course I'm here," he answered churlishly.

"Where'd you think I'd be on a day like this? Out on the golf course perfecting my putt?"

"How did you sleep?" I asked, ignoring his early morning grumpiness. By this time in our lives together, I was used to it.

"Oh, fine. Fine. Why should I let the incessant howling of werewolves disturb my slumber?"

I didn't take up the issue of werewolves with Chester just then, because I'd finished eating my breakfast and discovered the words "Have a Nice Day!" at the bottom of my dish.

"Chester, does your food dish—"

"If you're going to ask me to discuss the attack of cutes this place is suffering from, I refuse," Chester grumbled. "If I wanted my fortune told every time I ate, I could have gone to a Chinese restaurant." And with that, he let out a great sigh and went back to sleep.

I could tell that any attempts at further conversation would prove futile, so I fell back asleep, too, waiting for something else to happen and wishing I were back home.

* * *

BY THE TIME I woke again, the rain had stopped and the something else I'd been waiting for was about to happen. Harrison and Jill were going from bungalow to bungalow opening the doors.

"Okay, animals, let's go," Harrison was saying in a bored sort of way. "Exercise time."

"Thank goodness it stopped raining," Jill called out. "I thought I'd go crazy if I had to spend another minute working on those charts."

"There's still the office to clean," Harrison said, "and the storage shed."

"Harrison," Jill replied, "we don't have to do it *all* today."

"Oh yes, we do," Harrison answered with some urgency.

Jill put her hands on her hips and looked at Harrison with wonder. "You're really something, you know that, Harrison?"

"Am I? Gee, thanks."

"I didn't mean it as a compliment."

"Oh."

"I mean you blow hot and cold. Like yesterday, all you wanted to do was lie around and read your comic books all day. Today, you can't stop working, and you're driving me crazy. What's with you, anyway?"

"Who knows?" Harrison replied. "Maybe I'm getting ambitious. You'd like that, wouldn't you?" He smiled in Jill's direction, revealing the remnants of that morning's breakfast neatly lodged between his two front teeth.

In disgust, Jill turned away and poked her head inside my door. "Good morning, Harold," she murmured softly. "I hope you had a good sleep your first night at Chateau Bow-Wow." I allowed myself to be coaxed out into the muddy outdoors. I wasn't too thrilled with the condition of the ground, but was happy just to have the chance to stretch my legs and move about.

"Where is that storage shed, anyway?" Jill asked after a moment, continuing her conversation with Harrison as she unlocked Chester's door.

"Out back," Harrison answered, pointing to the far corner of the compound. "Right outside the fence near Howard's bungalow."

"Oh."

"But there's no entrance from here. You have to go around the outside wall," Harrison went on. "That's why it's such a pain to clean."

Jill groaned. "That's too bad," she said, picking Chester up and stroking him. Chester's face looked like a car accident. Obviously, he had not slept well at all. "Well, I guess we'd better get to it." She put Chester down and headed for the gate.

"Aren't you forgetting something?" Harrison asked.

Jill looked blankly around her, then quizzically at Harrison.

"Lyle," Harrison said simply. "You didn't let Lyle out of his bungalow."

Jill shook her head slowly. "Oh, of course," she said at last, "I guess I'm just so used to Lyle getting out all by himself, it doesn't even occur to me to unlock his door anymore." I watched as she opened Lyle's door and then walked to the gate, tripping over a small rock that was in her path.

Watching her, Chester dropped his head and moaned.

"All right, everybody," Harrison called out,

"hurry up and enjoy yourselves before it starts raining again." And then he too went out the front gate, carefully locking it after him.

Chester and I looked back to discover Max bounding spiritedly in our direction. With his natty turtleneck sweater and his square shoulders and jaw, he resembled the captain of a college football team.

I remarked on my observation to Chester, whose only response was a rather anemic, "Yea team. Rah. Rah. Rah." Then, he added, "If he says anything athletic, I'll scream."

Max stopped abruptly before us.

"Want to jog?" he blurted out.

True to his word, Chester let out a bloodcurdling screech and immediately turned on his heels. Max appeared to take it in stride.

"I'm Max," he said.

"I'm Harold," I replied politely. "And this is—uh, that was—Chester," I added, introducing Max to Chester's retreating hindside.

"Pleased to meet you both," Max said with a nod to Chester's tail. He returned his gaze to me.

"So, Harold, you want to jog?"

I remembered the one time I'd tried jogging with Pete and Mr. Monroe and had had to be carried home on the back of Pete's bike.

"Uh . . . well, no . . . uh, not really . . . uh . . ." I stated emphatically.

"Helps work out your aggressions," Max countered.

"I don't have any aggressions," I said honestly.

Max seemed disappointed. "So you don't jog, eh?" he asked a little sadly.

"No," I told him again, disappointed that he was disappointed.

"Well, then, now's the time to start. Come on." I could see that Max was not going to be a pushover. I, on the other hand, was and always have been a pushover, so before I could say anything more I found myself trotting, somewhat breathlessly, alongside Max.

"The thing is," Max said after a moment, "you have to get your exercise when you can around here. They only let us out for a few hours in the afternoon. Of course . . ." and he looked around him before he continued, ". . . it's easy to unlock the doors from the inside. Anybody can do it, Harold. Even you."

"Oh, thanks," I said. Or at least, I think that's what I said. I was having a little trouble getting my words out and breathing at the same time. In a burst, I asked, "Do the others know?"

"About getting out? Oh, sure. Everyone knows how to do it. I'll show you later. Lyle's the only one dumb enough to do it when Harrison and Jill are around. The rest of us wait until after supper, when they've gone home."

Suddenly, Max called out, "Taxi! Taxi!" I thought he'd completely flipped.

"Uh, Max," I said, "I'm not sure how to tell you this, but I don't think there's a cab for miles of this place. Besides," I went on between wheezes, "if you're getting tired . . . we don't . . . have to . . . ride. We could . . . just stop . . . running."

"You don't understand," Max said, without once stopping to catch his breath, "I'm not calling a taxi. I'm calling Taxi." He nodded to my right, and I glanced over to see one of the oddest-looking dogs I'd ever encountered, waddling frantically in our direction.

"What kind of dog is this?" I asked.

"Who knows?" Max replied. "I don't think poor Taxi himself knows for sure. He's one part of everything, I guess. He's a good mutt, though. A little on the slow side, if you get my drift, and he tends to be something of a clinging vine, but—"

"What do you mean?" I asked.

"I don't know what it is, but some days he sticks to me like glue. Seems to think the sun rises and sets on me," Max said, without apparent displeasure.

Taxi joined us then, falling into step beside Max. He regarded Max with a look that was one degree away from idol worship. I could see what Max had meant.

"Hi, Max," he said.

"Hey, Taxi, how're you doin'?" Max replied gruffly. "Taxi, I want you to meet Harold."

Taxi nodded absently in my direction. "How are

you feeling today, Max?" he asked.

"Not bad. Not bad. Taxi, I said I want you to meet Harold."

Once again, Taxi nodded his head in a vague sort of way, not really acknowledging my presence. Of course, at that moment I was wondering how much longer it would be before my presence became my past. I could barely catch my breath, and my tongue was hanging somewhere around my knees.

"Had enough?" asked Max, brimming with energy.

". . . uh . . . uh . . . uh . . . uh . . ."

"I guess you have. Come on, let's head for the cooler and take a break."

At the community water cooler, my breathing returned to normal and Taxi noticed me at last.

"Oh, hello," he said as if seeing me for the first time, "who are you?"

"I'm Harold," I replied.

"Harold, Harold," he said, a puzzled look on his face. "Where have I heard that name before?"

"I just introduced you," Max said.

"Oh."

I looked at Taxi. Max was right. He really was on the slow side.

"Are you okay, Max? You're really feeling all right?" Taxi asked.

"Sure, sure," Max snapped, a little irritably. "Why do you keep asking?"

"Well, after that fight last night . . . I mean . . ."

"Oh, *that,*" Max answered.

Taxi and I looked at Max as his face grew red beneath his hair. When he returned our gaze, he looked a little embarrassed and not just a little angry.

"Acchh, women!" he uttered. "What a nuisance they are sometimes. That Louise can be so unreasonable."

I glanced over at Louise's bungalow and saw that she was watching us. I felt a little sorry for her.

Max went on. "Just because Georgette and I have said hello a few times, she thinks we're going to run off together." He looked about him and

then in a low voice added, "As if we could get out of here even if we wanted to."

Taxi nodded his head in sympathy. He looked up at Max with wide eyes and sighed deeply. "It must be pretty hard sometimes," he said.

"Yup," Max grunted. "Women. Sometimes I think I'd be better off without them."

There was a moment of silence. All at once, Taxi's face lit up. "Oh, Max," he said excitedly, "you just reminded me of this television show I saw last week. The man said just what you did."

"What's that?" Max asked.

" 'Women. Sometimes I think I'd be better off without them,' " Taxi repeated.

"And then what did he say?" Max asked.

"Nothing. He murdered his wife."

I looked at Taxi. He looked at Max. Max stared straight ahead in the direction of Louise's bungalow.

"That's terrible," he said softly.

Taxi just shrugged his shoulders and began drinking again. He looked up after a moment, water dripping from his lips, and said, "I don't think so."

I looked at him in surprise. "How can you say such an awful thing?" I asked.

"Oh, I wouldn't!" Taxi said.

"But you just did."

"Did what?"

"Say such a thing."

"Did I?"

I was getting confused. "Yes, of course you did. You just said it wasn't such a terrible thing for a man to murder his wife."

"Oh," Taxi said, thinking it over. "Well, I guess I must have meant it then." I could see that holding a conversation with Taxi was definitely going to be a challenge.

"She wasn't a very nice person," Taxi added, as if that made everything okay.

"Still, that's no reason—" I started to say when Max cut me off.

"How'd he do it?" he asked suddenly, turning his gaze from Louise's bungalow to Taxi.

"Poison," Taxi answered simply. And then: "In her soup."

"Hmmm," was Max's only reply.

I observed him for a moment. He must have noticed me, for he laughed suddenly and said, "Well, that's one way of handling women, I suppose."

"I suppose," I replied, not at all sure I liked being part of this conversation.

"Yes," Max went on thoughtfully. "Murder is one way. Murder in its infinite varieties. Poison, stabbing, drowning, strangling—"

"Split pea," Taxi interjected.

Max and I looked at him. "He put poison in her split pea soup," he explained.

"Oh," I said.

"Ah," said Max.

"Yoo-hoo," called a new voice.

We all turned and saw a tiny white French poodle standing a few feet away.

"Georgette," Max whispered.

"Good afternoon, Max," Georgette cooed as she approached the water cooler. She smelled of honeysuckle and magnolias. She also smelled of trouble. "How're you doin' after that terrible fight? I just felt so awful-awful bad about it, I couldn't sleep a wink all night worryin' about you." And here she yawned, showing us, I gathered, how much she had suffered on Max's account.

"Don't believe a word of it," Taxi whispered to me.

Max started pawing the ground self-consciously. "Aw, shucks," he said at last. "I'm fine today. Thanks for asking."

"Oh, that's silly," Georgette replied.

"What is?" Max asked, grinning openly now.

"Thankin' me for carin' about you," Georgette answered.

"Aw, shucks," Max said again. It struck me that when Georgette came around, Max's vocabulary suffered.

It was then I noticed that Louise had joined us.

"Hah!" she exclaimed. " 'Aw, shucks,' says Monsieur Max. I come over here to tell you that I am—how you say—sorry that we have had our little fight. And what do I hear? 'Aw, shucks!' Well, *mon ami,* is this what you will say when I am no longer around? Eh? 'Aw, shucks'? Because if you are keeping this up much longer with Hester Prynne here—"

"Georgette," Georgette said softly.

"Georgette, Hester, what am I caring? If you think you can have your Louise and your Mademoiselle Aw-Shucks, too, you are sadly misshapen!" I think she meant to say "mistaken" but she was so overwrought at this point, it was understandable that the word came out wrong. I wanted to console her, but she left us with a grand flourish before anyone, including Max, could speak. Just as she was about to reach her bungalow, Lyle suddenly pounced on her back.

"Bombs away!" he cried.

Louise screamed. "What are you doing?! You are a very crazy cat, you nutty Lyle, you! Get off me this instant!"

Lyle didn't seem to be paying any attention to Louise's screams. In fact, it appeared that he was talking to someone else entirely.

"Ace-One to Four-Seven. Come in, Four-Seven. Have bombed the target area. Meeting resistance. Roger. Over and out."

Max ran over to Louise to help. "Lyle!" he commanded. "Stop this at once!"

"Don't you be helping me!" Louise cried. "I will take care of myself, *merci*-you-very-much." Max backed off, tucking himself as far into his sweater as possible.

Louise turned her head around so that she was staring directly into Lyle's eyes.

Lyle mumbled under his breath as if talking into a headset. "Enemy contact. Enemy contact. Standby. Mayday! Mayday!"

"Now you listen to me," Louise said in a low, threatening tone. Lyle's eyes went wild, and he stopped talking immediately. "We know all about you here. Do not think we are playing the fools. You have been driving us all—what is it?—ah, yes, pineapples . . ."

"I think she means bananas," Georgette whispered across the way to no one in particular.

". . . but I, for one, have had enough. Do you understand me, Monsieur Lyle? Enough pineapples you have driven me! You will not make me into a fruit salad, *n'est-ce pas?* Now, get off my back and do not ever again use me for a landing stripe!"

Lyle hissed at her and jumped off her back. He dashed to the other side of the compound and then he turned suddenly and faced her.

"You haven't seen the end of me, toots!" he shouted. "No one talks to Lyle like that and gets away with it!"

"You are not frightening me, Monsieur Bombs-Away!" Louise yipped back.

There was a sudden crash of thunder, which shook us all. No one spoke for a few seconds; then there came a deep, rumbling sound. I thought at first it was more thunder. Then I realized it was coming from Lyle's direction. I looked at him. He was growling at Louise.

From somewhere deep in his throat, he said, "I don't like being crossed, sister. Just . . . watch . . . out!" He stared at her coolly, and Louise, momentarily stunned, stared back. She looked frightened, and I wondered, for the first time, if indeed there was reason for her to be.

[FOUR]

The Storm Gathers

ALL AT ONCE Louise broke into a rapid-fire attack of barking. I wanted to check out Max's reaction, but Harrison's voice startled the thought right out of me.

"What's going on in here?" he asked, suddenly entering through the gate. Everyone froze. "What's all this noise? Now calm down, or back into your bungalows you go."

Jill appeared next to him, carrying a large bag of garbage. She was panting slightly. "What was it?" she asked.

"Oh, nothing. Just a dog fight, I guess," Harrison said. Dog fight, I thought, what a quaint expression. I wondered if people ever had dog fights.

As Harrison and Jill turned to go, Jill tripped on the very rock I'd seen her trip over before. The bag of garbage flew out of her hands, spilling its contents all over the ground.

Harrison jumped back as some of the debris landed on his shoe. "What a clumsy oaf!" he shouted. "Can't you do anything right?"

Jill's face turned red. I could see tears coming to her eyes as she spoke. "Well, aren't you Mister Perfect all of a sudden?" she asked, her voice quivering. "If you weren't pushing me so hard, I wouldn't be like this in the first place."

"Maybe if you weren't like this in the first place," Harrison retorted, "you wouldn't think I was pushing you so hard."

Jill's mouth fell open. After a moment, she spoke. "And *maybe* you'd like to work by yourself the rest of the day!"

"Okay, okay," Harrison replied in a softer voice. "I'm sorry. Come on, let's forget it and clean this up."

Jill, sniffling back her tears, knelt in silence and began shoveling tin cans and bottles back into the plastic bag. "I'm sorry, too," she said quietly. "I'm just tired. It's not your fault."

They finished their task in total silence. We all sat motionless, watching them. I guess people *do* have dog fights, I thought.

Just before they went out the gate, Harrison turned back to us and said, "Now, keep it down in here." And once again we were left to ourselves.

I turned to Max, but saw that he and Georgette had wandered off. Their heads were very close together. Taxi was watching them, too, and seemed to be annoyed. When he noticed me looking at him, he said, "A fine thing!" and walked away in a huff.

Suddenly, I found myself alone. I could feel that a light rain was beginning to fall. And a second crack of thunder announced that the storm was about to break again. Not knowing what else to do, I headed back to my bungalow in the hopes that Chester might be around to talk to.

I guess I was so lost in thought that I never saw them, but when I was almost to my bungalow, I tripped. Looking down, I discovered that what had

crossed my path were two long, low dogs, the likes of which I'd never seen before. As politely as I knew how, I spoke.

"Please forgive me for tripping over you," I said.

"Not at all. Not at all," said one. "Indeed, it was our fault for—"

"Yes, yes," said the other. "For walking in your way."

"We weren't watching—" said the first.

"—where we were going," concluded the second.

There was a moment's silence as I looked them over. They were almost identical, and though one had a slightly higher-pitched voice than the other, they spoke as if one mind were encased in two bodies. Their heads did not stop bobbing up and down.

"I'm Harold," I said.

"Howard . . ." said the one with the lower-pitched voice. He nodded his head once.

". . . and Heather," said the other. And she nodded her head crisply.

"We're out for a stroll," Howard continued, as if he owed me an explanation. "We do like a stroll. Of course, Heather here isn't up to—"

"Now, now, now," Heather said, cutting Howard off. "No need to go into all that, is there?" She smiled vaguely in my direction, and our conversation drew to a halt. The rain began to come down more heavily then. I was more than a little relieved to have a reason to excuse myself.

"Well, it was—" I began.

"Yes, yes, it was," Howard said eagerly. "So sorry we have to run, but—"

"Oh, I understand," I said.

"—but, I'm not feeling myself suddenly," Heather added. "Dear, mightn't we—?"

"Yes, yes, of course," Howard said to her. There was a look of great concern in his eyes.

"Goodbye, Harold," he said, as they turned to leave. "We will talk again, I am sure. Oh, and Harold . . . ?"

"Yes?" I asked.

"Beastly sorry about that noise last night. Frightful, what? But we just can't seem to—"

"—help it, really," Heather finished the sentence for him. "Come, dear."

"Quite," was all that Howard said then, and the two of them strolled off, rather more hurriedly, their heads bobbing like pigeons all the way home.

"CHESTER!" I cried as soon as I saw my friend waiting for me in my bungalow. The rain was really coming down by that time.

Chester sat licking a paw and staring into the distance. As he did not respond immediately to my calling, I concluded that he was once again in a state of advance mellowhood. I waited another moment before I spoke again.

"Guess what?" I asked.

Chester looked at me through half-lowered lids. "Harold, you know I hate it when you do that," he said.

"When I do what?"

"When you say 'Guess what?' " he replied with faint disdain. "How am I supposed to guess what, when I don't even know where you're coming from?"

"Oh, sorry," I answered. There was a pause.

"Harold," he said quietly after a moment.

"What?"

"I think we've established that I'm not going to guess what. So why don't you just tell me what's on your mind, hmm? I have a lot to think about, however, and I don't wish to be distracted by trivia."

"Oh, I don't think this is trivia," I said, though

I couldn't be sure since I didn't know what trivia was. "It has to do with these two strange dogs I just met named Howard and Heather. They said they were sorry about the noise last night. Do you think they were the ones who—"

"Is that all?" Chester said sharply, interrupting me. "I figured that out long ago."

"You figured what out?" I asked. I hadn't figured anything out, except that it was Howard and Heather who had been howling all night.

"That Howard and Heather are werewolves."

I couldn't help myself. I chuckled at the thought of those two little dogs being werewolves. To me, they looked more like sausages with legs, and I told Chester so.

"Dachshunds," he replied.

"Gesundheit."

"I didn't sneeze, Harold."

"Oh, but you said—"

"Dachshunds."

"Gesundheit."

"Harold, put the etiquette on the shelf for a minute and listen to me. Howard and Heather are not sausages. They are a kind of dog called dachshunds. Because of their long hair, I am assuming that they are what is known as wire-haired dachshunds."

"But you said they were werewolves."

"It is my belief," Chester went on (and here he drew out his words to give the impression that what he was saying was of the most crucial importance), "that Howard and Heather are a cross between a wire-haired dachshund and . . . a werewolf." He paused and looked at me to check out the impact of what he was saying. There was none. With a slight tremor in his voice, he added, "A most vile and dangerous combination."

I yawned. I knew Chester well enough to know when to respond and when to yawn. This was definitely a time to yawn.

"You don't believe me, do you?" Chester asked. "Well, it doesn't matter, Harold. This isn't the first time you've chosen to ignore my warnings, and I'm sure it won't be the last. Just let it be said that Howard and Heather are to be watched."

"If you ask me," I replied, "Lyle is the one to watch. Now, *there*'s a basket case."

Chester agreed that Lyle was worthy of observation, for he too had witnessed the scene earlier with Louise. "Indeed," he concluded, "I'd say *all* of the guests in this establishment deserve our careful attention. There is an undercurrent of tension here, Harold." He looked out at the pouring rain and the darkening sky. "An undercurrent that will one day erupt with a sudden and terrible force."

There was a loud explosion of thunder. I jumped.

"The storm gathers," Chester commented drily as I landed.

"What shall we do?" I asked.

"Nothing to do. Nothing to do but wait." He lay down then and closed his eyes. "Meanwhile, I'm going to get some sleep—while I still can."

"Mind if I join you?" I asked, not wanting to be alone.

"Not at all," Chester said, making room for me next to him on the rug. I was thinking how hospitable he was being, when I realized that we were in *my* bungalow.

"Just one favor, Harold."

"What's that, Chester?"

"When you dream?"

"Yes?"

"Try not to smack your lips all the time, will you? It drives me crazy."

So promising, I fell into a deep sleep.

THE NEXT THING I remember was the deafening crash of thunder that awakened us. Chester jumped up and ran to the door.

"It's dark!" he cried.

Max and Taxi were in the center of the compound, barking loudly.

"What's going on?" I called out.

"They're late with dinner," Max responded. He and Taxi began barking again, as Georgette ran out and joined them. I noticed how she cuddled up to Max's side and immediately my heart ached for Louise. Since my attention went rather quickly to my stomach, however, my heart didn't ache for long.

"What do you think has happened?" I asked

Chester. "I can't go without food. Dogs aren't meant to be starved. Cats are different. Cats can live off their own fat, but dogs are—"

"Try living off the fat on your brain," Chester said, cutting me off.

Just then, the door of the office swung open and Jill and Harrison rushed out. Jill was wearing an orange slicker, and Harrison carried an umbrella that quickly turned itself inside out, doing neither him nor our dinners any good. I made a mental note to complain about the service. But later. At the moment, all I cared about was that our food was here at last.

The storm was in full force, the wind lashing the rain against us. Harrison and Jill scurried about quickly, calling to each other across the compound. I couldn't hear everything they said, but I did pick up snatches of conversation.

". . . can't understand how we let this happen," Harrison was saying. "We've never been late before. It's your fault, you know. I told you to keep your eye on the clock."

"My fault?" Jill answered. "You were the one

who insisted that we clean the office after we finished the shed. Push, push, push."

"Okay, Jill," Harrison said, with an exasperated tone in his voice, "give it a rest, huh?"

"Give it a rest, he says," Jill muttered to herself. "He doesn't know the meaning of the word." Then turning her attention to us, she said, "Oh, you poor things, you must be starving. Sorry, sorry," she kept saying to everyone. "Sorry," as she put down the food dishes and scurried us back into our bungalows.

I was so relieved to get my dinner, I hardly noticed that I'd gotten soaked by the storm. I was glad, though, when Jill suddenly showed up at the door of my bungalow with a big white towel in her hands.

"Sorry to have to interrupt you, Harold," she said sweetly, "but let me dry you off a little so you can enjoy the rest of your dinner." Jill's hands felt good as she rubbed me down, and I would have happily rolled over for a complete MTR (that's "massage and tummy rub" to you laymen) had I not been so anxious to return to eating dinner. "I don't know where my head is these days," she said as she rubbed the hair along my back. "I completely forgot about feeding you guys tonight. And then we raced out here so fast, I left the towels inside and let the door slam shut behind me." She laughed to herself and shook her head. "I guess I need a rest, too," she said. "Dr. Greenbriar and I have been working so hard these past few weeks, I'm ready to drop. And Harrison —but I can't blame him," she said seriously. "That's no excuse. It would be awful if something happened just because I let myself get a little tired and careless."

"Jill," Harrison called, "I've finished drying the rest of them. I'm going back in."

"Okay," Jill shouted back above the din of the rain. "I'll be right there."

She turned to me and scratched me behind the ears. "Okay, Harold, that's it. Enjoy your dinner now. And get a good night's sleep. Night-night."

And she was gone.

I liked Jill, I thought, as I plunged back into my food. She was clumsy and forgetful it was true, but she seemed nice enough. As for Harrison, well, I wasn't sure what to make of him. There was something about him that made me nervous. Besides, anybody who preferred reading comic books to chewing on them was a little suspect in my eyes.

Later that night, I tried to sleep. But the raging storm and the determined howling of Howard and Heather kept startling me awake. And then I started thinking about what Chester had said earlier. What were his exact words? Something about an undercurrent of tension that would one day erupt with a terrible force. What could he mean? I wondered.

Little did I imagine then, tossing and turning in my sleep, that the terrible eruption Chester had predicted had already occurred.

[FIVE]

"She's Gone!"

THE NEXT MORNING, I was startled out of my sleep by the sound of Harrison's voice.

"Oh no!" he cried.

I moved quickly to the front of my bungalow to see what was going on. So did everyone else. Harrison stood in the center of the compound, shaking his head, as Jill flew out of the office door.

"What is it?" she shouted. "What's happened?"

Harrison pointed at Louise's bungalow. The door was wide open.

"She's gone!" he proclaimed.

Immediately, I shifted my gaze to Max. Our eyes met. His jaw fell open, as a look of shock and bewilderment swept over him.

"But how?" Jill asked. "This has never happened before, has it?"

"Not in the three summers I've worked here," Harrison replied. Slowly, he surveyed the entire compound, looking at each of us in turn. Then, suddenly, he called out, "Look!"

We all turned our heads sharply in the direction he was pointing. Unfortunately, I hit my nose on the wall of my bungalow and I couldn't see a thing except stars. So it took Jill's words to make clear what it was that had so astonished him.

"Oh no," she said. "The gate! It's open!"

"How can it be?" Harrison asked. "There's no way any of the animals could open that lock."

"I don't know," Jill said, her brow wrinkled in confusion and distress. "Unless one of us . . ." She stopped speaking then, and a strange expression came over her face.

"What is it?" Harrison asked. "What's the matter?"

"I did it," she said after a minute. Her voice was soft and a little wavery.

"What do you mean?" Harrison queried. His eyebrows came together to form a hedge across his forehead.

"I did it," Jill repeated. "I left the gate open. Don't you remember? When I ran in to get the towels, I accidentally let the office door lock behind me, so I had to go back by the gate. I was in such a hurry and it was raining so badly, I guess I just didn't notice . . . I . . ." Her shoulders slumped, and it was another moment before she spoke again. In the interim, a flash of lightning ripped through the sky, letting us know that the storm was not yet over. "Oh, I feel terrible," Jill went on. "It's all my fault. What are we going to do?"

Much to my surprise, Harrison came over to Jill and put his arm around her shoulders. "Don't worry," he said softly, "we'll find her. It was a mistake. It could have happened to anyone. Come on. Let's give everyone breakfast, and then you and I will go out looking for her."

Jill seemed as surprised as I was at Harrison's concern. She looked at him warily out of the corner of her eyes. "What if we don't find her?" she asked.

"Then she'll find us," Harrison said calmly. "She'll wind her way back home sooner or later." He smiled then and said gently, "Okay?"

"Okay," Jill replied, accepting Harrison's attempts at reassurance, and together they went back inside the office.

AFTER breakfast, Chester and I put our heads together to consider Louise's escape. Harrison and Jill had let us out early for exercise, since there was no way of knowing when the storm would start up again.

"What did I tell you?" Chester asked me.

"I give up," I answered, not at all sure what he was referring to.

"Didn't I say there would be trouble?"

"What trouble?" I countered. "Louise ran away. Makes sense, if you ask me."

"Oh, really?"

"Sure."

"Would you care to enlarge on your theory?"

"I'd be delighted," I replied. "Louise was very upset about Max's flirting with Georgette. Agreed?"

"Agreed."

"So, when she saw that the front gate had been left open last night, she seized the opportunity to run off and teach Max a lesson. She'll be back."

"And that's it?"

"Simple, really. Just opened the door to her bungalow, and out she went."

"Mmm-hmm," Chester replied, licking his paws. His long tongue moved slowly between each of his toes as he reflected on what I'd said. No doubt he was impressed with my powers of deduction. "And did she unlock Max's door, too?"

"Huh?" I asked, completely thrown. "What do you mean?"

"What I mean is that Max's door was open this morning, too. You may not have noticed that, but I did. You have to learn to be observant in this business, Harold."

"What business is that, Chester?"

"The business of crime detection," Chester answered, neatly snapping his head in my direction to look me squarely in the eyes.

"Crime detection?" I responded. I could feel the hairs along the back of my neck rise slightly. Chester has always had the ability to alarm me, often unnecessarily. I was hoping this was the case. "Chester," I said, "I think you're getting carried away."

"On the contrary," he replied, "it may well have been Louise who was carried away."

"Oh," was all I could say, for Max's voice suddenly bellowed throughout Chateau Bow-Wow.

"It's no good," he groaned, "no good!" Chester and I looked out to see him sitting in the middle of the compound, a forlorn expression smeared across his face like after-breakfast jam. The ever-present Georgette was at his side.

"Now, Max, you mustn't carry on so," she said softly.

"Hussy," I heard myself utter under my breath.

"I can't help it, Georgette," Max cried, his voice cracking. "It's all my fault this happened. I never should have spoken to her the way I did."

I could see Taxi moving in Max's direction; Max looked up and saw him coming.

"I'm sorry, Max, I—" Taxi started to say.

"Not now, Taxi!" Max fairly shouted.

"But, Max—"

"No, Taxi, I want to be alone!" And Max picked himself up and lumbered back to his bungalow. Georgette followed. He turned to her suddenly and said, "Please, Georgette. I need some . . . space."

"Of course," she answered, her feathery voice at its featheriest, "I understand. This is not the time for . . . us."

She turned and walked away, her spirit trailing behind her like a long shadow on a sultry summer day. Taxi, meanwhile, stood in the center of the compound. From the look on his face, he was not pleased that Max had dismissed him so abruptly. After a moment's deliberation, he moved away toward one corner of the compound and began to scratch himself behind the ears.

"Come on," Chester said to me, "we've got some exploring to do."

"Okay," I answered, "but I don't know what you expect to find. Anyway, if you're suspecting Max of anything, I guess you can rule him out now. Boy, is he upset. Poor fella."

"Is he?" Chester asked pointedly. "Perhaps he is a 'poor fella,' as you say. Or perhaps a poor actor putting on a good show."

We were walking in the direction of Louise's bungalow when we bumped into Howard and Heather. They both jumped in surprise.

"Sorry," I said, "I didn't mean to startle you."

"Oh . . . oh . . . it's nothing," Howard said. "No, it's nothing—"

"—at all," said Heather. "Oh my, I'm so jumpy today. I don't feel quite myself. No, I—"

"Sorry about that beastly howling last night, old chap," Howard said to me. He turned with a nod to Chester. "Certainly hope we weren't the cause of Louise's . . . uh . . ."

". . . departure," Heather added. She giggled suddenly. And then, just as suddenly, she gasped and tried to catch her breath.

"What is it?" Howard cried.

"Oh, it's nothing," Heather replied, after letting out a great sigh. "I'm having such trouble breathing today. I don't know what . . . it . . . is . . ." She looked at Howard, her big eyes wide in bewilderment. The two of them stared at each other a long moment, their heads bobbing up and down in unison.

"I think we'd better—" Howard began.

"—go home," Heather finished. "Yes, dear. I think we'd best. Do excuse us," she said, turning to us. "I'm just not—"

"—herself," said Howard. And they turned and left. Chester and I watched them go.

"Typical werewolvian behavior," said Chester, his voice full of authority. I'm sure I would have asked him to elaborate, if it were not for the fact that I didn't really care in the least what he had to say. So I changed the subject.

"Weren't we going to do some exploring?" I asked.

"Yes," Chester answered, snapping himself out of his pensive mood. "Follow me."

I followed Chester to Louise's bungalow, where

we stood for what felt like a long time, staring at the emptiness inside. "Just think," I said, feeling a tear come to my eye," last night she was here. Today, she's gone."

"Yes," said Chester slowly. "That's exactly the word. 'Gone.' "

"Escaped," I added. "But soon she'll be back with us."

"Nonsense," Chester said scornfully. "She didn't escape. And she won't be back. No one comes back from murder!"

"Murder?"

"Of course, murder," Chester replied evenly. "It's all falling into place, don't you see?"

"What's falling into place?"

"The suspects. The motives. And now the evidence," said Chester.

I was confused (which around Chester is a normal state of being, so it didn't alarm me). "What evidence?" I asked.

"Look for yourself," he said, with a nod toward the bungalow. "What do you see?"

I surveyed the interior. "A rug. A water dish.

A food dish," I said. "Just like mine."

"Ah, but it isn't just like yours, Harold, and that's the key."

"Why? I don't see anything so different."

"Look again. And this time use your powers of observation, such as they are. *Now,* what do you see?"

I scrunched up my eyes and looked carefully at each square inch of space as if studying for a final exam at obedience school.

"Well?" Chester prodded.

"A rug. A water dish. A food dish," I proclaimed.

Chester sighed and shook his head sadly. "Sometimes I despair, Harold," he uttered. "Allow me to fill you in on what you've missed."

"Please do."

"The rug. How is it different from yours?" I shrugged. "It's all jumbled up," Chester went on. "A real mess, in fact. And the food dish? Almost filled with food. These observations may seem insignificant, but wait, my friend. Now we come to the water dish, perhaps the most significant item of all. And yet it isn't really the water dish, but what lies around it that is so disturbing."

Thoroughly confused, I looked at the water dish and the floor around it. Nothing struck me as unusual.

"But don't you see?" Chester asked. "What is lying all around the water dish?"

"Water?" I ventured.

"Exactly!" he exclaimed triumphantly.

"But what else would you expect to find around a water dish?"

"Ordinarily, the appearance of water around a water dish would not be out of the ordinary in the least. But given the unusual combination of factors, it is most striking. And it will be given serious consideration in our investigation."

Suddenly, Lyle zoomed by us.

"Faster than a speeding bullet—" I heard him call out as he passed. "Able to leap buildings in a single bound!"

Chester shook his head. "That Lyle is a disgrace to the species," he said. Then, back on the track of his previous thought, he said, "Come on, Harold, I need to talk this out with you right now."

We found a quiet spot under a tree in a corner of the compound. The storm seemed to have abated for the moment, and I thought how pleasant it would be just to lie here for a while and commune with nature. But Chester had other ideas.

"The rug, the food dish and the water on the floor all add up to foul play, my dear Harold, don't you see? Signs of a struggle, old boy!" Old boy? I thought. "My guess—and it's only a guess, mind you—is that someone pushed Louise's head into the water while she was drinking. She resisted, which accounts for the spilled water and the wrinkled rug."

"And the food?" I asked.

"She never finished her dinner," Chester said simply. "She was . . . shall we say . . . interrupted."

I must confess Chester's deductions began to awaken in me the possibility that what he was suspecting was true. Still, I wasn't going to give up my theory of Louise's escape so easily.

"What if it happened just as Jill and Harrison

said?" I asked. "Isn't that possible?"

"Sure, it's possible," Chester answered. "But it's unlikely."

"Why?"

"If Louise had run away, it's only logical she would have finished eating her dinner first, since she couldn't have known when she'd be eating her next meal. And why the appearance of a struggle? And why," Chester added, "was Max's door open as well?"

"So you're saying Max did it?"

"I'm not saying anything—yet. Obviously, Max had the motive. And the strength to pull it off. Let us picture the scene: He comes to Louise's bungalow telling her he wants to apologize. She lets him in. He pushes her head into the water. She struggles, but he has the strength to hold her down. Afterward, he drags her body out through the front gate."

"But he's so upset today," I said, still not believing Max capable of such an act.

"Either that or, as I suggested before, he's pretending he is. To throw us off, you see?"

I allowed as how I did. "What about Georgette?" I asked. "She could have done it. I wouldn't put much past her."

"Yes, that's possible, too. The only problem there is that I doubt she has the strength to hold Louise's head down. What's more likely is that they're in cahoots, she and Max. She may have been his accomplice. Unless, of course," and here Chester thought for a moment, "I have the method of the murder itself wrong. Hmm, that will bear some thinking."

In the distance, Lyle dropped from the branch of a tree onto Taxi's head. Taxi, not in the mood to wear Lyle as a hat, shook him off so violently that he landed several feet away. Stunned, he picked himself up and screamed at Taxi, "I can tell when I'm not wanted! Don't think I can't take a hint!" And he stormed off.

"What about Lyle?" I asked. "Do you remember how he threatened Louise yesterday?"

"Indeed, I do," Chester answered, nodding slowly. " 'You haven't seen the end of me,' he said. 'Just watch out!' And you know, Harold,

Lyle is just crazy enough to do it. When you think about it, the murderer could be anyone here."

"Anyone?" I asked, puzzled.

"Anyone!" Chester affirmed. "We know, for instance, that Howard and Heather are part werewolf—"

"*You* know," I corrected.

"Oh, come on, Harold, no normal dog howls like that."

"That's true," I concurred, "*I* don't."

"True. Of course, you're not normal either, but we'll overlook that for the moment."

"Thank you," I said.

"Besides, werewolves are very hairy. Look at how hairy Howard and Heather are."

"They're wire-haired dachshunds. You said so yourself."

"They're very *hairy* wire-haired dachshunds," Chester countered, refusing to allow logic to blow his theory. "And if they are werewolves, they can change shape anytime they want."

"Huh?" I inquired.

"Werewolves can change into anything, anytime at all, in order to assist them in their pursuit of evil." I tried to imagine Howard and Heather changing shape. It was hard to picture Howard as a clothes hanger or Heather as a toaster-oven. I was about to mention this to Chester when he spoke again.

"You have to admit they were behaving strangely today," he said. "Guilt, Harold. They were consumed with guilt!"

I said, "I doubt werewolves feel guilty."

"The guilt comes from the wire-haired dachshund part of them. It's common to the breed."

"Oh," I replied. "And what about Harrison and Jill? Do you suspect them, too?"

"Of course," said Chester. "They're both a little on the shady side, if you ask me. Besides, we don't know the whole story on this Dr. Greenbriar yet. If you want my opinion, it's more than a little strange that he's gone off and left us in the care of these two. I wouldn't be at all surprised if they're acting on his orders."

"What are you implying?"

"I'm not implying anything," Chester answered

innocently. "I'm just thinking out loud. It's interesting, that's all, that while the doctor is away, Louise disappears. And neither Harrison nor Jill seemed too concerned about letting him know."

"Maybe they want to find Louise first," I suggested.

"Or maybe Greenbriar has ordered them to murder her."

"Oh, Chester," I said. This last was too much. "What about Jill? Didn't you see how upset she was?"

"Again, like Max, it could be she's faking. Or"—and here he paused a moment—"perhaps Harrison is in it alone with the not-so-good doctor. That's a possibility, too."

My head was spinning with Chester's theories. Then I thought of the one suspect he'd left out. "And Taxi?" I asked. "He's too dumb to concoct a murder like this." I didn't like saying it about poor Taxi, but it was true. Chester didn't agree.

"You don't have to be a genius to murder, Harold. No, it isn't Taxi's intelligence that troubles me. It's his strength. He's a timid little fellow.

I can't imagine him holding Louise down long enough to . . ." Here Chester drifted off into thought. Suddenly, his eyes lit up.

"Unless . . ." he said excitedly. "If we change the method of murder . . . then . . ."

"Yes?"

"We know that Taxi is always buttering up to Max, right?"

"Right," I agreed.

"And we know that his feelings were hurt yesterday when Max went off with Georgette instead of spending time with him. We also know he'd do anything to please Max to get back into his good graces."

"But murder?" I asked. I couldn't believe it of Taxi.

"Sure, why not? I was on the wrong track, don't you see? If we believe that Louise was drowned, then Taxi is pretty much ruled out. He wouldn't have the strength. And I doubt that he'd have the guts. But if the method of murder were less direct—if, for instance . . ." and he paused dramatically, ". . . Louise were poisoned—"

I felt a jolt go through me. "Chester!" I cried. "What is it?"

"I just remembered something Taxi said yesterday. Max had just gotten through telling us how sometimes he thought he'd be better off without women."

"Yes?"

"And Taxi told us about a television program he'd seen where a man, feeling the same way, murdered his wife."

"And the method, Harold? What method did he use?"

"Poison."

Chester and I sat very still for a moment. My gaze drifted to where I had seen Taxi sitting a few moments before. He was no longer there.

Could it be? I asked myself. Could Taxi have murdered Louise to please Max? What kind of warped mind existed within that peculiar little body of his?

I turned my head then and, much to my surprise, saw that Taxi was sitting a few feet away. He stared at me in such a cold way that I knew he'd heard every word Chester and I had said about him.

"Taxi!" I said, startled.

He didn't respond, but continued to glare at me.

I swallowed hard and tried to speak again. "I . . . I'm . . ."

Taxi cut me off with a menacing growl, and before I could get another word past my lips, he turned and walked away.

"He heard . . ." I said then to Chester.

"Yes," was all Chester said in reply. But there was something in the way he said it that sent a shiver down my spine.

[SIX]

The Cat Who Knew Too Much

WITHOUT warning, the sky opened and the rain came down. Lyle and Taxi ran for the shelter of their bungalows. Georgette ran to Max's, and he made no sign for her to leave. Interesting, I thought. Even more interesting was the fact that I was sitting in the middle of a pouring rain watching everyone else run for cover.

"Come on, Chester," I called out, "let's go."

"Don't be ridiculous," he shouted back. "Now is the perfect time for us to investigate."

"Perfect time?" I asked. "Investigate? Are you crazy? It's pouring."

"I know, I know. But Max and Georgette are together, and if we're clever about it, we can eavesdrop on them without their noticing. Follow me." I didn't budge. I couldn't believe Chester wanted to play detective in the middle of a storm. I was all set to return to my bungalow, but the next words he spoke got me.

"If not for me," he said, "do it for Louise."

As we approached Max's bungalow, Chester stopped and beckoned for me to bend down. He whispered, "If we could get up on the roof, we could lean over and hear everything. Give me a boost."

"How am I supposed to do that?" I asked. But Chester had already jumped up on my shoulders and from there to the top of the bungalow. "Oh," I said in answer to my own question. Seeing that I had no one's shoulders to assist me, I had little choice but to take a running leap.

"Softly!" Chester commanded as I landed next to him with a crash. "Nice move," he commented.

"I'm not as quiet as you are, Chester," I said. "I can't help it. I'm big."

"And clumsy! Well, never mind. If they heard us, I'll just go 'Ho! Ho! Ho!' and tell them Christmas is early this year."

We hung over the front of the bungalow, listening as best we could. The rain was coming down even harder now, making it almost impossible to hear what was being said inside. We couldn't see anything either because the door was just a little lower than either of us could reach with our heads.

"Listen," Chester said in a low voice, "I've got to get closer. If you hold me with your front legs, I'll be able to hang down to the top of the door and hear and see what's going on inside."

Well, I wasn't sure this was such a good idea, but as you may have figured out for yourself by now, once Chester has a notion in his head, there's no arguing him out of it. I held onto his back legs with my paws and lowered him to the front door. His tail brushed against my nose. It tickled.

"Chester," I whispered as loudly as I could, "move your tail."

"What?" he whispered back.

"Move your tail. It's tickling my nose."

"I can't hear you, Harold. Now be quiet. I think I can make out what they're saying in there. Lower me a little more."

I pushed myself forward an inch or two in order to lower Chester. With the rain coming down the way it was, the roof was getting pretty slippery and I didn't dare go much further.

"How's that?" I called out.

Chester couldn't hear me, so he didn't answer. Apparently it had worked though because I could see that his ears were standing up sharply, a good sign that he was able to hear something. Whatever he was hearing must have been good because his tail started twitching like crazy. Unfortunately, it was twitching like crazy all over my nose.

"Stop it!" I cried, as the tears started rolling down my face. Boy, did that tickle. "Chester! Chester!" I called out. But by now the rain was really coming down, and he couldn't hear a word I said. No matter which way I turned my head, Chester's tail found my nose. "Chester, you're making me laugh," I cried out desperately. I could feel myself starting to slip off the roof.

Finally, I couldn't stand it any longer. Without realizing what I was doing, I let go of Chester's legs and grabbed his tail. He plunged downward, pulling me with him. Off the slippery roof I tumbled, holding Chester tightly by the tail. Together we landed in a jumble right in front of the door to the bungalow. Max and Georgette turned to discover us lying in a puddle at their doorstep.

"Look, Max," Georgette said, "it's rainin' cats and dogs." She seemed to get quite a chuckle out of that, but Max hushed her immediately.

"Georgette, how can you laugh at a time like this?"

"But, sugar—"

"Enough now," he said emphatically. "Be still."

Chester glanced at me knowingly.

"So," Max said, turning to us, "to what do we owe the pleasure of your—shall we say, unexpected—company?"

"We were just in the neighborhood, so we thought we'd drop in," Chester replied smartly. I was impressed by the quickness of his wit. I tried to think of a quick comeback, too, but it takes me a while to think of quick comebacks. By the time I was ready, Chester had already strolled into the bungalow, casually shaking out the rain from his hair as he went. I followed his lead, but when I shook the rain out of my hair, there was nothing casual about it.

"Harold, sugar," Georgette cried, "you're makin' it rain indoors."

"Oh, sorry," I said, sheepishly.

"Well, it was nice of you to stop by, anyway," she said then. "I guess." She looked with uncertainty at Max, who glowered at Chester and said nothing.

After an awkward silence, Chester spoke. "We

were sorry to hear about Louise. If there's anything we can do . . ."

"Aw, shucks," Max said, his face softening. "That's really big of you."

"I mean, if we can help you *out* in any way," Chester added with emphasis. He looked meaningfully at Max. Max averted his eyes and pawed at the ground.

"Oh, I doubt there's anything anyone can do," he mumbled. "We'll just hope she comes back soon, that's all. Meanwhile, I'll just have to bear my sorrow alone."

Chester nodded sympathetically at Max. "Of course," he said, "we understand." And then, under his breath, he muttered, "Save it for the judge."

"What about me?" Georgette asked. "I'll bear it with you, Maxy."

"Gee, thanks, Georgette."

I noticed Chester's face out of the corner of one eye. He was taking it all in.

"Well, I suppose you're right," he said. "There really isn't anything we can do. Just wanted to let you know—" He paused dramatically and spoke with great intensity. "—that we're here if you need us."

"Right," Max said, sticking out his jaw. I gathered that for a bulldog, a stiff lower jaw was the equivalent of a stiff upper lip for the rest of us.

The rain was letting up, a perfect excuse for us to take our leave. We raced back to Chester's bungalow.

"Well, I couldn't hear everything," Chester said, as soon as we were inside, "but what I did hear was pretty incriminating."

"What does that mean?" I asked.

"It means it's not the kind of stuff you'd want your mother to know."

"Oh."

Chester bathed himself as he continued. "It seems," he said between licks, "that our friends Max and Georgette are planning to escape."

"Really?" I asked. I could feel my eyebrows take on a life of their own.

"Really," Chester replied. "The first voice I heard was Georgette's. She was saying something like 'We have to stick together and everything will be all right.' "

"Wow!"

"That's what I thought. Then Max said, 'But what if we're caught?' and Georgette said, 'That's why we have to be very careful. We'll go when it's dark. First we have to find a way out . . .' And that's all I heard."

"That's too bad," I said.

"Yes, it is," Chester agreed. "Unfortunately, a certain party who shall remain nameless dropped me right at that moment."

"Oh," I said, swallowing. I decided not to respond further. "Well," I went on, "obviously Max and Georgette are the guilty ones. They murdered Louise and now they're planning their getaway. Gee, it's hard to believe it's really happening. It's like something you'd read in a detective story."

"Not so fast," Chester cautioned. "It doesn't look good for them. But I'm still not convinced they did it."

"You're not?" I asked in surprise.

"Not at all," Chester replied. "They're not the only ones with a motive. *And* there's still a big piece of the puzzle that doesn't fit. Until it does, I won't know for sure who the murderer is."

"What's that?" I asked.

"Well, Harold, I don't know about you, but I had a lot of trouble sleeping last night. Howard and Heather were howling so much, I don't think I slept at all. If anyone had walked across the compound, much less dragged a body across it, I would have known. But I didn't see or hear anything. All night long. Doesn't that seem odd?"

I had to admit that it did. "What do you make of it?" I asked Chester.

"I don't know what to make of it," he confessed.

"Maybe whoever did it didn't want to get wet, so they waited for the rain to let up," I suggested.

"But that would mean early this morning, when it was light already. Nope. It would have been too risky."

"Then it had to be last night."

Chester was deep in thought. "Yes," he murmured softly. "Yes, last night." Suddenly, his eyes lit up. I was aware that at that moment the rain stopped. It was very still when Chester uttered his next words.

"That last piece of the puzzle, Harold?"

"Yes?"

"It just fell into place," he said.

"Huh?"

"I just figured it out, Harold." His voice became louder and more excited. "I don't know why, and I don't completely understand how, but I know who did it. Without a doubt, I know who did it."

"You know who did what?" Taxi's voice said sharply.

Surprised, I turned to see Taxi, Lyle, Georgette and Max gathered at the door of Chester's bungalow. It was Max who spoke next.

"Taxi tells us you and Harold are saying he murdered Louise," he said.

"Nonsense," Chester replied immediately. Nothing seemed to faze him.

"He said he overheard you talking."

"He may have overheard us talking, but he never heard us say he murdered Louise."

"You believe that Louise was murdered?" Georgette asked, her eyes growing wide. "How can you say such a thing?"

"I say it because it's true," Chester replied matter-of-factly.

"Oh, come on, mate," Max retorted. "You have an overstimulated imagination, if you ask me. Just like Lyle. I've always said that about cats."

Lyle was outraged. "Don't put me in the same camp as Chester," he cried. "I may be crazy, but I'm not *that* crazy! I never accused anybody of murder. He's a troublemaker. String him up! That's what I say. Let's string him up!" Hysterical, he dashed off, I presumed in search of rope.

Chester stared coolly at the three who remained. "Yes," he said, "I know who murdered Louise. I need just a little more information, and when I have it, I'll prove my case."

Max began to laugh.

"Go ahead and laugh," Chester snapped, cutting him off mid-chortle. "Yes, my friend, laugh today, for tomorrow you'll know the truth. And then, perhaps, you'll never laugh again."

I noticed that Howard and Heather had come up behind Taxi and were listening to what Chester had to say. I felt myself trembling as I beheld the five pairs of eyes staring penetratingly at Chester. It was so quiet you could have heard a doggie-pop drop.

And then, all at once, Heather threw back her head and let out an ear-splitting howl.

"Aaaah-ooooooooooooooooooo!" she cried. Gasps of shock went out from us all. She looked about her, an expression of great surprise on her face.

"So sorry," she said softly. "Just not myself. Oh, how embarrassing. I think I'd best—"

"—rest," Howard continued. "Yes, dear, I do think that's best." And off they went, their heads bobbing all the way back to their bungalows. We watched them go.

Then, without a word, Max, Georgette and Taxi followed, leaving Chester and me alone with each other and our thoughts.

I looked at Chester. A cool smile sat on his lips.

"How can you smile like that?" I asked. "Don't you realize what a dangerous thing you've done? Exposing yourself like that? Now the murderer knows you've found him out."

"Oh, I don't think I've done such a dangerous thing," Chester answered smoothly. He was quiet then, and I remember looking at him, hoping that he was right and feeling somewhere deep in my bones that he wasn't.

He was lost in thought for the rest of the day. In fact, the only time he spoke to me again was shortly before dinner.

"Just one word of warning," he said. "Keep awake tonight. The murderer may strike again. Remember: *do not sleep.* If you do, you may never wake again."

How it chills me to recall those words. Particularly when I think of them as Chester's last.

[SEVEN]

Good Night, Sweet Chester

I SHOULD have known something was wrong when tears fell on my breakfast. I looked up and saw that Jill was crying. She didn't say a word, but when she caught me looking at her, she burst into a fresh bout of sobbing. Shaking her head as if to deny something she knew to be true, she closed my door and moved on to feed the others.

I heard her move past Chester's bungalow and then I called out, "Chester, Chester." There was only silence.

"Chester," I called again. "Why is Jill crying?" Silence. "Answer me, will you? What's the matter? Cat got your tongue? Heh, heh, heh."

Again, no response. I was beginning to worry. But not so much that I let it stand in the way of breakfast.

When I looked up from my food dish, I saw that Jill was going back into the office. I knew it was risky, but I had to find out why Chester wasn't talking to me. I pushed up the latch to my door with my nose and cautiously crept over to Chester's bungalow.

A shadow fell across his door, making it hard to see inside.

"Chester?" I whispered. I strained my ears to pick up a sound. Any sound. I thought maybe he was still asleep and I'd hear his breathing. Or a rustle of movement.

"Chester!" I snapped impatiently. "Wake up!"

But then my eyes adjusted to the shadowy scene before me. I held my breath as I realized the truth.

Chester was gone!

Immediately my mind began searching for a logical explanation. He was out investigating, I told myself. He was . . . he was . . . But what

I saw next stunned me into the realization that not only was Chester gone, he might not be coming back.

The bungalow was entirely empty. No food dish. No water dish. No rug on the floor. Only a rag of a mouse hanging limply by its neck suggested that the place had once been inhabited.

I didn't know what to think then. I stood there, useless as a fire hydrant in a town without dogs, and felt the tears welling up in my eyes. Oh Chester, I thought, why didn't I listen to you? You told me to stay awake all night, and I didn't. I was so tired I fell asleep right away. And then *this* happened. It was all my fault.

Feeling thoroughly miserable, I turned my head away. And then I saw them. All the guests of Chateau Bow-Wow, their noses pressed against the fronts of their bungalows, were watching me. Their silent vigil reminded me of the scene the night before. I saw in their eyes the same look I'd seen when they'd stared at Chester, accusing him wordlessly of . . . of what? Of knowing too much, I realized. Yes, Chester had paid a price for his curiosity. And for his big mouth.

The sounds of Jill's renewed crying within the office shook me from my thoughts. Maybe Chester is sick, I thought, and they've taken him indoors. I decided to find out what I could by listening at the office window. As I crossed the compound, I thought of our eavesdropping on Max and Georgette yesterday, and a smile came to my lips. It was funny thinking of Chester's tail tickling my nose, of our falling into the mud puddle, of his saying to me—

And then I felt a lump in my throat, and I thought no more about it.

Placing my front paws on the windowsill and standing on my back legs, I was able to see inside the office. Harrison, his back to me, stood by the examining table. Jill sat in an old beat-up chair next to him. She kept dabbing her red eyes with a handkerchief. Chester, I observed, was nowhere in sight. I strained to hear as best I could.

"I can't believe it," Jill was saying, between sobs. "I just can't believe it."

"Neither can I," Harrison replied. "But it's the only explanation."

"How did it happen?" Jill asked. "That's what I don't understand. It doesn't make any sense."

"Sometimes life is like that," Harrison said, waxing philosophical. "Sometimes life just doesn't make sense."

"We're not talking about life, Harrison. We're talking about—"

"Yes, I know."

Jill stopped crying and heaved a huge sigh. After a moment of silence between them, she looked up at Harrison. "It's all my fault, you know. I did it."

"Of course you didn't, Jill," Harrison answered calmly. "You've got to stop talking like that. These things happen, that's all. It could have happened to anyone. Look, I make mistakes, too, you know."

"Maybe, but *I* was the one who cleaned out that part of the storage shed. I remember carrying that stuff out to the street for pickup. I just don't understand how it got inside the compound."

"Uh . . . well . . ." Harrison said.

Jill looked up at him. "What?" she asked.

"Nothing," Harrison answered quickly. His eyes flitted nervously from side to side.

"What were you going to say?"

"Nothing, really. I just—"

"Harrison . . ."

"Never mind, I don't want to upset you."

"I'm upset already. Tell me what you were going to say."

"Okay, if you insist. I was just remembering that when you came inside the compound, you were carrying that bag of garbage . . ."

"When Louise was barking, yes," said Jill, with a worried look. "And the bag broke. *That*'s how it got there." They both fell silent. "Harrison?" Jill said then.

"Yes?"

"May I take the rest of the day off?"

Harrison paused uncertainly. Then he said, "Of course you can. Why not? Maybe the rest will do you good."

"Yes," was all Jill said in response, and then she stood. She took off her smock and started toward the door to the front of the building. Turning back to look at Harrison (I could see her face clearly now and had to duck down so she wouldn't see me), she said, "How could it have gotten into Chester's food? Just tell me that."

This was the first I'd heard Chester's name, and I felt my stomach tighten. How could *what* have gotten into Chester's food? I listened carefully.

"I don't know," Harrison replied. "All I know is that I found the container near his bungalow, and when I tested his food—"

"Poison?"

"Poison."

Poison. The word went through me like an arrow.

Jill spoke again. "And now he's . . ."

"Gone. Yes," Harrison said.

"May I see him?" Jill asked.

Harrison stepped toward her. He put his arms out to take her by the shoulders. "Why upset yourself anymore?" he asked. "I'll take care of everything."

"And Dr. Greenbriar?"

"I'll call him. Don't worry. Just go home and rest."

What happened then I don't know. I dropped down from the windowsill, no longer caring about anything more I might hear or see. I'd heard quite enough. Slowly, I stumbled back to my bungalow. Everyone may have been watching me still, but I have no recollection of anything except the lump in my throat growing larger with every step I took. And the thought that my best friend in the whole world was gone. Poisoned. And all because he knew too much.

Back inside my bungalow, I curled up as tight as I could and fell into a deep sleep.

[EIGHT]

Harold X, Private Eye

I AWAKENED to the sound of cloth being torn. From the low growls that followed, I surmised that a game of Rip-the-Rag was in progress. Slowly, I opened my eyes and stared out into the bright sunlight. At last, the storm had passed, and from the sight of animals at play before me, it appeared that all was well with the world. Max, Georgette and Taxi tugged at what looked like an old towel. Heather sat sunning herself, while Howard dug at the earth in the far corner of the compound. Lyle was wrapped around a ball of some kind, kicking at it with his hind feet. The scene was so inviting that for one brief moment, I wanted to run outside and join in the play.

And then I remembered Chester. My heart sank. And the thought occurred to me: someone out there, some seemingly innocent frolicker, was really a cold-blooded killer. How could I play with a murderer? I asked myself. And who could it be? Who could it be?

I cast my eye over each in turn.

Georgette let go of the towel and, merrily darting back and forth, nipped at Max's ankles. Sure, I thought, she has reason to be happy. With Louise out of the picture, she's got Max all to herself now. He didn't seem so miserable either, I noticed. How quickly his grief had spent itself. Well, why not? After all, if he had bumped Louise off, no one but Chester knew. A little poison in Chester's food, and there was no more need to pretend. Soon he and Georgette would run away together. Everything was going according to plan. Why shouldn't he be happy?

And Taxi? I watched as he collided with Max's shoulder. He fell back onto the grass and rolled around, scratching his back. Max ran off with the rag, waving it in the air. Suddenly, Taxi lurched to his feet and, picking up the challenge, grabbed one end of the rag from Max. They tugged in opposite directions. How pleased Taxi must be, I thought, if he were the culprit. After all, he'd wanted so badly to impress Max, to be his best friend. And now, it appeared, he had given Max everything he could ask for . . . and more. And, in return, he'd gotten everything he'd wanted, too. It was not easy to forget Taxi's interest in murder by poison. How excited he'd been when he first mentioned it to Max and me. No, he might appear on the surface to be a little dumb, but Taxi was no dumb dog.

The sound of scratching drew my eyes to Howard. What was he doing, anyway? He seemed to be digging a hole. To bury a bone, I thought. Or perhaps something else. He kept looking furtively over his shoulder, as if he were afraid of being caught. My glance fell on Heather. How strange the two of them were. Perhaps Chester had been right, maybe they were werewolves. I vowed to keep my eye on them.

Suddenly, Lyle sprang up and attacked a leaf that happened to blow by in the passing breeze. "Gotcha, you little devil," he cried. "You thought you could escape the long arm of the law, eh? Well, take that. And that." And he bludgeoned the poor leaf into a fine powder. He was an oddball, no question about it. I remembered his threat to Louise. And then his words from the night before popped into my head. "Let's string him up!" he had exclaimed as he ran off. Lyle was just crazy enough, I concluded, to carry out his threats. Murder would be as natural to him as playing with a ball of yarn was to most cats.

Just then, the door to the office opened, and Harrison stepped outside, coming in my direction. "Hey, Harold," he called out cheerily, "it's about time you were up. You going to sleep all day?"

"Woof," I answered.

"Oh, yeah? What kind of thing is that to say?"

Frankly, I wasn't sure myself what I meant by it.

He opened my door. "Come on," he said, "it's

almost time for dinner. How about getting a little exercise?"

Leaving my bungalow, I observed Harrison out of the corner of my eye. He was whistling now. His cheeks were puffed out and red from the force with which he blew the melody (such as it was) through his lips. Gee, he seemed happy, I thought. There was a twinkle in his eye as he patted my head and said, "Good boy, Harold." From anybody else, such good cheer would have been normal behavior. From Harrison, it was definitely suspect.

What if he's the one? I thought. Maybe he's in cahoots with Dr. Greenbriar, as Chester once suspected. Maybe they're doing some kind of awful experiment in their laboratory and . . . A shudder went through me as I thought of poor Louise and Chester in the laboratory of a mad doctor. I didn't let myself think about it any longer.

Harrison went back inside, and I surveyed the scene before me. Georgette and Max had gone off by themselves, and Taxi was rolling on the ground playing alone with the remains of the towel. It was at that moment I decided to take matters into my own paws.

I remembered something Chester had once said to me when I had refused to go along with him to investigate another of his little hunches. I'd promised him I'd stay home and think about it.

"Sure, sure," he'd said, "you may *think* about it, Harold, but I'm the one who will *do* something about it."

"What do you mean by that?" I'd asked.

"Cats are doers. Dogs are not. That's what I mean."

"I think you may be overstating your case."

"Think what you will," he'd said as he'd walked away. "The fact is that *I* am the one who's trying to do something. While you, O passive pooch, wrap yourself around your food dish and do nothing."

Once more I felt the sting of Chester's accusation. Do nothing! I thought. I'll show him he's not the only one with a brain. And so, with gritted teeth and a sense of great determination, I set out to unearth the truth.

I decided to start with Taxi, and I figured I'd catch him off guard with a direct assault.

"What do you know, Taxi?" I queried.

Taxi looked at me blankly. Perhaps that had been the wrong approach. I tried again.

"How are you, Taxi?"

"Oh hello, Harold," Taxi said, as if seeing me for the first time.

"Some storm we've been having, eh?" I asked him.

"Oh, I'm all right, I guess."

"What?"

"Fine, thanks." There was a pause as Taxi and I looked at each other. "You asked how I am, and I'm telling you I'm fine."

"Oh. Yes. I see."

"How are you?"

"I'm okay, I guess."

"You're welcome."

"Huh?"

"Oh, I'm sorry. I thought you were going to say 'thank you.' "

"For what?"

"For asking how you are."

"Oh," I said, "I'm sorry."

"That's all right."

"Thank you."

"You're welcome."

I looked at Taxi a long time. Suddenly, I couldn't remember what I had wanted to ask him, or why. Knowing Taxi, I decided, was definitely one of life's more confusing experiences.

"You're probably wondering how I got the name 'Taxi,' " Taxi mumbled so softly that at first I thought he was talking to himself.

"Well, no, I wasn't really, I—"

"Then I'll tell you, Harold."

"Thank you," I said, wondering when the dinner bell would ring.

"You see, I was owned by these people in New York City who thought that when they took me out for a walk, it would be cute to call 'Taxi!' People who live in New York City think things like that are cute. It's the air pollution that does it to them, I think. Anyway, for a long time, whenever they called 'Taxi' I thought they were really calling a taxi, so I wouldn't come. And the taxi drivers thought they were calling a taxi, too, so they'd pull up. So all the time they were getting all these taxis they didn't want and taxi drivers were getting mad at them and meanwhile I was wandering off down the street 'cause I didn't know they were calling me . . ."

"What happened?" I asked.

"Oh, eventually I figured out that 'Taxi' was my name, but by then I think they'd gotten bored with the whole thing. They bought roller skates and gave me to their cousin who lives in town here."

"Air pollution is a terrible thing," I commented.

"Mmmm," Taxi murmured, as he rolled over on his back. Just then, I remembered why I'd started this conversation in the first place. Interesting, I thought, how neatly he'd gotten me off the track.

"Taxi, I want to ask you something."

"Oh, hello, Harold."

"Where were you on the night of . . . uh

. . . um . . . uh . . . last night?" I asked forthrightly.

"Huh?"

"Your whereabouts last night, Taxi."

"My what, Harold?"

"Your whereabouts!" Taxi looked up at me as if his brain had just gone out to lunch. *"Where . . . were . . . you . . . last . . . night?"*

"Oh, why didn't you say so?" He paused for a moment. Now, I had him! I could feel it. "In my bungalow, of course. Just like everyone else. Why do you ask?"

Oh, he was a slippery devil. But I wasn't going to be fooled so easily. I thought how proud Chester would have been of my investigatory skills.

"The truth now, Taxi!" I said. "Tell me the truth."

"Okay," he said.

"That's better," I replied encouragingly.

"I was in my bungalow."

"You said that already."

"I know."

"Why are you telling me the same story?"

"Because it's true. And you asked me to tell you the truth, didn't you, Harold?"

"Yes, I did . . ." I could feel myself beginning to falter.

"I'm sorry about Chester," Taxi said then in a voice full of sympathy.

"Me, too," I said, completing my falter.

"Want to play Rip-the-Rag?" he offered.

Downhearted, I began to walk away. "No thanks," I called back over my shoulder. "Maybe another time."

"Okay," Taxi called out lightly. " 'Bye, Harold." And he returned to his tug-of-war with himself.

Not feeling particularly encouraged by the results of my investigation thus far, I was almost ready to give up and go home when I saw that Howard had stopped digging and was now sitting next to Heather in front of their adjoining bungalows. As I approached, I watched their heads move up and down and couldn't help thinking how terrific they'd look on the back window ledge of an old Chevy.

"Good afternoon," I said.

They stopped talking immediately and stared at me as if they'd been caught chewing on a leg of the dining room table. Neither said a word.

I cleared my throat. "Uh . . . good afternoon," I repeated.

They glanced into each other's eyes. No one spoke for what felt like a very long time. In a tiny voice, Howard finally said, "Good afternoon."

There was a pause. I decided to plunge in.

"Where were you last night?" I asked.

"Not much in the mood for conversation at the moment, Harold old chap. Frightfully sorry. It's just that we're—"

"Now, now, now," Heather interjected crisply, cutting Howard off from saying another word.

I had no choice but to plunge right back out again. "Well, another time perhaps," I said.

"Yes, yes," Howard said with a crooked little smile.

"Another time," Heather said firmly. And then just to make certain I got the message, she added, "Goodbye, Harold."

"Goodbye," I said, walking away and muttering under my breath, "It was nice talking with you."

Fortunately, I had no time to brood further over my lack of success, for I saw that Max and Georgette were coming toward me. I felt a little nervous. After all, they were prime suspects, and I didn't want to blow my examination. I considered how best to approach them. Clearly, they were too smart not to recognize a direct attack. No, with them, I reasoned, I would have to be subtle. I would work my way into it slowly, craftily, never letting them suspect what I was up to.

"Beautiful day, isn't it?" I asked casually, as they stopped before me.

"Oh, yes," replied Georgette. She smiled sweetly.

"Right you are, Harold," Max added.

"Well, speaking of what a beautiful day it is, last night certainly wasn't, so where were you?" I was extremely impressed with myself. If only Chester could have been there, I thought, to see just how clever and subtle I could be when I put my mind to it.

"What?" Max asked, pretending to be confused.

I heard the dinner bell ring and saw Harrison making his rounds. Drat, what a time to be distracted by food. Just when I had them on the ropes!

I'd forgotten exactly what we were talking about, but I didn't let that stand in my way. "A likely story!" I snapped.

Georgette looked concerned. "Harold, do you think maybe you've been out in the sun too long?" she asked.

An interesting ploy, I thought, trying to make *me* look like the suspicious one.

"Harold, pal," Max said gruffly, "it's been terrific chewing the fat with you, but we've got to run. Chow time, you know what I mean?"

I do indeed, I thought. Any excuse to get away, eh? "Think about what I've said," I told Max and Georgette as they started to go. I wasn't going to let them off the hook so easily. "You know where you can reach me if you have anything you need to get off your chest."

Max gave me a puzzled look, just to keep me thinking he was innocent, no doubt. "Sure, mate," he uttered, "anything you say."

"Oh, Harold," Georgette said then, "there is something."

"Yes?" Ah, a confession at last.

"We're sorry about Chester."

I'll bet you are, I thought. Just like you were sorry about Louise. But "Thanks," was all I said.

"Hey, Harold, let's go," Harrison called out. "Soup's on."

As long as it isn't split pea, I thought.

AFTER checking my dinner out for any uninvited smells or tastes, I plunged in. I was starved, which was understandable considering the amount of energy I'd used up conducting a tough and unyielding criminal investigation. The only thing that bothered me about it was that I'd unearthed no new evidence.

What I *had* unearthed was doubt. Doubt in my own mind that anyone at Chateau Bow-Wow was the culprit. Or indeed that a crime had taken place. Perhaps Chester had conjured the whole thing up in his twisted imagination. It *was* possible, after all, that Louise had run away, just as everyone had said. And it may have been just an accident that led to Chester's poisoning. Perhaps all of it, I reasoned, was the unfortunate result of Jill's carelessness.

It was then that I noticed the writing on the bottom of my food dish. The letters were smudged so that it was hard to make out what it said at first. Boy, I thought, the least they could do is serve dinner in bowls you can read. I was definitely going to complain about the service. I strained my eyes and looked into the depths of my bowl.

The last word was "now." I had no trouble reading it because it was the only one that wasn't marked up. After a moment's consideration, I could see that the first word was "Hello!" The end of that word was messy, but "Hello!" it was. Of that I was certain. Because of all the black marks, the three words in the middle were harder to decipher. But having hung out around Toby when he did crossword puzzles on the living room floor,

I was pretty good at working my way around black marks. So, finally, I was able to figure it out. With a great sense of accomplishment, I uttered my findings out loud.

" 'Hello! How's your tummy now?' "

Fine, thank you, I replied silently, although my eyes are a little out of focus.

I went to the water dish, thinking what a cute thing that had been for a food dish to say. Too bad it had been so hard to read though. I thought of what a time I'd had trying to make out the word "tummy." It was almost as if someone had tried to cross it out deliberately.

Suddenly, my ears went up. I lifted my head from the water dish. What if . . . ? I asked myself. What if someone *had* tried to cross it out?

Again, I studied the bottom of my food dish, but this time with a new intent. How could I have missed it? This wasn't an old, worn-out bowl, and these weren't random smudges. Someone was trying to tell me something.

Looking at it this way, I saw a new message emerge. "Hello!" became "Help." "How's" became "Howls." The third word was a little harder to make clear, but I finally read it as "out." "Tummy" had been smudged out entirely, and "now" was left as it was.

"Hello! How's your tummy now?" became

"Help Howls out now "

The sky was getting cloudy. A low rumble of thunder made it clear that the day's sunshine had been only a brief respite from the storm.

Help howls out now, I thought, as I lay down to sleep.

"Help howls out now."

What did it mean?

[NINE]

And Then There Were Three

IT WAS useless trying to sleep. Even if I'd been able to get the message of the food dish out of my mind (which I wasn't), my eardrums were assaulted by Howard's and Heather's ceaseless caterwauling. It seemed worse than usual that night, with one taking up the howl as soon as the other had left off. With it all, the storm was again raging in full force, thunder and lightning exploding in the air like a giant fireworks display. In short, Chateau Bow-Wow was not exactly slumber heaven that night.

"Help howls out now." I turned the phrase

over and over in my head. I had already decided that "howls" referred to Howard and Heather. Someone was telling me to help them out. But who? And why? They seemed perfectly capable of taking care of themselves. The way they kept apart from everyone else, they probably wouldn't accept help even if it were offered. Unless—and here I stopped for a moment to consider this new thought—unless *they* had sent the message. Maybe they were saying, "Help *us* out now." Were they in trouble? Were they, in fact, the next victims?

A sudden crash of thunder startled me into the realization that it had become very still. For several minutes there had been no thunder. And no howling. Why? I asked myself. And then a flash of lightning revealed it all.

In that fleeting moment of illumination, I saw two figures scurrying across the compound. Howard and Heather are out, I thought. And then the words in the food dish took on a new meaning. What if, instead of "Help howls out now," it read "Help! Howls out now"?

A scene rapidly played itself out in my mind. Chester is eating his dinner. He looks up. Howard and Heather are staring at him through the wire mesh of his bungalow. He realizes that they have put poison in his food, and as he takes a last gasp of breath (I could feel the tears coming to my eyes as I imagined this part), he finds some way to scratch out the message on the bottom of his food dish, hoping that somehow it would reach me. A cry for help. A warning from beyond! That was it, I was certain.

Without giving a thought to what I'd do once I got there, I threw open my door and raced across the compound to Howard's and Heather's bungalows. Taxi must have seen me coming, because he called out, "Harold!"

I didn't answer.

"Harold, is that you? What are you doing? What's going on?"

I stopped dead in my tracks. Howard and Heather were gone.

"They're out again!" I cried. "On the loose!"

"What are you talking about?" Taxi asked. "Who's out?"

"Howard and Heather," I answered. "Have you seen them, Taxi? We have to find them before it's too late."

"Sure, I've seen them. Seems like I've seen everybody tonight."

"What do you mean?" I asked. "Who have you seen?"

"I just told you, Harold. Everybody. Well, everybody but you, that is. Until now, that is. Now, I've seen you, too. Boy, it's been some night. Try and sleep? Forget it."

"*Who* have you seen?" I demanded again.

"*Everybody!* First Howard and Heather were running around. I thought that was pretty silly. I mean, with the rain coming down like it is and all. Seems to me it's a good night to stay at home, you know what I mean?"

"Who else?"

"Oh, well, then Max and Georgette . . ."

"So they were out, too," I said under my breath.

"Yeah. I thought, boy, some night for a picnic. Then I got mad that I wasn't invited, so I went to the back of my bungalow and sulked."

"And Lyle?"

"I don't know if he sulked or not. He probably did, knowing him. But you'll have to ask him yourse—"

"No, no," I interrupted. "I mean, was he out, too?"

"Oh." Taxi paused for a moment to think it over. "Yes. No, no, I don't think so. Maybe. I'm not sure."

I glanced over at Lyle's bungalow. I heard him muttering to himself inside. And then I cast my eyes in the direction of Max's and Georgette's bungalows. They were both empty. Mystery upon mystery, I thought. What did it all mean?

I thought back to the message at the bottom of the food dish. If it read "Help! Howls out now," it might mean that Howard and Heather were the murderers and that they'd now killed Max and Georgette. Or if it read "Help howls out now," it could mean that Howard and Heather were next on the list of victims, that Max and Georgette were the killers and they'd struck again. Now they'd escaped, just as they had planned. My mind was spinning.

"Taxi," I said, scratching myself behind the ear.

"Yes, Harold?"

"What do you make of it?"

"Oh, I'd say it should let up by tomorrow morning."

"Huh?"

"I think it'll blow over soon. This is just a little squall. I don't think—"

"I'm not talking about the storm, Taxi," I said sharply.

"Oh."

"I'm talking about all these strange disappearances."

"I don't know what to make of it, Harold," Taxi said after thinking a moment. "But I'll tell you one thing."

"What's that?"

"I sure will be glad to get back home."

I looked around the compound. There were three of us left. Three out of nine who had started the week at Chateau Bow-Wow.

"So will I, Taxi," I said softly. "So will I."

* * *

BACK INSIDE my bungalow, I shook myself dry and lay down to think. I really didn't know what was left for me to do. Obviously, I'd been too late. Whatever the message had meant, Howard and Heather were gone, and there was no longer anything anyone could do to help. With a heavy heart, I shut my eyes and tried once again to sleep.

I shall never forget my dream that night. I was the only one left. In all of Chateau Bow-Wow, perhaps in all the world, I was the only one left. I went running from bungalow to bungalow, crying "They're gone! They're gone!" And then, from all around me, a terrible cry went up. It was like Howard's and Heather's howling, but echoing and coming from all directions. I tried to run from it. I ran in a big circle, round and round, attempting to escape the awful sound. "They're gone!" I cried again, as the howling reverberated in my ears. And then I felt myself being kicked. Over and over. It was Chester. Or the ghost of Chester. Kicking me and accusing me. "You blew it!" he snarled. "I tried to tell you, but you couldn't figure it out until it was too late. Boy, leave it to a dumb dog!" The kicking went on and on. It was so bad that it woke me up. "Chester!" I cried, thinking I was still in my nightmare.

"It's about time!" a voice replied.

I shook my head, trying to make clear if I was asleep or awake.

"Boy, Harold, nobody sleeps the way you do. Even for a dog, you're in a class by yourself!" I'd know that voice anywhere. And those insults! It could only be . . .

"Chester!" I cried.

"Well, give the little dog a big cigar!" he said.

There was no doubt about it. I was awake. And Chester was back.

[TEN]

Mystery, Mayhem and Mud

I COULDN'T believe my eyes.

"Was it all a dream?" I asked Chester.

"Of course it wasn't," he said. "Now, come on. We've got to move fast."

I was still blinking in disbelief when I heard a howl that sounded like the one in my dream. Echoing eerily, it sent a shiver all through me.

"Howard and Heather!" I exclaimed. "It's them, isn't it, Chester? They're the ones, aren't they?"

"Yes, yes, yes," he answered impatiently.

"It's been them all along, hasn't it?"

"Come on, Harold! Move!"

As I was pulling myself to my feet, I heard a voice call out, "They're gone!"

"Chester!" I cried in amazement, "This is just like my dream. The echo. The voice. Everything. What's happening? Who just said 'They're gone!'?"

"Harrison," he replied quickly, as he pushed against my hind legs (which were still sitting) with the top of his head. "No more questions, Harold. Just follow me. We've got to get the others."

"And help Harrison find Howard and Heather," I added, but Chester was already out the door and couldn't hear me.

By the time I found him, he was already scratching at the door of Lyle's bungalow.

Lyle was talking in his sleep. "Oh, yeah?" he was mumbling. "Says who? Think you're a tough guy, huh?"

"Psst, Agent 47X," Chester whispered.

Lyle's eyes popped open. He regarded Chester with a look of total befuddlement.

"Wake up!" Chester commanded.

Something inside Lyle snapped into focus. "What is it, Agent 37B1943X10YKLB97—" I think he would have gone on till morning if Chester hadn't cut him off.

"A secret mission. Follow me," he said.

Lyle flipped open his door and crawled out. He looked stealthily out of slitted eyes and kept low to the ground as Chester led the way to Taxi's bungalow.

"Don't let Harrison see you," Chester hissed back at us.

"But why?" I started to ask, when Chester cut me off with a sharp *"Sshhh!"* We continued creeping across the muddy compound until we arrived at Taxi's. He was wide awake and looked out at us as if he'd been half-expecting our arrival.

"Boy-oh-boy-oh-boy," he said in greeting. "Can't a soul get any sleep around this place? What is going on, anyway?"

"Ask Chester," I replied.

"Okay," Taxi said, and then with a start, he exclaimed: "Chester!"

"Sshhh!" Chester retorted.

"Chester!" cried Taxi again, but this time in a tiny voice. "You're back!"

"Yes, yes, I'm back."

"But how—"

"I'll explain later. Right now, we've got more important things to deal with."

"How do I know you're not a ghost?" Taxi went on. "Do something so I'll know you're not a ghost."

"How would it be if I bit your nose?" Chester hissed through clenched teeth. "Would that be proof enough for you?"

Taxi thought a moment. "Yes," he said then, "yes, I guess that would do it."

"Agent 35HBO7575NFL13YXX42—"

"Hike!" Taxi cried.

"What is it, Lyle?" Chester asked, turning his head.

"Can we get this operation underway? I was in the middle of a good dream."

Chester shook his head in dismay. "What a crew! I should have done this myself."

"Done what?" I asked. "I still don't understand—"

There was a crash of thunder and, in the accompanying lightning, I could see Harrison standing several yards away. Chester noticed, too, and motioned to us to huddle together and keep our voices down. Taxi crept out of his bungalow and put his head close to mine.

"Howard and Heather are somewhere nearby," Chester told us. "We have to get to them before it's too late."

"Help! Howls out now!" I thought.

"What should we do?" I asked, as the rain quieted to a steady drizzle.

"Just wait," Chester ordered.

"For what?" queried Taxi.

"For a sound that will tell us where they are."

Thinking he meant their howls, I was not at all prepared for what I heard next. Or for its significance.

My ears perked up as tiny yips resounded softly through the murmur of the rain.

"It's happened," Chester said softly.

"What has?" I asked.

"Sshh. Listen."

I did as Chester bade me, but what I was listening for, I didn't have a clue. The yipping sound continued, echoing as if from a great distance. And yet, I had the feeling it was coming from someplace very near.

"That's it!" Chester cried. "I know where they are! Let's go!"

At the very same moment, Harrison shouted, "I know where you are, you little devils! Now I've got you!"

Chester and Harrison both ran to the corner of the compound near Howard's bungalow. I was relieved to see that Chester no longer cared whether or not Harrison saw us. After all, if we were going to help him, he may as well know about it.

"Chester!" Harrison cried out, as he and my feline friend reached the same spot at the same time. "Where did you come from?" I imagined that it must have been quite a shock to Harrison's system to see Chester returned from the dead. But he appeared to be so determined to find Howard and Heather that he didn't dwell on it.

"Never mind," he muttered, as he began pulling at a plank of the back fence, "I'll deal with you later. Right now, I've got . . . to . . . get this . . . off." The plank, which was somewhat loose to begin with, tore off suddenly in Harrison's hands and fell to the side.

At first I couldn't see anything, but then Harrison shined his flashlight through the opening in the fence, and what I beheld on the other side amazed me.

There, inside the storage shed, their eyes gleaming in panic at the sudden intrusion, were Howard and Heather. A discarded rainpipe ran along the ground from where they sat to the opening in the fence. No doubt that accounted for the echoing effect of their howling, I reasoned. As for the yipping sound of moments before, that was quickly accounted for, too. For there, next to Heather, huddled five or six squirming newborn puppies. Their yips, no longer amplified by the rainpipe, were as tiny as they themselves.

In the glare of Harrison's light, Howard began to bark.

Harrison laughed. "Sorry, ol' boy," he said,

"but you're going to have to come with me."

"Jump him!" Chester shouted. "Taxi, go for his ankles. Harold—"

"But, Chester," I stammered, "I thought we were supposed to help Harrison find Howard and Heather. Weren't they the ones we were after?"

"Yes, yes, of course," Chester snapped. "But not because they're the murderers. Don't you see? Harrison's the one! And it's Howard and Heather he's been after the whole time!"

Well, I didn't see at all, of course, but I decided this was not the time for further discussion. Particularly not when I looked up and saw Harrison glaring down at me.

"What are you all doing here, anyway?" he uttered in a low, threatening voice. "Get out of here! All of you! Move!"

We sat, riveted to our spots. Suddenly, Harrison lunged at me. I didn't know which way to turn.

"Jump, Agent16IQ!" Lyle shouted in my direction, as he leaped onto Harrison's shoulders.

I jumped. Harrison lunged. And he landed, face first, in a big puddle.

"Mmmphhgrrux," he said (or something to that effect), as he lifted his head out of the mucky water. "Get off of me, you stupid cat!" He tried to shake Lyle loose, but Lyle was going nowhere.

"The game is up, NY7!" Lyle cried out. "Your spying days are over." He dug his claws in to get a firmer hold, and Harrison let out a yelp. He struggled to his feet; Lyle held on tight.

"Taxi!" Chester cried out. "The ankles! I'll join Lyle. And Harold—"

"Yes?" I asked. I wasn't very good at rough stuff, so I wasn't sure what I could do to be of help.

"Bark!" Chester commanded.

"But, Chester, you know how I hate the sound of barking."

"Bark!" Chester ordered again.

I wasn't sure what good it would do, but I did as I was told. Loudly, I barked. Howard joined in.

Chester jumped up onto Harrison's back and Taxi began nipping at his ankles.

"Hey, what's going on here?" Harrison cried. "Get off of me! Ouch!" Chester must have gotten in a good one. "What's with you animals all of a sudden? Ow, Taxi, get away from my feet!" Harrison kicked at Taxi, who fell over backwards.

"Are you okay?" I asked, concerned that he'd hurt himself.

"I'm fine," Taxi answered. He broke into a smile. "Isn't this fun?" he asked. And then he dove for Harrison's feet again.

"Break his thumbs!" Lyle was shouting gleefully. "We'll teach him a thing or two!"

"Attaboy, Lyle!" Chester said encouragingly. "Come on, Harold, what happened to the barking?"

Oh yeah.

"Woof! Woof!" I couldn't help thinking how dumb I sounded, but, unfortunately, a dog's vocabulary is limited. Just then, I heard a car pull into the driveway. Maybe "woof" wasn't so dumb after all; it seemed to have done the job.

The gate to Chateau Bow-Wow flew open, and Jill and Dr. Greenbriar rushed in. They were followed by Max, Georgette and—yes, it had to be, it was—Louise!

"Okay, Harrison, that's enough!" Dr. Greenbriar shouted.

Harrison froze to the spot. His eyes widened in amazement as his mouth fell open, and his flashlight fell to the ground. The light went out.

There was a long moment of silence, and then Jill's voice cut through it like a knife.

"Harrison, how could you?" she said at last.

Harrison mumbled something under his breath, as Jill and Dr. Greenbriar moved in closer to confront him face to face. Lyle and Chester hung stubbornly from Harrison's shoulders.

"I only hope, Harrison," Dr. Greenbriar said, "for your sake as well as theirs, that no harm has come to any of these animals."

"When I think of how I trusted you . . ." Jill interjected.

"How did . . . did you . . . how did you . . ." Harrison stuttered.

"Oh, I knew you were up to something after I called you tonight, Harrison," Jill answered. "You were so strange on the phone. Nervous and jumpy. I'd never heard you like that before. And then, well, I thought about how weird it was that you were here instead of home in the first place. I mean, *that* dedicated you're not."

"I never should have answered the phone," Harrison said weakly.

"Yes, that was your first mistake. And then on the way over here, we passed your house and found the dogs barking outside your window."

"I don't know what's going on," Dr. Greenbriar said, "but you and I have to talk, Harrison. First, I want to take a look at everyone and get them back into their bungalows. I'll check on Howard and Heather and the kids. If they're all right, we'll leave them where they are for the night. Harrison, wait inside the office until I come in. I want a full explanation. And then . . ." and here he paused dramatically, staring into Harrison's eyes, ". . . then we'll decide your fate."

Harrison hung his head as Dr. Greenbriar moved beyond him and through the opening in the fence. Jill stayed where she was.

"I just can't believe you'd do such a thing!" she said vehemently, her eyes connecting with the top of Harrison's unruly thatch of hair. "What got into you, anyway?" she demanded. "Was *this* how you were going to make a million dollars? By lying? And kidnapping?! And murder? And on top of everything, making it look like it was all my fault! I can't believe it, that's all! I just can't believe you're capable of such evil."

Harrison continued to stare at the ground, avoiding Jill's gaze.

"Well?" she asked after a moment. "Don't you have anything to say for yourself?"

Harrison shrugged and lifted his head slightly. In a soft voice, he uttered his defense. "You can't blame a person for trying."

Jill just shook her head slowly and watched as Harrison shuffled off toward the office door. Then, she moved away to join Dr. Greenbriar in the storage shed. Chester and Lyle jumped down from Harrison's shoulders. And Taxi came over to me with a piece of Harrison's sock hanging from his mouth. A souvenir of his night of bravery, no doubt.

When he reached the office door, Harrison turned back and sighed heavily. I almost felt sorry for him then and turned to Chester to tell him so.

"Don't waste your pity," Chester replied. "When I tell you about Harrison, you're not going to have such a soft spot in your heart for him."

Just then, Louise walked over to me. "Scott," she said to me softly. I wanted to remind her that my name was Harold, but she continued before I could say anything. "Scott, I know you have held out hope that we'd get together. But I am going back to Chip. He wants me . . . and, well, I am wanting him. I'm going to forgive and forget. No matter what has been between him and Liza. Forgive and forget, Scott, I hope you can understand." She walked back to Max's side.

Chester and I turned to each other.

"What terrible thing did Harrison do to Louise?" I asked in shock. "Mind control?"

"Worse," Chester answered. "Two days of afternoon television."

I looked back at Louise and a feeling of horror overwhelmed me. Chester was right. There could be no pity for Harrison.

[ELEVEN]

In the Days That Followed . . .

IN THE DAYS that followed, a calm fell over Chateau Bow-Wow. After that fateful night, the storm died down and was replaced by hot, sunny weather. Heather was moved indoors with her babies; and Howard, when he wasn't inside visiting, was proudly extolling the virtues of family life. He also handed out bones on which he'd written, "It's a boy . . . and a boy . . . and a girl . . . and a boy . . . and a girl . . . and a girl . . . and a boy." I was very moved by his gift. Chester was nauseated.

"Typical dog present," he grunted after Howard

walked away.

"What do you mean 'typical'?"

"You wouldn't catch a cat giving out used bones," he replied, as he rolled over on his back to bask in the sun. After a moment, he added, "Yuck! Just the thought of it—"

"Hello, Harold," a voice called out. It was Taxi, stopping by to chat. I told him I was sorry for thinking he might have murdered Louise and Chester, and he readily accepted my apology.

"Under the circumstances," he said to me, "it's understandable that you'd think I might have done it. After what I said about poison, I mean—"

"Yes," I replied, "and you seemed pretty upset about Max and Georgette, too."

"Well, I was a little jealous, I'll admit. But, Harold, do you really think I'd murder someone just because I was jealous?"

I was embarrassed that such a thought had ever crossed my mind. Chester, naturally, wasn't embarrassed in the least.

"It happens all the time," he said. "Besides, just because you look like you wouldn't hurt a fly doesn't mean you aren't capable. I checked into your file while I was being held in the office, and I found out a thing or two."

"Really?" Taxi asked in surprise. "What kinds of things?"

Chester just smiled.

"You read the files?" I asked.

"Yup," he said. "Harrison and I pored over every single one of them that evening. And let me tell you, there was some pretty interesting stuff in there."

I started to panic. I was hoping there was nothing in my file about the incident with the geranium. I mean, it had been in poor taste (and it tasted pretty poor, too) to eat Mrs. Monroe's favorite plant. I didn't sleep too well after that one, but whether that was from an unclear conscience or an unsettled stomach, I wasn't too sure.

Chester must have been reading my thoughts. He looked into my eyes with a knowing little smirk.

"Geranium?" I inquired innocently.

He nodded his head. Was nothing sacred? I

thought. Boy, you make one mistake in life and they never let you forget.

"There was also mention of the episode with Mr. Monroe's electric shaver," he added.

Boy, you make two mistakes in life and they never let you forget. That one wasn't really my fault anyway. Could I help it if I thought he was being attacked by an oversized bumblebee? It was a perfectly logical error.

"Clever of you to grab the shaver with your teeth and toss it in the toilet the way you did," Chester commented.

Taxi looked at me with a queer sort of expression on his face. I couldn't tell whether he was appalled that I had done such a stupid thing or appalled that he hadn't been as clever under similar circumstances. He just shook his head slowly and said, "You're some dog, Harold."

I decided to take it as a compliment. "Thanks," I replied.

"Yeah, you're some dog, all right," Chester joined in. "So clever you couldn't even figure out the message I sent you until it was too late."

"So it *was* from you," I said.

"Of course it was from me, you ninny. What did you think it was, a fan letter from Taxi here?"

Taxi looked puzzled. "What message?" he asked.

"Oh, just a little after-dinner reading I sent Harold," he answered.

"Huh?"

I was getting fed up. I had tried and tried to get Chester to tell me the whole story, but he kept pleading emotional fatigue. "Come on, Chester," I said. "Tell us what really happened."

"Okay, okay," Chester said irritably. "I'm still suffering from mental exhaustion, of course—"

"Would you like to suffer from physical exhaustion as well?" I asked between my teeth.

He picked up his tail with one paw and began to bathe it. "Boy, talk about impatience," he said.

Taxi whispered to me, "Is he going to tell us the story or take a bath?"

"I know Chester," I answered quietly, "and he always bathes his tail before he settles down. Don't worry."

"If you two boys in the back row will stop whispering," Chester said then, dropping his tail, "I'll begin." And so it was that I learned the true story of the strange events at Chateau Bow-Wow.

"AS I WAS eating dinner the other night," Chester began, "I felt myself growing drowsy. Oh, no, I thought, how could I be so dumb? I was so worried about staying awake that I hadn't even considered the obvious. And here it was, right before me."

"Here what was?" I asked. Chester stopped and gave me a look through half-closed eyelids.

"The food, Harold," he said.

"Oh."

"After all, we knew Louise hadn't eaten all of her dinner the night before. And we knew there was a good chance she'd been poisoned. By that time, I had figured out that Harrison was the culprit, so I—"

"How did you know that?" I asked.

"Patience, Harold. You can't rush a great mind."

"Oh. I'm sorry, Chester."

"That's all right. Now, where was I?"

"Something about a great mind," I said.

"Before that, you dolt."

"Oh . . . uh . . ."

"Oh, yes. So it stood to reason that if Harrison had poisoned Louise, he might pull the same trick on someone else. As I say, this thought didn't occur to me until I'd already eaten some of my dinner and was beginning to drift off. I tried to call out to you, Harold, but my voice was fading. You couldn't hear me."

I felt awful thinking of my poor, dear friend calling out for help in the bungalow next door and me being unable to heed his plea.

"Of course, you were slurping your food so loudly," he went on, "you wouldn't have heard me if I'd used a microphone and loudspeakers. Anyway, before I knew it, I was asleep."

"Then what happened?" Taxi asked.

"I slept."

"Oh," Taxi said, taking it in. "That makes sense."

"When I woke up, it was dark all around me. I didn't know where I was or how I had gotten there. After a while, my eyes made out a window, and with the help of the little bit of light coming through it, I could tell that I was inside a cage of some kind. I tried to undo the latch, but there was a heavy padlock on the outside. Seeing that there was no way to escape, I had no choice but to wait it out till morning.

"When I awoke again, it was light in the room, and I realized I was inside Greenbriar's office. Suddenly, Harrison's face appeared before me. I felt my heart pounding in my chest.

" 'Good morning, Chester,' Harrison said. I wasn't fooled by his pleasant tone of voice. 'I'm sorry, but I'm going to have to put you downstairs for a while.' And he picked up my cage, carried me down into the basement and left me there all alone. Now the thing is, I must have been near a heating duct or something because I could hear what was going on upstairs in the office. Jill had arrived and—well, it doesn't matter everything that was said. The important thing was—"

"I know," I said, interrupting. "I heard it, too. Harrison told Jill you were poisoned."

"Exactly," Chester said, looking at me with a puzzled expression. I smiled. Chester wasn't the only sleuth in the joint, and I wanted him to know it.

"Anyway," he continued, "he gave her the rest of the day off, came downstairs to get me and brought me back up to the office.

"Later, he took me out of the cage and put me on the examining table. I didn't know what was going to happen next. But I kept my eye on the window, which was open slightly, planning my getaway as soon as he came near me with any

funny-looking instruments. But he didn't do anything. Just sat down next to the table and stared at me.

" 'Are you the one?' he asked after looking me over from head to tail. 'I don't see what's so special about you.' Well, the insult aside, I found what he had to say very interesting. I wanted to know what he meant. So I began to purr. I sashayed over to him and bumped my head against his shoulder. I looked up at him with big, soft, mushy eyes, and just when I had him hooked, I got the purr going a little deeper in my throat so that it sounded like I'd just fallen in love. People are suckers for that stuff. Harrison was no exception.

" 'Aw, you're a nice kitty,' he said, patting me, 'but you don't seem very special.' I almost stopped purring at that, but remembered that I was after something. 'I was sure you were the one. Doc says you're special. I heard him tell your family. And your file has got some pretty interesting stuff in it. Still, you look like a pretty ordinary cat to me.' I wanted to bite him then, but resisted."

Knowing Chester, I had to admire his restraint.

"Well, then Harrison let out a big sigh and shook his head. 'Maybe I'm just not cut out for this racket,' he said. 'First I thought it was Louise. After all, she's pretty fancy-looking. But then once I got her home . . . I don't know . . . she didn't look so unusual. And *then* I looked back in her file and found out she's not even a purebred. So I figured I had the wrong one! Well, it's not so bad with her. I mean, I made it look like she escaped. I can just bring her back anytime I want. Meanwhile, she's not having such a bad time of it over at my pad. Watching TV all day, eating leftover Chinese food. What could be better? So, I went back to the files, and I read up on you, see? And I remembered what Doc said about you. And I figured *you*'re the one. But, now, I don't know . . .' And he just stared at me some more, his face growing more and more perplexed.

"And then he said something that really frightened me. 'Too bad I made it look like you'd been poisoned. After all, I can't bring you back from the dead, can I? If you're not the one, we're both in trouble. Of course,' he added with a chuckle, 'you'll be in more trouble than me, but . . .'

"Well, I felt like running for the window then and there, but I was determined to see it through. What did he mean by 'the one'? Who was he after and why? I purred even more loudly. 'Hey, you're real friendly, aren't you?' he said. And then, reflecting back on his problems, he added, 'If only I'd heard the rest of that phone conversation.' He paused a minute and then looked me squarely in the eyes, as if he'd heard me asking him to explain.

" 'See, Chester, it's like this. I heard Doc saying to somebody on the phone that they shouldn't worry, that he knew how valuable they were and he'd take good care of them. But I never heard who he was talking about. I figured once I knew, I'd kidnap whoever it was, see? Make a mint, blackmail or something. You know? But how am I going to make a penny if I can't figure out who it is I'm supposed to kidnap?' Well, naturally, I knew right away who he was talking about."

"You did?" I asked.

"You did?" Taxi echoed. "Who was it?"

"And how did you know?"

"The thing about criminals is, no matter how smart they are, they're always just a little bit dumb. And that's where they get tripped up. Harrison hadn't even noticed that Greenbriar had said 'them.' So, obviously, he was talking about more than one animal. And since I knew that Howard and Heather were purebred wire-haired dachshunds (with the possibility of having been crossbred with werewolves, of course, which would only increase their value), I knew that they were the ones he was after.

"Later that afternoon, when Harrison was busy putting food into the dinner bowls, I made a run for the window, hoping to get out and warn Howard and Heather. Unfortunately, it wasn't open wide enough so I got stuck halfway through. Harrison pulled me back in and closed the window.

" 'Nice try,' he said to me, 'but you aren't going anywhere.' It was then that I had the inspiration to scratch out the message on the bottom of your food dish, Harold. I could only hope that you would be having one of your rare fits of intelligence when you ate dinner that night.

"Anyway, after he fed everyone, he put me back inside the cage and went home."

"But when . . ."

"I'm getting to it," Chester said. "He came back later that evening in a state of great agitation. 'I've got to find the answer,' he said. He pulled out all the files and started to look through them. I went into my purring number again, hoping he'd take me out of my cage so I could read over his shoulder. It worked. 'Just don't try to go anywhere this time,' he said. He needn't have worried. I was much more interested in finding out what more I could from the files. When he got to Heather's, there it was in nice, bold print: 'PREGNANT. DUE TO DELIVER SOON.' I looked at Harrison. How could he miss it? I thought.

"Then the phone rang. It was Jill, calling to remind him about the very thing we'd just read in the file. 'Yeah, I know she's going to give birth soon, Jill,' he said. 'Don't worry, it's a natural thing. Happens all the time.' Then she said something that stopped him dead in his tracks. He just stood there, his mouth hanging open. When at last he spoke, he said, 'Yeah, yeah. I heard you. Valuable. Of course, I know they're valuable. Don't worry. They'll be fine. Just fine.' He hung up the phone and ran for the door. 'That's it!' he cried. 'It's them! And all those little puppies in the bargain. I'll make a fortune selling them off!' He was so excited he ran out of the door without noticing what had become of me. Naturally, I was fast on his heels."

"And that's when you woke me," I said. It was more a statement than a question.

"That's when I *tried* to wake you," he answered. "It wasn't so easy."

Taxi looked dumbfounded. "He was going to sell Howard's and Heather's babies?" he uttered. "But what about *them?* What was he going to do with Howard and Heather?"

Chester shrugged. "Who knows? Maybe sell them, too. Maybe keep them locked up somewhere. Or perhaps, once he'd made his money selling the kids, dispose of the evidence."

"Wow," Taxi said, "that Harrison isn't such a nice guy."

"You can say that again," I concurred.

"Wow, that Harrison isn't such a—"

"Chester," I went on, "there are still some things I don't understand."

"For instance?"

"Well, for instance, what about Max and Georgette? If they didn't murder Louise, why were they planning to escape? Weren't they going to run away together?"

To my surprise, it was Taxi who answered. "If you hadn't been so busy suspecting everyone, Harold, you could have figured that one out a long time ago. They were planning to go look for Louise and bring her back. Max was convinced she'd run away because of him. Georgette felt terrible, too, so she suggested they go look for her together."

"You mean there was nothing between them?"

"No, of course not," Taxi said.

"Georgette is a bit of a flirt, that's all," Chester added, as if it had never been his idea in the first place that she and Max had murdered Louise.

So Harrison took Louise," I said softly, letting it sink in. "But how? You said you never saw anybody cross the compound that night."

"That's right," replied Chester. "That was what had me stumped. Then you said something that made it all fall into place. And that's when I knew Harrison was the culprit. Do you remember? You said that whoever did it would have gotten very wet."

"Yes, I remember saying that," I said, "but I don't see what that has to do with—"

"It made me think of the towels Harrison and Jill had used to dry us off."

"So?" I asked. "I still don't see—"

"Harrison wrapped Louise in a towel right while she was eating dinner and took her inside with him. No one saw her disappear. All they would have seen if they'd bothered to look was Harrison carrying a used towel into the office. And because it was already dark, no one even knew Louise was gone until the morning."

"And he made sure that her door and the gate were left open. Hmm, pretty clever," I admitted. "He really made it look as if Louise had escaped.

And that it was all Jill's fault. I was even beginning to think it was her."

"Sure. And do you remember that day they were cleaning the storage shed?" Chester asked. Taxi and I nodded. "Well, Harrison remembered, too. And he remembered that Jill had dropped some garbage inside the compound. He was able to use that later when he told her he'd found a container of rat poison near my bungalow. Just as he wanted her to, she believed she'd dropped it. And that her carelessness had resulted in my death."

There was a long moment of silence as Taxi and I tried to take in everything Chester had told us. It was an incredible story. Even more incredible when I thought how close I'd come to never seeing Chester again.

I looked at Chester and then up at the blue sky above. The storm was over, I told myself, and everyone was safe at last.

[TWELVE]

Howie

AT THAT MOMENT, I was attacked from behind.

Thump!

I felt the blow between my shoulder blades. "Help!" I cried out as I went sprawling onto my belly.

"No mercy!" the voice above bellowed. "The game is up. Your days are numbered. Resist, and you'll walk the plank!" I recognized the voice. Lyle had dropped by to say hello.

"Get him off of me!" I hissed at Chester, thinking he might know how to communicate cat-to-cat.

"Agent 11½D!" Chester shouted. "Release your captive!"

I felt Lyle's claws loosen. "Why?" he asked.

"You have the wrong dog," Chester shot back.

"Oh," Lyle muttered softly. He jumped off my back onto the ground before me. Calmly, he looked into my eyes. "Sorry about that," was all he said. And then he strolled off as if nothing had happened.

"There goes a great all-American twit," Chester said in tribute as he watched Lyle walk off. He shook his head sadly. "What a shame he has to be a cat."

"Now, I wouldn't have been surprised to find out Lyle was the murderer," Taxi commented. "I wouldn't put anything past him."

Chester shook his head again and sighed. "Lyle's had a rough life," he said. "You want some excitement? Read *his* file!"

"I think we've had enough excitement around here," I said to Chester. "And I think we can be grateful for one thing."

"What's that?"

"That with everything that's happened, no real harm has come to anyone."

I looked up and saw Max coming toward us. On his right was Louise. On his left, Georgette.

"Right!" he blurted as he came to a halt before us. "Just came over to see how you were doing, Chester. Must have been pretty tough for you, behind bars."

"I've been through tougher," Chester replied with typical modesty.

"It was a nightmare," Louise said dramatically. "I shall always forget my days and nights at the Chateau of Bow-Wow. How my heart it will ache when I am thinking of everything that has happened here. But, *alors,* in the end, everything is fine and we all live happily ever—oh, what is that word?"

"After?" Georgette offered.

Louise turned to Georgette and smiled sweetly. "Thank you, Camille."

Georgette started to correct Louise, then stopped herself. "You're welcome, sugar," she said instead.

Max smiled. "These gals have become great friends," he said happily. "Louise knows my heart belongs to her and her alone. And she knows that without Georgette, I never would have figured out how to break out of here and find her."

Georgette blushed. "Thank goodness Dr. Greenbriar and Jill came along when they did and heard our barking. By the way," she added, lowering her voice, "you can't imagine what a dump that Harrison lives in."

"Please!" Louise interjected. "I do not wish to be speaking of it. It was simply—" She pursed her lips as if searching for just the right word. *"—abdominal!"* she proclaimed at last.

Well, it was close to the right word.

"Jogging?" Max suggested. I started to crawl away.

"No joggin', Max," Georgette replied. "How about Rip-the-Rag?"

"I have gotten it!" Louise announced. "Let us play Knock-Each-Other-Down!"

"Good!" Max snorted. "You fellows want to join us?"

"Maybe another time," Chester said. "Tennis elbow."

"Harold?" Max asked, turning to me.

"Uh, no thanks," I replied. "Coward cramps."

"I'll play," Taxi said brightly.

"Right! Let's go then."

Chester and I watched as the four of them hurried off into the distance to play Knock-Each-Other-Down. Before they had gotten too far, Louise ran back and whispered in my ear.

"Barry's been hitting the sauce again," she uttered. "I didn't want to tell you in front of the others. You have no idea what it's doing to Marcia. She's making a fool of herself over Ron. And all because of you, Todd." Todd? "It's no good, can't you see? How many times do I have to tell you? No, no, don't say anything. Just remember: when this nightmare is over, I'll still have Mike. All you'll have is a pocketful of memories and lint." She sobbed and ran off to join the others.

I turned to Chester. "You know what I said before?"

"What's that, Harold?"

"About no harm coming to anyone?"

"Mm-hmmm."

"Forget it. I only hope there's a cure for day-time television."

Howard howled in the distance. "Kids are great!" he called out, with a wink in our direction.

"Harold?"

"Yes, Chester?"

"This place is a loony bin."

"Yes, I know, Chester."

"I want to go home, Harold. I don't know how much more I can take of Lyle and Louise and Taxi and that crazy werewolf."

"Wait a minute, Chester," I said, "do you still believe Howard and Heather are werewolves? They've probably been acting strangely because they were nervous about having their babies."

"Werewolves can't get nervous about having babies?"

I had to admit the thought hadn't occurred to me.

"Uh-uh," he went on. "Nothing will convince me that they couldn't be part dachshund and part werewolf. Stranger things have happened." Howard let out another howl. "Besides, just listen to that. If that isn't the call of a werewolf, nothing is. No, I just want to get out of here. That's all I care about. Get me home, where I'll never have to listen to that terrible sound again."

I was about to answer him when the gate flew open and Toby and Pete bounded into Chateau Bow-Wow. As soon as he saw me, Toby came running in my direction.

"Harold!" he cried, throwing his arms around my neck. Boy, was I happy to see him! I started drooling like crazy.

"Chester!" Toby squealed, as he swooped the cat up off the ground and hugged him. Chester showed how overjoyed he was by not having a fit.

"Hey, guys," Pete said coolly.

"Boy, did we have a neat vacation," Toby said excitedly. "Wait'll I tell you about it."

"Yeah," Pete joined in. "Dad lost our travelers' checks and everything. Just like on TV."

"Yeah, and then we had a flat tire, and Dad had forgotten to put the spare back in the car before we left home, so we had to sit in the rain until the tow truck came."

"And then we were on this picnic and Dad fell out of the tree and now he's wearing this cast, see—"

"Yeah, and it's real neat, Harold. I wrote my name on it and everything."

"Me, too!"

"Anyway," Toby said, "sorry you had to be stuck *here* the whole time. I'll bet it was real dull."

Chester and I exchanged knowing glances.

"But now we're going home, boy. Come on, let's get your things."

What things? I wondered. I didn't remember having packed a toothbrush.

"Wait a minute," Pete said, "let's go ask Dad about you-know-what first."

"Oh, yeah, I forgot," Toby replied, dropping Chester to the ground. "We'll be back, you guys. Oh, here, Harold, here's a chocolate cupcake I brought for you. With cream in the center." And off they ran. The cupcake was a little smushed, which made sense since Toby had been carrying it in his back pocket. But it tasted delicious, especially after seven days of chocolate deprivation. That Toby was really a good kid.

A few minutes later, Dr. Greenbriar and Jill came out of the office door. I felt the blood pumping through my veins as they approached.

"I think the judge handled it very well," Dr Greenbriar was saying, "don't you?"

"Mm-hmm," Jill replied. "It might set Harrison straight after all. Even if he doesn't continue, a year of college can't hurt anybody."

"Pretty smart sentence, all right," the doctor said, smiling. "But what I liked best was the job he came up with for Harrison. To pay for school."

Jill smiled now, too. "Yes. Working at the zoo. I think that should suit Harrison just fine."

They laughed at the thought. I didn't think it was so funny. What if he tried to steal an elephant?

"Well, you boys are going home," Jill said, leaning toward us. "You must be glad about that, aren't you?"

"Bet your boots, sweetheart," Chester uttered under his breath.

We walked toward the gate, and we never looked back. We were going home at last.

MR. MONROE stood by the end of the station wagon, waving his good arm in our direction.

"Hey, Harold! How ya doin', Chester?" he called out.

Mrs. Monroe cooed her greetings, and then Pete and Toby came running over to us. I noticed that Toby was carrying something small in his arms.

"Harold! Chester! Wait'll you see the surprise we have for you," he sang out. I looked up and saw that he was carrying a little brown puppy. Chester's eyes went berserk. "Guess what!" Toby continued. "There were puppies born here a few days ago and one of them was the . . . uh . . . what'd ya callit . . ."

"The runt of the litter," Jill said helpfully.

"Yeah, right. And we're getting to keep him. 'Course, he has to stay with his mom for a while. But then we get to bring him home to live with us. Dad said we could, right, Pete?"

"Right," Pete chimed in. "And *I* got to name him."

"Yeah, but it's a good name anyway."

"Yeah, see," Pete went on, "the puppy's

father's name is Howard. So I named the puppy Howie."

Chester and I stared at Howie. He looked into my eyes, then into Chester's. And then, lifting his head slightly, he let out a tiny, tiny howl.

"aah-oooooooooo."

"Gee, that's neat," Toby said.

"Yeah, neat," echoed Pete.

I turned to Chester and commented, "Before you know it, he's going to sound just like his mom and dad."

But Chester didn't hear me. He'd fainted dead away.

[EPILOGUE]

CHATEAU Bow-Wow was an adventure, and I suppose in some ways, Mr. Monroe was right: adventure *is* good for the soul. But what I like best about adventures is that they come to an end.

It's fall now, and I'm glad to be home. Fall means long walks in the woods with Mr. Monroe and Pete, late-night snacks of roasted chestnuts and pumpkin pies with Toby, and rolling in the leaves with Howie. Oh yes, Howie is living with us now. And since it's his first fall, there's a lot I have to teach him.

Of course, Chester is sharing in his education. Right now, he's teaching him how to meditate. Even as I write, I can hear them in the living room.

"Ommmmm . . ."

"Omm-oooooooooooooooo . . ."

"No, you dumb dog. *Ommmmmm . . ."*

"Omm-oooooooooooooooo . . ."

"Not 'ooooo,' you numbskull, *'ommmmm,*

OMMMMMM!' Can't you hear the difference? Don't you want to learn? Meditation is good for you. It'll make you mellow. Keep you cool. Like me. Don't you want to be like your Uncle Chester? Howie? Howie! Come back here! Where are you going? Get down from there! No, no . . . not the—Harold!"

Excuse me. I think I'm needed in the living room.

"Harold, get in here! I'm not a nursemaid!"

"In a minute, Chester!"

"He's going after the geranium! He's—he's—"

"He's what, Chester?"

"He's eating the geranium!"

"Coming, Chester!"

Well, I've got to go. It was quite an adventure, but when all is said and done, there's no place like . . .

"Ommmmmmm . . ."

BUNNICULA
strikes again!

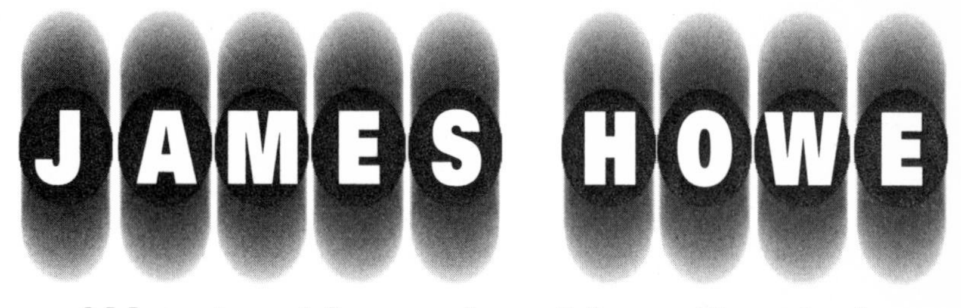

illustrations by Alan Daniel

atheneum books for young readers

Atheneum Books for Young Readers
An imprint of Simon & Schuster Children's Publishing Division
1230 Avenue of the Americas
New York, New York 10020

Book design by Ann Bobco

The text of this book is set in Berkeley

The illustrations are rendered in pencil

Printed in the United States of America

Library of Congress Cataloging-in-Publication Data
Howe, James.
Bunnicula Strikes Again! / by James Howe.
p. cm.
Summary: When Bunnicula the rabbit starts acting strangely, the Monroe dogs and cat renew their suspicions that he is a vampire.

[1. Dogs—Fiction. 2. Cats—Fiction. 3. Rabbits—Fiction. 4. Vampires—Fiction.] I. Title.
PZ7.H83727But 1999
[Fic]—dc21
99-20419

Contents

To Harold's Editors Extraordinaire—
Jonathan J. Lanman
and
Jean Karl

[EDITOR'S NOTE]

LOOKING back on my years as an editor of fine literature, I can name many honors and associations of which I am proud. Yet one stands out as the apex of my career—the unique privilege of having edited the work of Harold, canine author extraordinaire. How many in my position have received a manuscript from the clenched jaws of its creator? Who else has known the pleasure of reading a novelist's new work for the very first time while the novelist himself lies at one's feet, snoring contentedly? What publishing professional has successfully entertained an out-of-town author with a handful of doggie biscuits and a bowl of cocoa? Other editors may dream of such things, but I have known them!

And yet, numerous books and countless doggie biscuits later, the unanswered questions remain: Where did Harold learn to type and how does he manage it with those big paws of his? What does he do with the early drafts of his work—bury them in the backyard? Doesn't anybody notice all that missing typing paper? If a tree falls in a forest and there is no one around to hear it, does it still make a sound?

Alas, these questions are destined to remain unanswered—small mysteries within the greater mystery of life itself. For although Harold is able to communicate via the written word—and, in ways that are incomprehensible to mere humans such as you and I, to speak to his fellow animals—he remains mute (other than the occasional "woof") in face-to-face contact. As delighted as I am to see him when he drops by my office, I don't count on much in the way of scintillating conversation.

Thus it was that when he last appeared at my door with a manuscript gripped between his teeth, I invited him in, proffered the usual cocoa and dog biscuits, and—without a word exchanged between us—proceeded to read his latest book as he curled up at my feet and went to sleep. First, I read the note that accompanied the manuscript, which read:

My dearest friend and esteemed colleague,

We have come a long way together since my first book, Bunnicula: A Rabbit-Tale of Mystery. *Little did we know that my life, which until Bunnicula's arrival had been decidedly unremarkable, would thereafter be filled with ad-*

ventures and that each adventure would translate into yet another book. Odd, that I, whose greatest ambition has always been the uninterrupted nap, should after all these years find himself the semi-famous author of several books!

And now we may have reached the final chapter. I must warn you that the story you are about to read is chilling, but it is one that nonetheless had to be told. I hope it will not disturb you or your readers too much, for it has never been my intention to disturb, merely to entertain. I trust you will find the entertainment value sufficiently present to warrant publication of this book as you have the others in the past.

I look forward to your response and, as always, I send you my good wishes.

Yours sincerely,
Harold X.

A curious letter, I thought. Then I began to read. And at once I understood why Harold had warned me the book would be disturbing. There on the very first page was another question. Would it remain unanswered? Read for yourself and ask as I did: Is this the end?

BUNNICULA
strikes again!

[ONE]

The End

HOW unexpectedly the end can come. Had I even thought such a thing was possible, I might have noticed the warning signs that Friday night one May when, ironically, I was feeling so at peace with the world. I remember the feeling well, for although a general sense of contentedness is part of a dog's nature, keen awareness of just how fortunate one is comes along less frequently than you might imagine. This was one of those rare moments.

I was stretched out on the bed next to my master, Toby. I call him my master because while there are four members of the Monroe family, it is the youngest who treats me with the greatest kindness and consideration. On Friday nights, for instance,

Toby, who is allowed to stay up late to read, shares his stash of treats with me. He knows how much I love chocolate, and so he's always sure to have at least one chocolaty delight ready and waiting for me. (Some of my readers have written expressing their concern about the potentially detrimental effects of chocolate on dogs, to which I can only say that while it is true some dogs have been known to become ill from eating chocolate, others have not. Luckily, I fall into the latter category. Also, I hasten to remind my readers that I, like the books I have written, am a work of fiction.)

Parenthetical digression aside, I return to that Friday evening in May when I lay happily snuggled up next to my favorite boy, my mouth blissfully tingling from the lingering taste of my favorite food—a chocolate cupcake with cream in the middle, yum. Toby's hand rested on my head, which in turn rested on his outstretched legs. The warm spring breeze wafted through the open window, gently carrying Toby's voice as he read to me. Toby is the kind of reader who devours books—and long books, at that—unlike his older brother, Pete, whose reading is limited to a series of truly gross horror novels called FleshCrawlers. (Believe me, I know they're gross; I chewed on one once and the cheap glue they use on the bindings made me sick as a—you should pardon the expression—dog. Give me Literature any day!)

Lulled by Toby's voice, I remember thinking how perfect my life seemed at that moment. My best friend, Chester, had undoubtedly settled himself in on the brown velvet armchair in the living room below and was now contentedly sleeping or shedding or reading. He, like Toby, is a voracious reader, which may surprise you, given that he's a cat; but, again, in the world of fiction, anything is possible. Consider the other two members of the Monroe menagerie: Howie, a wirehaired dachshund puppy who Chester maintains is part werewolf, and Bunnicula, a rabbit with fangs. While Chester doesn't concern himself much with Howie's howling, seeing it as irritating but harmless, he does work himself up into a fancy frenzy from time to time over the dangers he imagines Bunnicula poses to our vegetables, our family, the town in which we live, and, when he's really on a roll, Civilization as we know it.

Now all of this may seem very strange to you,

but to me it is just life. I couldn't picture it any other way. Over time, the eight of us in our family—four people, four pets—have settled into the comforting rhythms of a song without end. Or so I thought.

I had been only vaguely listening to the story Toby was reading. I knew that it was about the famous detective Sherlock Holmes and his friend Watson because those stories were all that Toby had been reading for weeks. I had grown fond of Holmes and had often thought that his friendship with Watson was something like mine with Chester. I was therefore unprepared for the terrible event that concluded this particular tale, in which Watson tells of the final confrontation between Holmes and his archenemy, the evil Professor Moriarty.

"'As I turned away I saw Holmes, with his back against a rock and his arms folded, gazing down at the rush of waters. It was the last that I was ever destined to see of him in this world,'" Toby read.

I lifted my head and woofed. Was it possible? Would Holmes perish? Could an author be so cruel as to kill off his most beloved character?

As if he could read my mind, Toby looked down at me with a forlorn expression on his face. "Are you worried about what's going to happen?" he asked. "I wish I could tell you the story has a happy ending, boy, but . . . Well, I guess I'd better just finish reading."

I listened attentively to every word. You may imagine my shock when it was revealed that Holmes and Moriarty, locked in a deadly embrace, tumbled from the precipice overlooking Reichenbach Falls into "that dreadful cauldron of swirling water and seething foam," where they were lost forever.

I couldn't believe it! The author had really done it! He had killed Sherlock Holmes! I would have written him an irate letter then and there if I'd known where the Monroes kept their stamps—and if it hadn't occurred to me that the author had been dead for three-quarters of a century.

I began to whimper and Toby, whose own eyes were glistening, bent over me and crooned, "There, there, boy. It's only a story." But Toby is a sensitive lad, and I knew that for him, as for me, there was something more here than a story. There was the painful recognition that all too quickly things can change. I didn't like it. I wanted my world to go on as it always had. I wanted to be sure that Friday nights would always mean treats with Toby, that Chester would always be my friend, that Bunnicula would always be in his cage by the living-room window, and that Howie would always, for reasons no one understands, call me Uncle Harold and Chester Pop.

I jumped down from Toby's bed with an urgent need to check downstairs and be sure that everything was in its proper place.

"Hey, where're you going, boy?" I heard Toby call. I turned back to give his hand a quick lick, then bounded from the room and down the stairs.

"Chester!" I cried out as I turned the corner from the hall into the living room. His chair was empty!

"Chester! Where are you?" I called into the darkened room.

As my eyes adjusted, I could see that Howie was not curled up under the coffee table where he should have been. Where was everybody? Thank goodness, Bunnicula at least was where he belonged, sitting in his cage, gazing out at the empty living room.

I trotted over to his cage and said hello. Slowly,

SHERLOCK
HOLMES
STORIES

he turned his head in my direction, and had I known then what I would later learn, I would have seen the listlessness in the movement, might even have detected the lack of luster in his normally sparkly eyes. Do I only imagine it now, or was there something behind that glassy gaze that was saying, "Help me, Harold"? How easy it is to look back and see everything so differently.

At the time, I was just relieved he was there. I didn't pay him any more mind at that moment because the door to the kitchen creaked open just then and through it appeared Chester, licking his chops.

"Where *were* you?" I said, trying to sound less alarmed than I felt and failing miserably. "I called you and called you."

Chester parked himself next to me and nonchalantly turned his tongue's attention to the tip of his tail. "For heaven's sake, Harold, get a grip on yourself. I was in the kitchen having a little snack. Knowing your inability to go without food for less than five minutes at a stretch, I assumed you'd be joining me. Now what's all the excitement about?"

"Well, I, that is . . ." I let my sentence drop, feeling foolish all of a sudden to be so worked up over a mere story. I might have reminded myself of the many times Chester had not only worked himself up but practically turned the house upside down from his hysterical overreaction to something he'd read—but then Chester *is* a cat and prone to overreacting.

"It was just—just something I read," I told him.

He snickered. "I understand. The list of ingredients on candy wrappers can be alarming."

He chortled to himself as I tried to think of a speedy comeback. Unfortunately, I am notoriously slow at speedy comebacks, so I gave up the effort even as I silently rejoiced that this exchange was proof that life in the Monroe house was proceeding as usual.

If further proof was needed, Howie came skipping down the stairs, his toenails clicking wildly. He raced to our sides and skidded to a halt.

"Boy," he said breathlessly, "that was *so* scary!" The poor kid was quivering.

"What happened?" I asked.

I noticed that Chester had stopped bathing his tail and was staring intently at Howie. His eyes were sharp. His ears were perked. He was ready to make his move on whatever had so frightened the impressionable young puppy.

"W-well," Howie stammered, "there was this giant p-p-potato, see, and he ate up everything in the refrigerator and when seventh grader Billy-Bob Krenshaw went to get milk for his cereal—"

"Hold it right there!" Chester snapped. Howie, who always does what Chester tells him, froze, his jaw dropped open, and his tongue unfurled like a flag hanging off a porch on a windless Fourth of July.

"Are you talking about what I think you're talking about?" Chester went on.

We waited.

"You can move your mouth now," Chester said.

"Thanks," said Howie. "I was talking about FleshCrawlers number nineteen, *The Potato Has a Thousand Eyes*. I was reading it over Pete's shoulder. Until he told me I had to leave because I had breath like the bottom of a garbage pail, which I resent because I haven't been near the garbage for a whole week, not since that time the baby-sitter left the lid off, which reminds me—"

"Howie!"

"What, Pop?"

"Do you have a point to make here? Do you know what I mean by a point?"

"Yes, I have a point to make!" said Howie. "And what was your other question? Did I know what a point meant? Of course I do. I had an appointment just last week with the vet. Get it, Pop? Get it, Uncle Harold?"

Howie chuckled merrily while Chester began to fume. I could have cried at how normal everything was.

"My point," Howie said, "was that the story was really scary. Especially the part where Billy-Bob's pet is transformed into a french-fried poodle."

Chester shook his head in disgust. "Who writes this drivel?" he asked.

"Drivel?" said Howie. "I don't know what drivel is, but I can tell you one thing. M. T. Graves does not write drivel! Besides, it could really happen—you said so yourself, Pop."

"What could really happen?"

"Vegetables can be dangerous."

"I've always said that about spinach," I interjected.

"Don't you remember when you were worried that Bunnicula was attacking vegetables all over town, draining them of their juices, and you said the vegetables would turn into vampires, too? Remember, Pop? You had us going around staking them through their little veggie hearts with toothpicks!"

"Well . . ." said Chester. I couldn't tell if the memory was making him proud or embarrassed. He's often poised between the two. You know how cats are—you never know if they're going to make a cool move or a fool move, and most of the time neither do they.

Howie pressed on. "You *do* still think Bunnicula's a vampire, don't you?"

"Of course," Chester said.

"And you *do* think he's a danger to vegetables, right?"

Chester hesitated before speaking. "Let's just say, he used to be a danger. I don't think we have to worry about that any longer."

"What do you mean?" I asked. Then I remembered. "Oh, because the Monroes feed him a liquid diet, he no longer drains vegetables of their juices. Is that it?"

Chester's face took on an odd expression. "Let's just say the matter is under control, Harold. At last."

"But, Chester," I said, "Bunnicula hasn't attacked any vegetables since he escaped that time. Surely you're no longer worried about him."

"Oh, I'm no longer worried about him. No, I'm not worried at all."

And with that, he jumped up on the brown velvet armchair, bid us good night, and, after circling and pawing at the seat cushion for a good five minutes, proceeded to fall into a deep and seemingly untroubled sleep.

Howie and I meandered over to Bunnicula's cage.

"What do you think Pop meant about everything being under control?" Howie asked as we regarded our lethargic chum.

"Chester just likes to hear himself talk sometimes," I told Howie. "And he likes to believe that Bunnicula is a threat. But I don't think he'd do him any real harm. After all, he's one of the family."

Howie smiled. "My brother, the bunny," he said. "Hey, that reminds me, Uncle Harold. Did you read FleshCrawlers number thirty-three, *My Sister the Pickled Brain*? It is so cool. See, there's this girl named Laura-Lynn O'Flynn who has this twin sister, and one day she asks her to help her with this science experiment and something goes way wrong and the next thing you know . . ."

As Howie nattered on, I thought about what I'd said to him. Although I was pleased to find life carrying on as usual in the Monroe household, I was troubled that something might once again be fanning the spark of Chester's suspicions and animosity toward an innocent rabbit—one we called a friend. Did I really believe Chester would do Bunnicula no harm? After all, he *had* tried to destroy Bunnicula once. How far would he have gone? How far would he go now? I had no answers and I did not like where the questions were taking me.

It was only later that night when I was fast asleep that the pieces came together as they do in dreams—the lifeless look in Bunnicula's eyes, Chester's mysterious comments, and the disturbing scene from the story Toby had read to me earlier. Was it one thing in particular, or was it all of the pieces floating dreamlike through my slumber, that put the questions into my mind that would not go away: Might Chester and Bunnicula be headed for their own fateful plunge from the precipice? Could this be the end of Bunnicula?

[TWO]

The Terrible Truth About Chester

IF Saturdays at your house are anything like Saturdays at our house, let me offer you a little advice: Do not fall asleep at the bottom of the stairs. After all my Saturdays with the Monroes, you would think I would have known better. But now that I'm well into my middle years, I take the position that if you can't live recklessly on occasion, what's the point of it all? Unfortunately, sometimes the point of it all is that you get trampled.

As was the case on the Saturday morning in question. I had little time to think of the dreams that had disturbed my sleep the night before when I was startled awake by the sound of Pete and Toby yelling at each other. The accompanying rumble told me a stampede was in progress, and, sure enough, when I looked up and saw the Monroe brothers scrambling down the stairs, there were Pete's bare and dirty feet heading straight for me. As far as I could tell, this morning's altercation had something to do with a large piece of cardboard Pete was waving around over his head, which Toby was trying to get from him.

For the record, I do not move quickly in the morning.

For the record, Pete and Toby do.

It was no contest.

Oomph!

"Watch it, Harold!" Pete shouted as he landed on a part of me that was blessedly not fully awake yet.

"You could say you're sorry!" Toby yelled at his brother, stopping to pat me on the head.

"I just did!" Pete shot back. Apparently, Toby had forgotten that "Watch it!" is Pete's idea of an apology.

Chester wandered in as Pete and Toby continued their morning exercises.

"Give me that poster!" Toby shouted. "I made it!"

Pete waved the poster at Toby. Toby grabbed at it

and missed. Pete called his brother a word of one syllable. Toby volleyed with a compound noun. Pete retorted with a backhanded insult. Toby lobbed a high string of colorful adjectives capped by a perfectly executed oxymoron.

"Boys!" Mrs. Monroe shouted from the top of the stairs. "Enough!"

"Breakfast!" Mr. Monroe called cheerfully and obliviously from the kitchen.

"And the match goes to Toby," Chester commented as he licked a curled paw. "Nice wordplay."

"People are fascinating, aren't they, Chester?" I asked as we followed the boys and the enticing aroma of bacon into the kitchen. "All those words and they actually imagine they're communicating."

"I swear," said Chester, "if you waved a sign in their faces that said FEED ME BEFORE I FAINT, they'd ask if you needed to go outside. Speaking of signs, what did the poster say?"

"Speaking of feed-me-before-I-faint," I replied, "who cares what the poster said?"

In the kitchen, I joined Howie at Mr. Monroe's side to pant and whimper and look as pathetic as possible while Mr. Monroe forked bacon onto a plate.

"Subtlety, thy name is dog," Chester observed sarcastically.

I chose not to engage in what I knew would be yet another futile round in one of our oldest debates—Getting the Food from Their Hand to Your Mouth: Shameless Begging versus Haughty Disdain. Besides, now that I was feeling a little more awake (helped by the strip of bacon Mr. Monroe slipped me on the sly; one point for shameless begging), my dreams started coming back to me. Questions were forming themselves in my mind, questions I needed to ask Chester as soon as the opportunity presented itself.

"No more, Harold," I heard Mr. Monroe say. I was unaware that he had seated himself at the table, and I had moved from whimpering at his side to laying my head on his lap and looking up at him plaintively. It's amazing the things that happen on automatic.

"If you want more breakfast," he said, scratching the top of my head, "go look in your bowl. There's a surprise waiting for you."

Before you could say, "For me?" I was at my bowl, where I found freshly ground meat! One thing

I have to say about the Monroes, their lives may get busy, but they always think of their pets in special little ways. I've always said I have the best family anyone could have. Even if I do get stomped on by a certain person's dirty, smelly feet occasionally.

"We won't be home until late," I heard Mrs. Monroe saying. "Toby, will you be sure to leave Bunnicula's carrot juice for him so he'll have it when he wakes up?"

"Okay," said Toby, chewing. Then, "Bunnicula hasn't been looking so good, Mom. Do you think there's something wrong with him?"

"Now that you mention it," said Mrs. Monroe, "there has been a real change in his energy lately. Maybe we should take him to the vet."

"He's just fat and lazy," said Pete.

"Oh, that's nice," Toby said.

"Boys," Mr. Monroe murmured in that way he has of letting you know you're about to sail into treacherous waters and you'd better change course.

For a moment everyone fell silent. Then Mr. Monroe said, "He doesn't seem seriously ill. Maybe we'll take him to the vet on Monday. I don't see how we can fit it in today. We've got so much to do, what with the rally at the movie house and all."

"Like this dumb rally is going to make a difference," said Pete. "I don't see why we're wasting our time. They're going to tear the theater down on Tuesday whether we protest or not. It's a lost cause."

"Your mother and I have put months into fighting this demolition, Pete, you know that. That theater is not only very convenient, it's architecturally important and is a local landmark of sorts. We're not going to stop now. Decisions can still be overturned."

"Besides, if the theater *is* torn down," said Toby, "tonight's movie will be the last one shown there. Ever! We don't want to miss *that,* do we? It's so unfair. Now we're going to have to go all the way out to the mall to see movies."

"Big wazoo!" said Pete, rolling his eyes. If eye-rolling were an Olympic event, Pete would be a gold medalist.

I didn't stick around to hear the rest of the conversation. Having thoroughly cleaned my dish, I retired to the living room to begin the important task of wondering where my next meal would come from. Howie and Chester joined me.

"Chester," I said.

"Are you going to tell me you're worried the Monroes will forget to put food in your dish before they leave?" he asked.

"I most certainly was not!" I replied indignantly. How did he always know?

There was something else I wanted to ask him, of course—something about what he'd said the night before—but I couldn't bring myself to ask it just then. I don't know why. Perhaps I didn't want to have to face the answer I suspected he would give me.

In any event, we weren't left in peace for long. Mr. and Mrs. Monroe began bustling about, which mostly meant piling things into their car, and it struck me that most Saturdays were composed of piling a lot things into the car in the morning and taking a lot of things out of the car in the afternoon. I never noticed if they were the same things or not, but I'd concluded long ago that it was just one of those bizarre human rituals destined not to make a great deal of sense. Meanwhile, Pete applied himself seriously to the task of finding ever new and creative ways to be annoying, while Toby took Howie and me out for a morning romp. When we got back I went into immediate nap mode.

I was awakened some time later by the sound of Toby's voice, soft and close, and the feel of his arms around my neck.

"I'm worried about Bunnicula, boy," he whispered in my ear. "Keep an eye on him, will you? Gee, if anything ever happened to him . . ."

I whimpered sympathetically and Toby sighed.

"Good old Harold," he said. "At least I'd still have you."

A tennis ball bounced off the top of my head.

"Nice catch, Harold!" Pete shouted.

"Mom!" Toby bellowed.

Mrs. Monroe emerged from the kitchen, her arms full of posters similar to the one Pete had been carrying earlier. "Come on, you two," she said. "We're going to be late for the rally. And will you please stop fighting? What happened to that promise you made me on Mother's Day? It's not even two weeks and the two of you are going at each other like cats and dogs. What am I saying? Harold and Howie and Chester get along better than you do."

The car horn honked.

"Let's go," Mrs. Monroe said. "Your father is getting antsy."

Toby gave me another squeeze, and the family was gone.

Chester glared at me.

"What?" I said.

"Why did Toby say, 'At least I'd still have you,' Harold? Why didn't he say, 'At least I'd still have you *and Chester*'?"

"May I remind you that just yesterday you deposited a hairball in his sneaker?"

"That was hardly my fault! I thought it was Pete's sneaker."

"Good point," I said. "But still you can understand—"

"Yes, yes," said Chester, dropping to the floor and stretching out. Cats have more ways of changing the subject than kids have excuses for not doing their homework.

Seeing that the subject was changed, however, I decided this was the moment to find out the truth.

"Chester, you said something yesterday," I began.

"Yes, and I'm sorry, Harold. I never should have called you a mindless mutt."

"Oh, that," I said. "I wasn't talking about that."

"But it was unkind of me," Chester went on. "Not to mention redundant."

"It's all right, Chester. I don't even hear your insults anymore."

"You don't?"

Ignoring Chester's wounded look, I persevered. "You said that there was no need to worry about Bunnicula anymore, that the matter was under control. What did you mean by that?"

Chester smiled slyly. "I think you know what I mean. Sometimes it's best to leave certain things unsaid."

"But—"

Just then, Howie came bounding into the room. "Don't go in the yard!" he cried out, his voice full of alarm.

"What is it?" I woofed, racing to the window to see what was going on.

"I just finished reading FleshCrawlers number fifty-two, *Don't Go in the Yard.* It's about this boy named Skippy Sapworthy, who moves with his parents into this creepy old house and he's told never to go into the yard, but one night he—"

"Howie," Chester said.

"Yes, Pop?"

"The best way to overcome your fear is to face it. Why don't you and Harold run along and play outside for a while?"

"In the yard?"

"In the yard."

Howie looked at me. "Want to, Uncle Harold?" he asked.

"I wouldn't mind a little fresh air," I told him. "Coming, Chester?"

"Not just now," said Chester. "There's something I need to do. But don't let me stop you. Run along and play."

It was only moments later as Howie and I were tussling over an old rag in the backyard that Chester's words hit me.

"What fools!" I exclaimed. "Every day for the last few weeks, Chester has told us to run outside and play and, being the obedient dog-types we are, we do it! Howie, don't you see?"

Howie looked surprised by my question. "Of course I see, Uncle Harold," he said. "And I hear and I smell and I taste and I—"

"No, no. I mean, don't you see what Chester is up to? He's gotten us out of the house so he can, so he can . . ."

"So he can what?" Howie asked.

I looked at him blankly. "I don't know," I said, "but there's one way to find out."

As stealthily as we could, we made our way across the yard, through the pet door and into the kitchen, where we were stopped in our tracks by the strangest sound emanating from the living room.

Slurp, slurp, slurp.

Was it Bunnicula, sucking the juice out of vegetables? It couldn't be—he was never awake during daylight hours. Suddenly, the terrible truth hit me—it was Chester! Chester had become a vampire! He was sucking the lifeblood out of Bunnicula! That's why he said there was nothing to worry about anymore. That's why Bunnicula had become so listless! It was all too beastly to believe, too awful to face, yet I knew I must face it, must fling open the door that separated us, and put an end to Chester's hideous deeds!

"Be brave," I told young Howie, without explaining why he would need to be. How could I tell him what lay on the other side of that door, what violation of all that was good and decent accounted for those seemingly innocent slurping sounds?

"Now!" I said, and with Howie at my side, I butted the door open, charged into the living room, and cried out in wild desperation, "The game is up, Chester! I know you're a vampire! Let the bunny go!"

[THREE]

Do Not Litter!

"HAVE you completely lost your mind?" Chester asked.

Had I not worked myself up into such a state, I might have asked him the same thing. There he was inside Bunnicula's cage, all hunched up next to the sleeping rabbit, the hair and whiskers around his lips slick and matted with . . .

Carrot juice?

"Fine, so you're not a vampire," I said, trying to sound calm despite my heart's pounding reminder that I was anything but. "You *are* drinking Bunnicula's carrot juice, though, are you not?"

"Past tense, Harold. I just finished."

"Gee, Pop," said Howie, "there must be some

way to let the Monroes know you like carrot juice, too. You don't have to drink Bunnicula's."

"I don't like carrot juice, Howie," Chester said, gingerly stepping over the inert bunny and out of the cage. Carefully locking the door behind him, he jumped down and joined us. "I do not drink it for pleasure. I drink it because I must."

"Is that why you eat string?" I asked.

"I ate string once in my life, Harold. Leave it to you to remember."

"How could I forget? There you were with this little piece of string dangling from your lips and Mr. Monroe went to pull it out and he kept pulling and pulling, and the next thing you know he was clear across the other side of the room holding one end of a twenty-foot piece of string with your mouth still holding the other end. You looked like a tape dispenser."

Howie cracked up. Chester did not.

"But that's beside the point," I said. "The point is, why are you doing this?"

Chester sighed heavily. "Harold," he said, "you have a touching belief in the goodness of all creatures great and small. But how many times do I have to tell you? Bunnicula is not like other rabbits. He is evil."

"Now, Chester," I said.

"Tut, Harold, don't interrupt. You asked me for the truth, and now you will hear the truth."

Howie lowered his rear end to the floor, an indication that he was settling in for a good story. I wondered if he understood the distinction between fiction and reality. Then again, I suspected that for Chester there was no distinction at all.

"It began about a month ago," Chester said. "It was a Saturday. I remember it particularly because Mr. and Mrs. Monroe had received phone calls that morning from both their mothers that they would be coming to visit on Mother's Day. And although Mother's Day was still two weeks away, the family spent the rest of the day in a frenzy of cleaning and fixing up and telling us we were underfoot and—"

"Piling things in the car and taking things out. Yes, I remember," I said.

"And we ended up getting kicked out of the house," Howie put in, "and they forgot about us and it started to rain and—"

"Yes, it was a memorable day," said Chester. "Well,

Bunnicula slept through the day, of course, as he always does, but in the middle of the following night I was awakened by a clicking sound in the kitchen, followed by a light appearing under the door."

"Refrigerator," I surmised.

"Precisely. I might have made nothing of it had I not happened to glance in the direction of Bunnicula's cage and seen that it was empty. Well, what was I to think, Harold? He was at it again! He was in there, I had no doubt of it, attacking artichokes, sucking squash, biting broccoli, sinking his fangs into fennel—"

"Stop!" Howie cried. "It's too horrible!"

Chester pressed on relentlessly. "I tried to catch him in the act, but, oh, he's a tricky devil, that one, and he outmaneuvered me. By the time I entered the kitchen, he was gone. He had left his victims behind, though, carelessly scattered about the floor like so much litter on a public beach."

"Uncle Harold," Howie said, "when you write a book about this, will you find a way to remind your readers that they should never litter?"

"I definitely will," I promised. "Now go on, Chester."

"What was I to do? Should I leave those poor victimized victuals on the floor for the Monroes to discover in the morning? Remembering how dense they had been the first time this happened and, seeing no reason to think they'd grown any additional brain cells since then, I decided on a different course of action. I buried the pallid produce under some other garbage in the pail and made a vow to myself once and for all to take matters into my own hands."

"Paws," Howie said.

"Why?" asked Chester. "Do you need to go get a drink of water?"

"Take matters into your own paws. You don't have hands."

Chester pulled his lips back into a strained smile. "Has anyone ever told you you're a bright little whippersnapper?" he asked.

"Gee, no," Howie said, beaming.

"Well, there's a reason for that," Chester said, and then he went on. "Every night for the next two weeks it was the same thing. Out of his cage, into the kitchen, drain the veggies, and back before dawn. But I detected a puzzling difference from times past when Bunnicula had sucked the juice out of vegetables. This time he didn't always finish the job. It must be, I thought, that he isn't all that hungry. After all, he was still drinking the juice the Monroes gave him every day. What then was his motive? It almost appeared that he was playing a game, that attacking vegetables was a form of sport for him. I thought about it, and it occurred to me that Bunnicula was unusually frisky and playful at that time."

Although I wondered why neither Howie nor I had come upon any evidence of these nighttime escapades, I knew the last part of what Chester had said was true. I remembered how on several occasions when Toby and Pete had taken Bunnicula out of his cage, he'd frolicked about with enormous energy and had appeared especially contented when he'd cuddled into the crook of Toby's neck. As best one can judge the emotional state of a rabbit, I would have said he was the happiest I'd ever known him.

"But he's not like that anymore," I pointed out. "When did it change? And why?"

"This is where the story becomes truly curious," Chester replied. "A couple of weeks ago, I was all set to prevent his midnight runs on the refrigerator when—"

Howie interrupted. "How were you going to do that, Pop?"

"Garlic," Chester said matter-of-factly. "It immobilizes vampires and, as Harold can tell you, it's worked on Bunnicula in the past. In any event, I never got to use it because all of a sudden he stopped."

"No more sinking his fangs into fennel?" Howie asked.

"No more attacking artichokes," said Chester.

"So why didn't you just leave him alone?" I inquired.

"At first, I thought I might. Then it occurred to me that he was probably well aware of my watching him. What if he was trying to lull me into a false sense of security? Perhaps he had something really *big* planned. Ha! I thought. I'll show him a thing or two! And with that, I began sneaking into his cage every day and drinking that disgusting potion the Monroes concoct for him. And as you can see, he's gotten weaker and weaker."

And you, Chester, I thought, have gotten weirder and weirder.

"Do you intend to continue to deprive him of his food until he starves?" I asked.

Chester just gazed at me slyly.

"Let me just repeat: The matter is now under control," he said.

So at the very least Chester planned to keep Bunnicula at bay by weakening him. Yet I couldn't help thinking that there was another reason Bunnicula had stopped his attacks, a reason beyond lack of food, that he had suddenly become less frisky, a reason that had nothing to do with Chester. However, my dog's brain, which is to a cat's brain what a corridor is to a labyrinth, could not begin to sort it all out. No, it would take Chester to do that—and although the conclusion he would draw would be based more on a hunch than hard, cold fact, it would prove to be correct. Just as the consequences would prove to be nearly catastrophic.

[FOUR]

A Rabbit's Tears

I DID not sleep well that night. Toby tossed and turned, and I, tethered to the end of his bed by inertia, allowed myself to be rolled this way and that until shortly before dawn when he sat up and whispered in the dark, "Harold, are you awake?" Not waiting for an answer, he climbed out from under his covers and wrapped himself around me in a full body hug.

"I had bad dreams, boy," he said in a hushed tone. "Did I tell you what movie we saw last night when we went to the last show at the theater? *Dracula.* Not the new one we saw the time we found Bunnicula, but the old one with Bela Lugosi. It wasn't even in color and the special effects were totally lame. I didn't think it was scary at all when I was watching it, but, boy,

Harold, it sure was scary in my dreams."

I looked him in the eye and panted to let him know I understood.

"Aw, you understand, don't you, boy?" he said.

Works every time.

"I'll tell you one thing, Harold," he said, yawning. "You'd better stay out of Mom and Dad's way today. They're pretty bummed out about this theater thing, losing the battle and all. You know what's going to happen on Tuesday? Boom! They're coming in with a wrecking ball and down it goes!"

He yawned again. "Well, I'm going to try to get some more sleep. What are you going to do?"

He ruffled the hair on the top of my head, then crawled back under the covers, and before I'd had time to find out if his question was multiple choice or essay, he was sound asleep.

Looking out the window, I could see that the sky was beginning to grow light. Bunnicula, whose sleeping and waking hours were at odds with everyone else's in the house, would be going to sleep soon for the day, and that meant it was time for his old buddy Harold to sing him a lullaby.

As quietly as I could, I removed myself from

Toby's bed, stretched out my aching muscles, and lumbered down the stairs.

On first encountering the familiar scene in the living room, I felt immensely reassured. Bunnicula was in his cage, Chester was curled up in his armchair, Howie lay sprawled under the coffee table. Each was in his proper place. Serenity was spread over the room like cream cheese on a bagel.

Now for those of you who haven't read my first book, *Bunnicula,* the idea of my singing a lullaby to my little furry friend in the language of his native land (a remote area of the Carpathian Mountains region) may strike you as peculiar. For those of you who have read the book, the idea probably strikes you as just as peculiar, but at least you've been warned. You see, soon after Bunnicula's arrival in our home, I discovered that this particular lullaby soothes him, and so I have sung it to him regularly ever since. Roughly translated, it goes something like this:

The sheep are in the meadow,
The goats are on the roof,
In the parlor are the peasants,
In the pudding is the proof.

Dance on the straw
And laugh at the moon
Night is heavy on your eyes
And morning will come soon.

So sleep, little baby,
There's nothing you should fear,
With garlic at the window
And your mama always near.

Admittedly, it sounds better in the original. I only regret that I cannot record the melody here, for there is a wistful melancholia about it that would touch you, I'm certain, as it touches me when I croon it in my throaty baritone. And I know it touches Bunnicula as it carries him off to dreamland. On this occasion, however, I noted a new response on Bunnicula's part—one that struck me as curious and, under the circumstances, somewhat alarming.

"Do rabbits cry?" I asked Chester after Bunnicula had fallen asleep.

Chester had roused himself from his night's slumber and was in the middle of doing that stretch cats do where they extend their front paws out on the floor in front of them as if they're praying and

raise their rear ends up high like they're waiting for the whole world to notice and say, "Hey, that's some nice tush you got there."

I explained that as I was singing the lullaby to Bunnicula—the same one, I pointed out, that I'd sung him many times before—tears were rolling down his fuzzy little cheeks.

"Rabbits don't have a sentimental bone in their bodies," Chester said, dismissing the whole thing categorically. "Especially vampire rabbits."

And with that he marched into the kitchen for breakfast. End of discussion.

I glanced out the window. The sky was gray, and a misty rain was beginning to fall. The perfect sort of day for serious napping, I thought, and that was exactly how I intended to spend it.

And that was exactly how I *was* spending it until some time later when I heard Chester's voice buzzing in my ear like a gnat.

"Harold, Harold," he buzzed. "I know you're in there, Harold!"

What next? I thought. We've got you surrounded?

"Okay, fine," he went on, "it takes you time to open your eyes, I know that. I wouldn't want you to strain yourself, have a heart attack or something, from the effort of pushing up your eyelids too quickly, so just listen."

Do I bite him now or later?

"I've got it all figured out, Harold."

"He does, Uncle Harold, he really does."

Oh, joy. The junior detective is also on the scene.

"Howie, let me handle this, will you?" Chester said.

"Sure, Pop."

I began to snore.

"Stop trying to pretend you're asleep, Harold," Chester pressed on relentlessly. "Okay, here's my theory. First, when was it that Bunnicula started acting frisky and playful and when, not so coincidentally, did he start his most recent assault on vegetables? Right after Mr. and Mrs. Monroe received calls from their mothers, that's when. Now, when did everything change? Two weeks later, on Mother's Day, Harold! When he heard the other mothers were coming, he must have gotten it into his little hare brain that *his* long-lost mother might be coming on Mother's Day, too, and when she didn't . . . it was down-in-the-dumps for our little furry friend."

"I'll bet he thinks she doesn't love him anymore," Howie chimed in. "And you know what they say—you're no bunny till some bunny loves you."

Fascinating. I could actually *hear* Chester gritting his teeth. "What more evidence do you need, Harold? Think about it. He *cried* when you sang him that silly lullaby. He cried, Harold. He misses his mother! But that's not the half of it. He has plans, Harold, I'm sure of it. Some of those tears were because his plans were not fulfilled. Come on, let's go. I know that you know that I know what must be done!"

Slowly, I raised my eyelids. "Do you talk that

way just to drive me crazy?" I asked. "Or do you actually *think* in sentences like that?"

"If there's any chance Bunnicula's mother has returned, we've got to find her before he does," Chester said.

"Before he does," Howie echoed.

"It can't all be coincidence, Harold. Just think about it. Mother's Day . . . and what movie was playing at the theater? *Dracula,* Harold, *Dracula!*"

I looked at the two of them. I looked out the window. I thought back to Chester's description of Bunnicula's half-finished attacks on the vegetables, as if it were a sport. Maybe he was celebrating in his own way the possibility of being reunited with his mother. There was some logic to that.

"But it's raining," I pointed out.

"So?" said Chester. "You're waterproof. If Bunnicula's mother is out there, who knows how many more vampire rabbits are on the loose?"

"Okay, okay, I'll go with you," I said. "Just give me a minute to look for my mind, will you? I seem to have lost it."

Luckily—at least, luckily for Chester and

Howie—the Monroes were all in other parts of the house, so they didn't see us sneaking out the pet door into the rain.

"This is so cool," Howie yipped excitedly as we rounded the corner at the end of the block. "It's just like FleshCrawlers number twenty-four, *My Parents Are Aliens from the Planet Zorg*. See, there's this girl named Tiffani-Sue Tribellini, and she's trying to find her mother because the person she thinks is her mother is really an alien. How the girl knows is that every time her mother goes near the microwave she glows. Which is not your normal mother thing to do. So one day—"

"Will you two get a move on?" Chester scolded.

"Chester!" I shouted back. "Do you have a clue where you're leading us?"

"More than a clue! We're going to the last place Bunnicula saw his mother and where I believe we will now find her, waiting for her sonny boy! The movie theater!"

"Oh, goody!" Howie cried out. "Can we get popcorn? Can I sit on the aisle? Will there be coming attractions?"

I didn't have the heart to tell Howie we weren't actually going to see a movie. As it turned out, we never even got to the theater. With the disaster that would soon befall us, I couldn't help thinking I'd been right in the first place. It was a perfect day for napping.

[FIVE]

Surprise Encounters

A BIT of an explanation may be useful here. Those of you whose memory, like mine, is as full of holes as a garden hose after Howie's played Let's-Pretend-This-Long-Green-Thing's-a-Snake with it may not recall the exact circumstances of Bunnicula's coming to live with us. One night a couple of years ago, the Monroes went to the movies and on one of the seats discovered a dirt-filled shoebox holding a tiny white-and-black bunny. A note in a foreign language read TAKE GOOD CARE OF MY BABY. Because the movie *Dracula* was playing there that night, Mrs. Monroe had the bright idea of combining "bunny" and "Dracula" to come up with the rabbit's name: Bunnicula. This was after she'd had the anything-but-bright ideas of naming him Fluffy or Bun-Bun. She means well, Mrs. Monroe, but sometimes her taste is decidedly *Brady Bunch.*

Now I was not convinced, as Chester clearly was, that Bunnicula's mother—if she in fact had been the one to leave him at the movie theater in the first place—would still be hanging around there. After all, how long could anybody take a diet of stale popcorn and gummy bears? And if she had not stayed there, what would make her want to return? Remorse? But I did find his argument compelling that Bunnicula, for whatever reason, seemed to miss his mother and had gone on his recent rampage out of excitement over Mother's Day. So perhaps it was worth trying to find her. I didn't let on that my motives were different from his. He may have been out to undo some vague grand plan he imagined was under way. He may have been determined to destroy vampire rabbits. *I* was intent on reuniting them.

Luckily, the rain stopped, the sun came out, and soon the sweet smell of spring blossoms and fresh earth permeated the air. Not to mention certain other aromas of infinitely greater interest to dogs.

"Do you two have to stop at *every* hydrant?" Chester snapped at one point.

"We're investigating," I explained.

"Yeah," said Howie, "maybe we'll pick up Bunnicula's mother's scent."

"Unless she's a volunteer firerabbit, I don't think that's too likely," Chester retorted. "Now, come on!"

"How do you know where the movie theater is?" I called out.

"I don't!" Chester shot back.

I would have protested, but what difference would it have made? Chester never allows a minor detail like not knowing where he's going to get in his way. Besides, it really was shaping up to be a beautiful day and, to my surprise, I was glad to be out in it. I didn't even mind that the streets we were trotting along no longer seemed familiar.

After some time, we came to a street that was lined with stores. A new scent caught the attention of my nostrils. I lifted them to the air and sniffed.

"Pizza!" I cried. "Lunchtime!"

"No anchovies on mine," said Howie. I doubted he knew what anchovies were. He just said it, I think, because Pete always says it when the Monroes order pizza.

"Will you two get your minds off your stomachs for once?" Chester said impatiently. "Look at those two dogs over there. They seem perfectly content just to be lying in the sun. Why can't the two of you—"

Chester was cut off by Howie's yipping, "It's Bob and Linda!"

I looked closely. A caramel-colored cocker spaniel in a Mets cap. A West Highland white terrier with a lavender bandanna knotted jauntily around her neck. The bandanna may have been different, but otherwise the two looked exactly the same as when we'd last seen them.

"It *is* them!" I exclaimed. "Chester, it's Bob and Linda from Chateau Bow-Wow."

I don't know whether it was Bob and Linda in particular or the memory of the boarding kennel where we'd met them, but Chester muttered, "Oh, no," and rolled his eyes. If Pete was an Olympic eye-roller, Chester could have been his coach.

Howie ran on ahead of us.

"Well, look who it is," I heard Bob saying. "Linda, it's little Howie from that dreadful place the kids left us last summer." "The kids" was what Bob and Linda called their owners.

Linda raised herself to her haunches. "Well, so it is!" she remarked. Looking in my direction, she called out, "Yoo-hoo, Harold, is that you?"

"And Chester," I called back. Chester was muttering under his breath as we approached.

"Well, for heaven's sake," Linda went on, "whatever brings you to Upper Centerville? This is just too quaint."

I noticed that the two dogs were tied to a parking meter in front of a coffee place called ESPRESSO YOURSELF. Bob's leash was bright green with the word POLO printed repeatedly in purple letters along its length. Linda's was lavender (perfectly matching her bandanna) with HALSTON repeated on it in black. Next to them was a ceramic trough with *Pour les chiens* written on its side. It was filled with water with slices of lemon floating in it. I later learned that *pour les chiens* means "for the dogs."

So this was Upper Centerville.

"Well," I said, trying to come up with an answer to Linda's question that would not immediately

POLO
POUR

qualify us for the loony bin, "we're out for a stroll, actually. We, we . . ."

"We're looking for the movie theater," Chester said.

What a relief! He wasn't going to say . . .

"Because . . ."

Oh, no.

". . . we're looking for a vampire rabbit. Have you seen one?"

"Uh, not lately," said Bob. He looked over his shoulder as if to say, "I wonder what's keeping the kids."

"We don't get many vampire rabbits in Upper Centerville," Linda said, regarding Chester with a mixture of sympathy and distaste. "What exactly would we be looking for?"

"Black and white," said Chester. "Red eyes. Fangs. Strange eating habits."

They thought for a moment. "We *do* know a dalmatian who's awfully fond of Tofutti," Linda offered.

"But then who isn't?" said Bob.

Linda nodded her head as Chester began muttering to himself again.

"I wish the kids would get out here with our cappuccino," Bob said. Then, "Say, here's a coincidence. We ran into two other inmates—I mean, guests—from Chateau Bow-Wow just the other day."

Linda wrinkled her nose. "Those two *cats*," she said. "No offense to you, Chester."

"None taken," said Chester. "I assume you're referring to Felony and Miss Demeanor."

"Indeed," said Bob. "Seems they were up to their old tricks. The kids were walking us in downtown Centerville. They hadn't taken us there in years, but now it's so 'out' it's 'in' again, if you know what I mean."

I didn't have a clue.

Linda picked up the story. "We had just passed the movie theater when we spotted these two cats scurrying out from behind a garbage pail in the next alley. I referred to them as riffraff—a little loudly, I'm afraid—and one of them said, 'Hey, you remember us!' and that's when I knew it had to be—"

"Felony and Miss Demeanor," said Bob. "They seemed genuinely pleased to see us. They asked where we lived."

"We told them we'd just moved and couldn't remember the address," Linda said. "After all, they *are* cat burglars. They were on their way to a so-called caper even as we spoke. Shameful."

Bob shook his head sadly. "They have too much time on their hands, that's their problem. They need a hobby. Anyway, they told us they lived down there."

"In the alley?" Chester asked.

"No," said Linda, "somewhere nearby. They just use the alley as their office."

"Wow," said Howie, "do they have a fax machine?"

Bob smiled indulgently at Howie. "I don't think so," he said. "Maybe you'll see them when you go to the movie theater."

"There's something to live for," said Chester.

As he was getting directions to downtown Centerville, Linda suddenly remembered something.

"Last night," she said, "we saw a black-and-white animal rummaging about in the garbage behind that new vegetarian restaurant. Just caught a glimpse of it really. Maybe it was the rabbit you're looking for."

Chester's ears perked up. "Vegetarian, did you say?"

"Yes, it's right down the street here between

Maison de Wallpaper and Amour de Hair; you can't miss it."

"In the French Quarter, eh?" said Chester. "Well, thanks for the tip. We'll check it out before we head downtown to the theater."

Bidding Bob and Linda goodbye, we headed off down the street.

"If it *was* Bunnicula's mother," said Howie as Maison de Wallpaper came into view, "wouldn't she be asleep now?"

"Making it all the easier for us to find her," said Chester, a satisfied smile creeping across his face. "Who knows? Maybe we'll get lucky and find more than one sleeping vampire rabbit! There, that must be it!"

VICIOUSLY VEGGIE, the sign on the restaurant read. POWER FOOD FOR THE POWER HUNGRY. I was learning a lot about the people who lived in Upper Centerville.

A narrow passageway ran between the two buildings. We could make out a glimpse of garbage cans and what looked like a Dumpster at the far end.

Chester went into his skulking position.

"Oh, do we *have* to?" I whined. "You know I hate to skulk."

"You're a hunter!" Chester snapped. "Now let's go!"

Chester began to slink along the building's edge, his body tight and as focused as a missile homing in on its target. I would have taken him a little more seriously had I not seen him assume this same position stalking a butterfly the week before.

Howie was directly behind Chester, imitating his every move. For sheer entertainment value, there's nothing quite like watching a dachshund try to slink like a cat.

But who am I to judge? After all, was I not soon third in line? If I wasn't exactly skulking, I was doing some sort of vague interpretation of your basic hunting stance. Not that I've ever *been* a hunting dog, mind you, regardless of what Chester may think about my canine instincts. The Monroes don't believe in hunting, for one thing, and as for me, just the thought of carrying something dead and uncooked between my teeth . . . *brrr.*

As we got closer to the back of the buildings, Chester slowed to a near halt.

"I see something," he hissed. "Look there, between those two garbage cans."

I didn't see a thing until the sun bounced off something shiny. Was it metal? No, it glistened and moved as if it was alive.

"I'm going to go in for a closer look," said Chester. "Cover me."

"Okay," Howie said. "Do we have a blanket, Uncle Harold?"

"I don't think that's what Chester has in mind."

"Oh."

Chester was moving as cats do when they're closing in on their prey, which is to say I could have napped between steps. When he got close, however, his demeanor—and his tempo—did an abrupt change.

"Run!" he shouted as he turned and sped past us back up the alleyway.

"What is it?" I cried out.

Well may you ask why I cried out instead of following Chester's (for once) wise advice. Suffice it to say that those three little words kept me in the wrong place for three little seconds too long.

And then it was all over. All over Howie. And all over me.

We hightailed it out of there as fast as we could, but the damage was done. My eyes were stinging. My throat was burning. My nostrils were begging for mercy.

"Chester!" I shouted. "I'm going to get you for this!"

But Chester couldn't hear me. He was far off in the distance, heading for home. So was Howie. And so was I.

And so was the stench of a *skunk*.

[SIX]

Tomato Juice, Togas, and Trouble

IF Pete said "Gross!" once, he said it a hundred times.

I tried not taking it personally. After all, it *was* pretty gross. Not to mention humiliating. Especially when Mr. Monroe bathed Howie and me in tomato juice. Chester had managed to escape the skunk's assault, but Mr. Monroe considered giving him a regular bath just to be on the safe side. Knowing how much Chester hates baths, he spelled it out.

"I think I should give Chester a b-a-t-h, too," he told Mrs. Monroe.

To which Chester's response was, "I'm out of h-e-r-e," and he was gone.

The Monroes haven't figured out that Chester can spell.

Cats, in case you don't know it, do not care to be bathed by anything other than their own tongues. Dogs, on the other hand, have an entirely different philosophy of life. Simply stated, it's this: Never do for yourself what you can get others to do for you. I call this "conservation of energy." Chester has a less exalted name for it. "Laziness," I believe it is.

In any event, after our tomato juice baths, Howie and I were plunked in the tub for a nice long soak. Howie got to practice his backstroke and I got to practice my lifesaving skills each time he sank to the bottom.

It was after Mr. Monroe had left us swathed in towels to dry off that Chester poked his head around the bathroom door, looked to the left and right, sniffed the air to be sure we no longer stank, and cautiously entered the room.

"Chester," I said, "I'd like a few words with you."

"All right, all right," he said, "so Plan A didn't exactly work out."

"It didn't exactly work out?" I repeated. "Is that all you have to say for yourself?"

"No," said Chester. "I also want to tell you about Plan B."

I am not normally prone to violence, but at that moment I might have been tempted to tie Chester's whiskers in a bountiful array of knots had I not been so tightly wrapped in my towel. At the very least I would have pressed for an apology, but I was beginning to see that there were more similarities between Chester and Pete than I'd ever noticed before. Being a cat or an eleven-year-old boy, I surmised, must mean never having to say you're sorry.

"Okay, lads, here's what I'm thinking," Chester said as he began to pace in front of us. Howie loves it when Chester gets going like this and he panted appreciatively. I, on the other hand, tried rolling my eyes but only succeeded in noticing that my bangs needed trimming.

"Let's say I'm right about Bunnicula's mother," Chester said, "which of course I am. My guess is that Bunnicula hasn't figured out where she is. Maybe he hasn't even made the connection between his mother and the movie theater. Otherwise, he would have broken out of this joint a long time ago.

So he's still waiting for her to come to him. Fine. Here's what we've got to do."

He paused to look at us.

"Why do I feel like I'm addressing the Roman Senate?" he asked.

Howie and I looked blankly at each other.

"Is that a trick question?" Howie said.

Chester shook his head wearily. "Togas," he said. "You look like you're wearing togas. The way they did in ancient Rome. Don't you two ever read?"

He should have known better than to ask.

"I read a book about ancient Rome!" Howie piped up enthusiastically. "*Screaming Mummies of the Pharaoh's Tomb*. FleshCrawlers, number twenty-eight. There were these twins, see, Harry and Carrie Fishbein, and they found this time-travel machine in their grandfather's attic. They were just fooling around with it, but before you knew it—*poof!*—they were in ancient—"

"Egypt!" Chester snapped, cutting Howie off. "They were in ancient Egypt, Howie, and the two of you look like ancient Romans, and there is an actual difference between ancient Egypt and ancient Rome, and why I even bother to bring up historical or literary references with you two dolts is beyond me!"

Chester kept on ranting, but I'm not sure what else he had to say. Drowsy from my bath and the room's warmth, I nodded off somewhere around "historical or literary references." When I regained consciousness, he was carrying on about Plan B.

"So we've got to keep our eye on him at all times," he was saying, "because if he does start making connections, there's no stopping him. Either we have to prevent their reuniting entirely or, better yet, use Bunnicula to lead us to his mother. He may still be weak, but even so I'm going to need your help. Maybe we should work in shifts."

"We have to put on *dresses?*" Howie whined.

Chester grimaced. "We'll *take turns,* okay?"

"Oh."

Just then, Mr. Monroe came into the room to give us a final rubdown. He looked at us and smiled.

"Chester, you look like you're addressing the Roman Senate," he said.

"Uncanny," Chester commented after Mr. Monroe had left.

"Yes," I said, thinking of yesterday's breakfast, "it was nice having fresh meat for a change, wasn't it?"

"Hey, Uncle Harold," Howie said. "I get it. Fresh meat. Uncanny. That was pretty good."

"Thanks, Howie," I said, leaving it at that. It's embarrassing when you make a joke and don't even realize it.

The night watch began. Why I was supporting Chester's harebrained scheme I don't know. Sometimes you just find yourself doing things Chester expects you to do. So I volunteered to take the first shift, figuring that it would be better to get it over with and have the rest of the night for uninterrupted sleep. What I hadn't counted on was the discovery I would make while I was on duty, one that would keep me awake—and alert—the whole night.

Bunnicula was sick. Really sick. Far weaker than he would be from Chester's depriving him of his carrot juice. He wasn't moving at all. When I talked to him, his ears didn't twitch or stir as they normally did. At times, it seemed he wasn't even breathing.

Not wanting to alarm Howie, I let him sleep through his shift. As for Chester, well, I tried to convince him that Bunnicula was in trouble, but he wasn't having any of it.

"Either he misses his mother or he's faking" was his unscientifically arrived at diagnosis. "Neither one is fatal, Harold. And if it is—"

"Chester! What are you saying?"

"I think you know what I'm saying, Harold."

Desperately seeking some way of comprehending Chester's devious mind, I asked, "Chester, are you still drinking Bunnicula's juice?"

"Not all the time," he answered, "although I have developed a taste for the stuff. No, I have other ways of foiling his plans now."

"But, Chester, he may be really sick," I said.

"Harold, once and for all, you've got to understand. Bunnicula is *not* the Easter bunny. He's a spinach sucker! The bane of broccoli! A bad rabbit with bad habits! If he can lead us to his mother, we may be able to put an end to this race of terrorizing hares once and for all!"

"But, Chester, you said yourself, he probably hasn't made any connections yet, and he certainly isn't going anywhere. He can barely move. How is he going to lead us to his mother when he can't lift his head?"

Chester narrowed his eyes to slits. "Don't underestimate his vampirical powers. Believe me, Harold, if he can't lead us to his mother, he will somehow manage to bring his mother here to him. You can lead a horse of a different color to water but it's still a horse."

Don't ask.

As it turned out, Bunnicula did go somewhere, but it was not under his own powers—vampirical or otherwise.

Unable to stand it any longer, I woke Toby just

before dawn and dragged him by the sleeve of his pajamas downstairs to Bunnicula's cage. It didn't take him long to get the picture.

"Mom! Dad! Come quick!" he shouted. "Bunnicula's really sick! I think he's going to die!"

Mr. and Mrs. Monroe raced down the stairs. Mr. Monroe, still half asleep, tumbled over the armchair, which sent Chester flying. Chester's indignant screech in turn woke Howie, who bolted from under the coffee table just in time to get tangled in Mr. Monroe's legs. Nobody, other than Chester, seemed to notice or care, though. All eyes were on Bunnicula.

"Oh, Robert," said Mrs. Monroe, touching her husband's arm as he opened the cage and lifted the limp, languid rabbit from it. "I *knew* we should have taken him to the vet on Saturday. We've waited too long."

Mr. Monroe held Bunnicula close to his chest. "His breathing seems normal, if a bit slow," he said, stroking the bunny lovingly. "But there's definitely something wrong with him. I'll call Dr. Greenbriar right away and leave a message that I'm bringing

Bunnicula in on my way to work this morning. I'm pretty sure his downtown office is open early on Mondays."

"Can I go with you, Dad?" Toby asked.

Mr. Monroe shook his head. "You have school today, young man."

"But I could miss it, couldn't I? What's one day of school?"

"You have tomorrow off because of teacher conferences. That's enough days off for this week. Besides, it's Bunnicula who's sick, not you."

"But what if Bunnicula d—" Toby stopped himself from completing his sentence. I bumped up against his leg to remind him that his pal Harold was there for him. I felt his hand come to rest lightly on the top of my head.

"Now, son," Mr. Monroe said in a soft, soothing voice, "I'm sure Bunnicula will be fine. Maybe there's a problem with the food we've been giving him. Or maybe it's some kind of virus. Whatever it is, Dr. Greenbriar will figure it out and have him all fixed up in no time flat."

"Promise?" Toby said.

I looked up at Mr. Monroe's face. There was

something in it that told me he wasn't entirely comfortable with his answer.

"Promise," he told Toby.

Later that morning, after Mr. and Mrs. Monroe had gone to work and Toby and Pete to school, the phone rang.

Howie jumped up from where he was napping and began running in circles. "I'll get it! I'll get it!" he yipped.

The answering machine picked up.

"Boys," Mr. Monroe's voice said. Howie stopped yipping at once. "I just wanted to leave you this message since you'll get home before I do today. Dr. Greenbriar is keeping Bunnicula overnight. He needs to run some tests. The important thing is not to worry. Bunnicula will be fine, guys. Okay? Bunnicula will be . . . fine."

The machine clicked off.

"Mr. Monroe didn't sound like Bunnicula would be fine," Howie said.

"No, he didn't," I agreed.

Chester said nothing, and the three of us fell into an uneasy silence. The only sound was the ticking of the grandfather clock in the hall. The space by the window where Bunnicula's cage had been sitting only that morning was empty, save for the fine layer of dust that held a few white and black hairs. I sniffed at them, sneezed from the dust, then felt my eyes grow wet with the thought that these few hairs were all that remained of Bunnicula. I'd never even said good-bye.

I turned. Chester was staring intently at the empty space.

"Plan C," he said, and then fell silent again.

[SEVEN]

Plant, See?

I DIDN'T see Chester for most of the rest of the day. I assumed he was keeping himself busy with Plan C, whatever that was, but since Bunnicula was now safely out of the house, I didn't worry about it much. Surely Dr. Greenbriar would find out what was wrong with him. And there would be no crazed cat around to suck down his vegetable juices while he slept, so at the very least Bunnicula would be able to eat properly again.

By the time the boys came home, I had begun to wonder where Chester was, however. On Mondays, Toby and Pete get home about a half hour before their father arrives from the university where he teaches. Howie and I always rush to the door to greet them and Toby always says, "Hi, guys, I'll bet you're hungry!"

Does he know dogs or what?

Now Chester may harp at me and Howie about our thinking with our stomachs, but it's a known fact that cats are every bit as meal-minded as dogs. It's just that dogs are more obvious about it. You take one look in our eyes and you know what we're thinking.

Feed me.

Pet me.

Love me.

Even if I did turn your new catcher's mitt into an unrecognizable glob of leather and dog slobber, I'm still your best buddy, right?

Cats, on the other hand, like to keep you guessing. They'll rub back and forth against your legs (I've observed that Chester likes to do this most when the Monroes are wearing black pants), meowing like crazy until you finally get the message, and then they start doing this little dance that you *think* is saying, "Yes, yes, that's it! Food! That's what I want! Give me food!" You bend down to put the bowl on the floor, and they practically knock you over trying to get at it. And then what happens? One sniff and they walk out of the kitchen with their tails in the air, as if to say, "Is *that* what you thought I wanted? You *must* be joking!"

I'm sure you have observed, however, that when you return to the kitchen fifteen minutes later, the bowl is empty. I'll let you in on a little secret: When it comes to food, cats are the same as dogs. They just don't let you see it.

In any event, normally when Toby and Pete get home from school, Chester comes out from wherever he's been hiding to rub up against Toby's legs and go into his little feed-me dance. This time, however, he was nowhere to be seen.

Once Howie and I had finished our afternoon snack with Toby and Pete, we set off in search of Chester.

We sniffed out his usual hiding places—under Toby's bed, on top of the computer in the den, in the laundry basket. All to no avail.

Howie even nosed Chester's favorite catnip mouse under several pieces of furniture where we wouldn't be able to fit but Chester might. Nothing.

As we trotted down the stairs after our second

search of all the bedrooms, Howie said, "Gee, Uncle Harold, maybe Pop went out the pet door while we were sleeping. Maybe he's gone after Bunnicula."

"I've already considered that," I told Howie. "The only problem is that there would be no way for him to get into the vet's office once he got there. No, I don't think that's what he—"

It was then that I heard it. Mewing. Pitiful mewing. It was coming from inside the front hall closet.

Moving quickly, I nudged the door open with my nose. There, atop a jumble of winter boots and fallen jackets, lay Chester. He looked worse than he sounded.

"Chester!" I cried out. "What's wrong?"

He responded with a deep-throated cowlike moan.

Alarmed, Howie and I went into a frenzy of barking.

Ordinarily, Chester might have told us to put a lid on it, but I noticed he wasn't complaining. I also noticed that he looked a lot like Bunnicula had been looking lately—glassy-eyed, lethargic. Maybe Mr. Monroe had been right. Maybe Bunnicula had a virus of some kind. Maybe Chester

had it now. Maybe Howie and I were next!

Just as Toby and Pete came running in from the kitchen, the front door swung open and in walked Mr. Monroe.

"What's going on?" he asked, dropping his brief-case to the floor.

"I don't know," Pete told his father. "The dogs started barking like crazy and we just got here and—"

"Look!" Toby grabbed his father's arm and pulled him toward the closet. Howie and I stopped barking as Chester, who now had all eyes upon him, filled the void with a mewling that sent chills down my spine.

"Pete, get Chester's carrier from the garage!" Mr. Monroe commanded. "We've got to get him to the doctor right away! And while we're at it . . ."

I started to slink away, but made it no farther than the bottom of the stairs before Toby had me by the collar.

". . . let's take Harold and Howie in, too, and have them checked."

I'll spare you the details of my trip to the vet. Suffice it to say it involved a lot of panting, drooling, shaking, and shedding. Fortunately, the vet knows enough to recognize normal canine behavior when he sees it, so Howie and I each received a clean bill of health and were sent home. Chester wasn't so lucky.

Of course, as I would learn later, luck had nothing to do with it. Chester was sick, all right, and he was going to have to spend the night at the vet's, but that was exactly what he wanted.

"Plant, see?" said Howie, calling out to me from inside the hall closet later that day. He had crawled in there to be close to Chester's scent and had quickly made an important discovery.

You've heard the expression "Take time to stop and smell the roses?" Well, for cats, it's "Take time to stop and eat the houseplants." So the fact that Chester had eaten Pete and Toby's Mother's Day gift to Mrs. Monroe was not altogether shocking—although he did usually exercise a little more restraint. What was surprising was the fact that he'd hidden the plant's remains in the back of the hall closet. And when I say remains, I'm talking about a few stems.

Why had he done it? It didn't take me long to figure it out.

"Plan C," I said to Howie.

"That's what I said. Plant, see?"

"No, Howie, this was Chester's Plan C. Making himself sick was his way of getting inside the animal hospital. He's gone after Bunnicula!"

"What does this mean?" Howie asked.

"It means," I said, aware that I was about to sound remarkably like Chester, "that we have a job to do, Howie."

"Oh, goody," Howie said. "Is it washing the dishes? I love that job. Although the last time I licked all the plates clean, Mrs. Monroe came into the kitchen and got all upset as if I'd left some food on them or something. Which I happen to know for a fact I did not. So this time—"

"Howie!" I snapped. Now I *really* felt like Chester. "Not that kind of job. A mission, a duty! We have to catch up with Chester before it's too late!"

"Then let's go!" Howie yipped enthusiastically. "We can wash the dishes later!"

Luckily, the Monroes had gone out for the evening, so it was easy to let ourselves out the pet door and be on our way. And although I hadn't thought so earlier, it was also a piece of luck that we'd been to the vet's that day and I had paid attention, because now I knew how to get there. The only problem was how we were going to break in. And then a third piece of luck fell into place. Howie said something that gave me the answer.

"Wait a minute, Uncle Harold," he said, coming to a sudden halt after we'd been walking for a few minutes. "We're not going back to where that skunk was, are we?"

"No," I said. "That was Upper Centerville. We're going in the opposite direction."

"Good, because that skunk makes me think

about counterfeit pennies, you know why?"

"Why?"

"Bad scents. Get it, Uncle Harold? Huh, do you get it?"

I chuckled indulgently. "Yes, Howie," I said, "very funny."

Encouraged, Howie went on. "Do you know what the judge said when the skunk walked in? Odor in the court! Odor in the court! Hey, Uncle Harold, what did one skunk say to the other skunk when he bowed his head? Let us spray! I got a million of 'em, Uncle Harold."

"Well, save some for a rainy day," I told Howie, but he went on anyway. I wasn't listening, however, because his mentioning the skunk had brought to my mind Bob and Linda. And thinking of Bob and Linda gave me the answer to my problem.

[EIGHT]

Friends and Traitors

"WHAT are we doing *here?*" Howie asked a short time later. "I thought you said we were going to the vet's, but here we are at the movies. Can I get some popcorn?"

"I'm afraid we're not going to the movies—or the movie theater," I explained to Howie. "We're looking for—"

I stopped myself when I spotted them coming around the corner of the alley they called their office. There was no mistaking that scrawny gray cat and her fat tabby sidekick. It was Felony and Miss Demeanor, all right. Sisters in crime. Cat burglars. If anyone would know how to break into a locked building, those two would.

"Felony!" I called out. "Miss Demeanor!"

They stopped in their tracks, Miss Demeanor clumsily stumbling into Felony's backside, nearly toppling her over. Felony turned and snarled at her companion, who responded with, "Oh yeah, you and who else?" Ah, they'd lost none of their charm!

Felony looked in my direction. "Who wants us?" she called out in a voice she probably picked up from watching old gangster movies on cable.

Howie ran to them, yipping happily. "It's us, it's us! Howie and Harold! Remember? From Chateau Bow-Wow last summer?"

As I loped along behind Howie, I could see Felony's eyes giving us the once-over. When she did it again, I wanted to ask if it was now called a twice-over but thought better of it.

Suddenly, recognition lit up her eyes as if someone had turned on a switch.

"Hey, Miss D.," she shouted over her shoulder.

Miss Demeanor, who was maybe an inch behind her, shouted back, "What?"

"It's two of those three bozos we met at Chateau Bow-Wow."

Miss Demeanor, who looked like she'd have to be completely rewired before anything lit up her blank eyes, drawled, "Uh-huh."

Felony scowled. "We ain't got all night, Miss D. Let me give ya a little hint: Cute Whiskers."

"Ooooo," the fat tabby purred. Cute Whiskers is what she had called Chester. "Now I remember. So where is he?" She looked on either side of us as if we might be hiding him somewhere.

"That's why we came to see you," I said. "You see, Chester is missing."

"I always said he was missing," Felony quipped. "Missing half a deck!" She chortled merrily and Miss Demeanor joined in.

"No, no, I mean he's really missing," I persevered. I explained that it was imperative we break into the animal hospital and rescue Chester right away. I didn't go into too many details. I was afraid they'd end up siding with Chester and want to help him instead of me. Besides, I had the feeling Felony and Miss Demeanor weren't exactly cut out for handling more than a few details at a time.

"I dunno," Felony said when I'd finished. "We

wuz on our way to a big caper. We haven't got a lotta time to spare."

"It won't take much time," I promised. "All you have to do is find a way in. We'll take it from there."

Felony turned up a corner of her mouth and made a strange sucking sound. I gathered this was an outward manifestation of some deep inner mental activity.

"Well *(slurp, snap, suck)*, I guess *(snap, slurp, pop)* we could consider it *(slurp, suck, sizzle)* . . ."

In desperation, I turned to Miss Demeanor. "Don't do it for us," I pleaded. "Do it for Cute Whiskers."

I couldn't believe I actually referred to Chester as Cute Whiskers. The words curdled in my mouth. But they worked.

"Yer right, Harold," said Miss Demeanor. "Come on, Felony, we gotta help out our fella feline. After all, he helped us out once."

"Yeah, yeah, yeah *(smack, slurp, smack)*." Felony lowered the corner of her mouth, then turned her head in either direction to make sure she wasn't being overheard. "We're breakin' into the Big Belly

Deli, see, and we gotta time it just right. We can't be late, got it?"

"I got it," I said. "Then you'll do it?"

"Yeah, we'll do it—seein' as how it's fer Chester an' all."

As we walked away, Miss Demeanor began to purr loudly. "We're gonna sneak inta the Big Belly Deli at closin' time and party all night," she said. "I'm havin' a corned beef and sardine on rye, and that's just fer starters."

"And I'm havin' bologna and herring on pumpernickel," said Felony, "with mustard and maybe a little Tabasco sauce. And then I'm havin' . . ."

By the time we reached the animal hospital, I wasn't sure if I was starved or never wanted to eat again.

It was just starting to get dark. Luckily, there were very few people around, so it was easy to check out the premises without being noticed. The problem was, the premises appeared to be sealed tight.

Staring at the heavily bolted back entrance to the building, I sighed. "What was I thinking? There's no way we can get in."

Felony cleared her throat. "I did not come all

this way to be insulted," she said. "You are dealing with professionals here, Harold. If you thought this was going to be a piece of cake, would you have called in professionals?"

"Oh, yeah," said Miss Demeanor, "and that reminds me—and then I'm gonna have a piece of marble pound cake with a side of potato salad."

"Did you ever read *The Potato Has a Thousand Eyes*?" Howie asked.

Miss Demeanor's eyes took on the dull luster of tarnished brass. "Read?" she said.

I sensed we were getting a wee bit off course.

"Felony," I said, "how do you imagine—"

"Window!" Felony snapped.

"But—"

"I was thinkin' we'd have to go in through the ducts, but looky there, Harold."

I raised my head in the direction Felony indicated. There, not two feet above my head, was a window. It was open only a crack, but if the two cat burglars could jimmy it all the way, the opening would be large enough for both Howie and me to fit through easily.

"That's lucky," I said.

Felony turned to Miss D. "Crowbar," she said.

"Crowbar," Miss D. repeated.

Within minutes, the two cats had come up with a makeshift crowbar and had the window halfway open. I had to admire their dexterity and skill.

From the other side of the window, I heard a familiar voice call out, "Who is it? Who's there?"

"Oh, yoo-hoo, hunky boy!" Miss Demeanor called out. I cringed on Chester's behalf. "We're comin' to get ya, Cute Whiskers!"

"Cute Whiskers?" I heard Chester repeat from inside. "Is it . . . is that . . . ?"

"One, two, three!" Felony commanded. The two cats arched their backs against the half-open window and forced it all the way up. We were home-free.

"It is I! It is me! It is we! It is us!" cried Miss Demeanor in a bravado display of grammatical insecurity.

I too became insecure at that moment, worrying that the two cats would jump inside and free Chester before I could stop them. I was saved by a remarkable stroke of luck.

A clock tower chimed eight times.

"It's closin' time at the Big Belly Deli!" Felony shrieked. "We're gonna be late!"

"Aw, can't I just say hello to Cute Whiskers?" Miss Demeanor whined.

"Pastrami and lox on an onion roll!" was Felony's reply.

Miss Demeanor jumped down from the windowsill. "Gotta run," she said. "Say hi to Cute Whiskers for me, will ya, Harold?"

"Thank . . ." I said to the two cats as they streaked off into the night, ". . . you."

"Harold, Harold? Is that you?" Chester called out. "What's going on out there?"

With the help of a garbage pail, I leaped up onto the windowsill, then lifted Howie up by the nape of his neck. The two of us dropped down into the dimly lit back room of the veterinarian's office. I felt like a hero in a war movie.

As my eyes adjusted to the light, I saw Chester staring down at us from a nearby cage.

"Chester!" I cried. "How are you feeling?"

"Greenbriar gave me some kind of medicine that made me sleep most of the day. Right now, my mouth feels like somebody lined it with mouse fur, but other than that I'm feeling a lot better. You've got to get me out of here, Harold!"

It suddenly occurred to me how quiet the place was.

"Where is everybody?" I asked.

"I'm the only one here."

"But where's Bunnicula?" Howie inquired.

"He's gone."

Howie began to whimper. "Gone? To the big carrot patch in the sky? The bunny beyond? The hareafter? The hoppy hunting ground? The—"

"He escaped!" Chester exploded.

"Oh," said Howie.

"That's why you've got to get me out of here! I've got to stop him before it's too late."

"Was this his cage?" Howie asked. He was looking in at a ground-level cage next to him.

"As a matter of fact, yes," said Chester. "Why do you ask?"

"Look, Uncle Harold," said Howie. "Look at the newspaper lining the bottom."

I looked. It was Saturday's paper. There was a big ad in the middle of the page:

CENTERVILLE CINEMA—THE LAST PICTURE SHOW!

SEE THE MOVIE THAT OPENED
THIS LANDMARK THEATER IN 1931!

***DRACULA*, STARRING BELA LUGOSI**

TRANSYLVANIA COMES TO CENTERVILLE!

BE THERE . . . IF YOU DARE!!

If Bunnicula hadn't thought before of looking for his mother at the movie theater, there was no question in my mind now that that is where he had gone. I knew what I had to do.

And I knew what I couldn't do.

"Come on, Harold, get me out of here. It can't be that hard to unlock this cage. I'll talk you through it."

I looked up at my friend, my best friend, my oldest friend in the world, and I said, "I'm afraid I can't do that, Chester."

"Oh, now, Harold," Chester said, "of course you can. I'm sorry for all the times I've called you a dunce or a simpleton—"

"Or a dolt," I said.

"Or a dolt," Chester went on, "but I know you're not really *that* dumb. I'm sure you can figure out how to open the door and get me out of here."

"It's not that I can't do it, Chester," I said. "It's that I *won't* do it."

I looked away, but I could hear in the silence that Chester understood what I was saying.

"I thought you were my friend," he said at last.

My heart lay heavy in my chest. "I am your friend, but I'm Bunnicula's friend, too, and I can't let you hurt him. I've stood by you in all your crazy attempts to do him in in the past, but I . . . Well, I just can't do it anymore, Chester. I'm sorry."

Chester's voice was like a shard of ice that cut through me. "Sorry?" he said. "That's what you have to say after all the years we've been friends? Sorry? Well, here's what I'm sorry about, Harold. I'm sorry that I can't be your friend anymore."

I looked up. "Chester," I said.

But he turned his back on me and said nothing. Nothing, that is, but one word, which he spat out at me as Howie and I made our way back out through the open window.

"Traitor," he said.

When Howie and I emerged into the outside world, the air felt different. Where it had been warm and springlike before, now all I felt was a chill. All I wanted was for everything to be the way it once had been. And all I knew was that it never would be. I had lost my best friend. How I ached to go home and curl up in a dark corner where I could sleep for days. But I couldn't go home. I had to find Bunnicula. How was he to know that the newspaper in his cage was from two days earlier? There would be no movie shown tonight, just an empty, dangerous theater perilously close to being destroyed.

As we set off to find Bunnicula, Chester's final word repeated itself over and over in my mind.

Traitor. Traitor. Traitor.

[NINE]

The Last Showdown

BY the time Howie and I reached the movie theater, the night sky was not only chilly but dark. I could make out several large trucks parked out front, one of which held a tall crane with an ominous steel ball hanging from the end of it, and everywhere there were police barricades and banners bearing the words DEMOLITION SITE, DO NOT CROSS. All I could think was that somewhere inside that darkened, haunted-looking theater was a weak and sickly bunny searching for his mother. Was she even in there? Or was Bunnicula pursuing a memory, a wish, a phantom?

"Are w-we g-g-going in there?" Howie stammered next to me. "It looks scary, Uncle Harold. Like *Night of the Living Gargoyles.*"

"Excuse me?"

"Number eighteen. There's this boy, see . . ."

"Howie," I said, "we have to get Bunnicula out of there before the building is torn down tomorrow."

"What about his mother?"

"Yes, well, we'll get her out, too, of course." I didn't tell Howie that I had serious doubts Bunnicula's mother was in there.

I also had serious doubts we would be in there anytime soon. This was a challenge that would have stumped Felony and Miss Demeanor. It was too dark to find a way in—and even if we did get past all the barricades and doors locked with chains, it would probably be pitch-black. Besides, I told myself, if we looked for Bunnicula now, the Monroes would miss us. No, it would be better to return first thing in the morning, when there was light.

Howie didn't give me an argument. He was as glad as I was to be out of there. And the Monroes were glad to see us when we returned.

Howie, being young and without worries, slept soundly that night. I did not. When I wasn't worrying about whether we'd be able to rescue Bunnicula before the wrecking crew did its work, I was thinking about what had happened between Chester and me. I kept thinking how only days before I had been so happy that things were normal around our house and how quickly everything had changed. Not everything, perhaps, but the friendship that mattered most to me in the world had been destroyed. And by my own doing. Had I been right to do it? I couldn't let Chester harm Bunnicula. I had to draw the line somewhere. So why was it that every time I licked my lips that night I tasted salt?

Just before dawn I fell asleep, only to be awakened a short time later by Toby's cry of "Do I *have* to go?"

"No," I heard Mrs. Monroe say, "you don't have to go. You can go over to Jared's house if you want."

"You're such a wuss," Pete said to his brother. "Don't you want to see it get knocked down? It's going to be *so* cool!"

"If you're going to cheer," Mrs. Monroe said then, "maybe you should go to Kyle's house, Pete. Our committee is going to register one final protest. No, it won't stop the wrecking ball at this point, but it's important for us to be there as a voice, as a conscience, Pete. The movie house is the most beautiful and architecturally interesting building in

Centerville. It should be preserved, not torn down. We live in a throwaway society. Someone has to be there to say, 'This is wrong.' Do you understand?"

"Can I have chocolate milk for breakfast?" Pete asked.

Mrs. Monroe sighed. "It's 'may I,' and yes, you may," she said.

"I want to be a conscience," Toby piped up. "Like you and Dad. I'll go."

Conscience. There was something about that word—and then my fuzzy, half-awake brain remembered.

"Howie!" I cried.

Howie jumped up from where he was sleeping and bumped his head on the underside of the coffee table.

"Ouch! What?" he asked.

I answered with one word: "Bunnicula!"

We were out of the house in ten minutes flat. Okay, we might have been faster if we hadn't stopped off in the kitchen to have breakfast first. But we needed our strength. Besides, we didn't want to make the Monroes suspicious.

By the time we got to the theater, a crowd was already beginning to gather. There were even a couple of reporters and TV cameras. And there, standing near the trucks, were several burly men glancing at their watches.

"They're going to start tearing the building down soon," I said to Howie. "I hope we didn't wait too long!"

Making sure we weren't being watched, we sneaked down the alley next to the theater until we came to a door marked STAGE ENTRANCE. Luckily, it was open, probably to allow the workers to make their final preparations.

"Okay, Howie, this is it," I said. "We've got to move fast. Are you nervous?"

"Wh-h-h-h-ho, m-m-m-m-me?" Howie replied. His tongue was hanging out of his mouth, his breath was coming in quick, short pants. "N-n-n-no, I'm n-n-not n-n-n-n-n-nervous!"

I decided this was no time for a debate. "Good," I said, "then let's go."

The theater was dark and cool inside. Enough light leaked through from cracks and windows here and there to help us see where we were going, but we still managed to bump into things with every fifth or sixth step. Every time we did, Howie would yip excitedly.

STAGE
ENTRANCE

"Ssh!" I admonished him. "We don't want to scare Bunnicula."

And then softly, softly I called out his name: "Bun-nic-ula! Bun-nic-ula!"

"Bunnicula!" Howie echoed. "It's us, Howie and Harold."

The farther we crept into the abandoned theater, the creepier the shadows became, the eerier the silence. At one point, I thought I heard something moving. I stopped and listened and realized that all I'd been hearing was the pounding of my own heart.

We were in the middle of a very large and very empty room. Having never been in a movie theater before, I couldn't make much sense of it. Then I remembered Mr. Monroe saying that all the seats were being taken out before the demolition began. Apparently, this was the room where people came to watch the movies. There at one end was a big white wall. And there at the other end was a wall with two doors in it. Very high in the center of that wall was a small square opening neatly framing the silhouette of a figure—a figure with two tall ears.

"Bunnicula," I said in a hushed voice.

Howie heard me and looked up, too.

"But, Uncle Harold," he said, "How can Bunnicula be awake? It's daytime."

"There's no sunlight in here," I pointed out. "Bunnicula must think it's still night. Now come on—we don't have a moment to lose."

As we made our way cautiously out of the large, empty room, through one of the doors, and up a set of stairs that would take us—I hoped—to the small square opening in the wall that held our friend Bunnicula, I heard the same clock I'd heard the night before. Only now, it chimed nine times.

Nine o'clock. Why, I asked myself, did that seem significant?

And then I remembered. The demolition was scheduled to begin at nine o'clock this Tuesday morning.

I picked up the pace, and Howie scampered after me. At the top of the stairs, we came to a half-open door. Behind it was a small room—and there on the wall to our left was the opening we'd seen from below. In the shadowy light, I could make out a pair of eyes glistening. Red eyes. Frightened eyes.

"Bunnicula!" I cried.

I was all set to leap up and grab him by the neck

when another set of eyes stopped me dead in my tracks.

"Uncle Harold!" Howie called out in alarm. He too had seen them. I could hear him panting rapidly behind me.

"Is it B-Bunnicula's m-mother?" he sputtered.

Was it? I asked myself. Or was it someone else? Some*thing* else? Had Howie's FleshCrawler books gotten to me? Was I imagining some sort of creature who lived in the movie theater, some beast who was about to leap out from the shadows and attack?

There was no time to waste. Either the beast would get us or the wrecking ball would.

"Who are you?" I demanded. "What do you want?"

"Oh, I think you know who I am," a familiar voice said. "And I know you know what I want."

"Chester!" I cried. "But how—"

"How did I get here?" Chester said, stepping out into a pale pool of light. His eyes looked unnatural, possessed. "Oh, it was easy enough, thanks to last night's handiwork of a couple of criminal kitties. When Greenbriar opened my cage this morning, I made a dash for it before he spotted the open window. I got here moments before you did, Harold. Oh, and by the way, whatever you had planned, forget it. Bunnicula is mine!"

"But what are you going to do?"

Chester bounded up to the opening in the wall with a single leap. Bunnicula barely budged. I could tell the poor thing was terrified.

"What am I going to do? I'll tell you what I'm going to do," Chester said.

But that was all he had time to say, for suddenly there was a thunderous roar, and before we knew what was happening, the wall to our right exploded.

"Run!" I heard Chester cry.

I looked up at the opening in the wall and to my horror watched as Chester and Bunnicula, locked in a deadly embrace, tumbled from the precipice. The scene from the story Toby had read to me flooded my mind, its words, its images exploding within me even as the room seemed to be exploding around me. I thought of Chester, my dear friend, who had so recently called me traitor, and the words of the story came back to me: "It was the last that I was ever destined to see of him in this world."

Before the terrible wrecking ball could strike again, I ordered Howie to run for his life. I ran, too. And I didn't look back.

[TEN]

One of the Family

"HAROLD!" Toby cried out. "Howie!"

Frantically, I raced toward my young master even as I searched the onrushing crowd for signs of Chester and Bunnicula, hoping against hope that they had miraculously escaped and were somehow already out there in front of the theater. But as Toby threw his arms around me, I knew that the only ones to have escaped were Howie and me.

"Are you okay, boy?" Toby asked. "What are you doing here?"

Mrs. Monroe had picked Howie up and was trying to comfort him, but Howie was squirming to be free.

"We've got to go back, Uncle Harold!" he yipped. "We've got to rescue Pop and Bunnicula!"

Mrs. Monroe seemed to understand. Perhaps people were more intelligent than Chester and I had been willing to give them credit for.

"Stop the demolition!" she cried out. "There may be other animals inside!"

"Stop the demolition!" someone echoed.

The trucks and the noise came to a sudden halt.

Breaking free of Toby's embrace, I charged down the alleyway to the back of the theater. Howie, who must have leaped from Mrs. Monroe's arms at the same time, was fast on my heels. Barking for everything we were worth, we led an impromptu rescue team, complete with flashlights and TV news cameras, into the partially decimated movie house.

"Be careful!" someone warned.

"Just follow the dogs," another voice called out. "They seem to know what they're doing."

A fine thing, I thought. Does that mean most of the time we *don't* seem to know what we're doing? I didn't dwell on the thought, however. I had more important matters to attend to. Matters of life and death.

There must have been a second blow of the

wrecking ball as Howie and I had been fleeing the building, because the wall that had held the small square hole where we'd first spotted Bunnicula and from which he and Chester had tumbled was gone. In its place was a large pile of rubble.

I stared at the pile with a sick, sinking feeling in my stomach.

"Chester!" I woofed.

At first there was no response. But then I heard it. The same sort of pitiful mew I'd heard coming from the closet only—was it possible?—the day before. This time it was not a sickly mew, but a frightened one.

"There!" I heard Mr. Monroe call out. "Let me have that flashlight!"

A beam of light bounced off the walls and floor and fallen pieces of plaster and concrete and wood, and then suddenly it caught something. Something alive! It was Chester, wide-eyed and panting!

Howie and I bounded across the room. "Chester!" I cried. "You're all right!"

He didn't respond, but just kept staring at all of us.

"What about . . . What about Bunnicula?" Howie asked.

Chester did the strangest thing then. He howled. Or so it seemed. He lifted his head high and let out the most piercing cry. Was he hurt?

"Chester, it's all right, boy!" Mr. Monroe said, brushing against me as he extended a hand to Chester. "Come here, boy," snapping his fingers. "Come on, it's all right, Chester. Everything will be fine."

But Chester didn't go to Mr. Monroe. On the contrary, the closer Mr. Monroe got, the more Chester hissed and spat.

"Maybe he's been injured," another man said.

"He might be in shock," said Mrs. Monroe. "That's possible, isn't it?"

I felt Toby's hand stroke my head. "Is he going to be all right?" he asked his parents. "Is Chester going to be all right?"

A big man who looked like he might have been a member of the wrecking crew worked his way through the small crowd that had followed us inside. "I'll take care of this," he said brusquely.

He walked up to Chester and started to grab him. "Come on, kitty," he said, "you're coming with me now."

He didn't know who he was messing with. Chester swiped him with his claws.

"*Yeeouch!*" the man said. "Hey, what gives?"

Chester turned to me. "Help me, Harold," he said. "You're my friend, aren't you?"

"I never stopped being your friend," I said.

"Then help me save Bunnicula."

"*Save* Bunnicula?" I repeated.

"You heard me," Chester said.

And then I understood. Bunnicula was somewhere in the pile of rubble Chester was sitting on. And Chester wasn't moving until Bunnicula had been found.

"Come on, Howie," I said, "we have one more job to do. A dog's job."

We moved toward the pile of rubble and sniffed. It didn't take long to catch Bunnicula's scent. Once we had it, we began to bark.

"The dogs are trying to tell us something," a woman said. "There's something else in there." Turning to the Monroes, she asked, "Do you have any other pets?"

"A rabbit," said Mr. Monroe, "but why would *he* be here?"

"There's something strange going on, Robert," Mrs. Monroe said to her husband, and then she said to the others, "Our vet called us this morning to tell us Bunnicula—that's our rabbit—wasn't in his cage when he arrived this morning. And soon after that Chester escaped."

"Well," said the big man Chester had lashed out at a few minutes earlier, "it looks to me like there may just be a rabbit in that rubble."

All at once, everyone began to dig.

"I see eyes!" someone called out. "Red eyes!"

"Bunnicula!" Pete shouted when the bunny came into view at last. "This is so crazy! What are the animals doing here?"

I don't know if the Monroes ever got that question answered to their satisfaction. I don't know if they really cared. All that mattered was that we were all safe and sound—even Bunnicula, who had miraculously survived because of a large beam that had fallen in such a way as to create a little cave in the debris where he had hidden. He didn't appear to have even a scratch. But you could see that his little heart was beating rapidly—and those red eyes had never looked more terrified.

The only thing predictable about Chester is his unpredictability, and in the next moment he did the most unpredictable thing I'd ever seen. He jumped down—and began to lick Bunnicula!

"What are you doing?" I cried.

"For heaven's sake, Harold," he said. "Use your brain, such as it is. I'm letting him know it's all right. Can't you see how scared he is?"

There was a flash of light as a camera recorded the moment. And *that* was the image that made the evening news and the next day's front page in the *Courier:*

CAT SAVES RABBIT—THE LAST SHOW

AT THE CENTERVILLE CINEMA

For the record, Howie and I were given some credit, too, but it was the picture of Chester wrapped around the terrified Bunnicula, licking him, that got the most attention. I had to chuckle to think that Chester had earned his brief moment of fame because of his kindness to a rabbit. And not just any rabbit—his archenemy, the vampire rabbit Bunnicula!

* * *

It was some time before things returned to what passes for normal at the Monroe house. Our odd behavior, strange disappearances, and reappearances in unexpected places took some sorting out, and to this day I don't think the Monroes have all the answers. Truth be told, I'm not sure we do, either. I think we were right about Bunnicula's missing his mother, although of course he never said a thing. That was why he had run to the theater when he saw the ad in the newspaper. But was she really "out there" somewhere as Chester suggested? I doubt it. I suspect once she had left her baby bunny at that theater years earlier, she had gone on her way, trusting in the kindness of strangers and hoping for the best.

Now the theater itself no longer exists, and so

for Bunnicula there truly is no going home again. But then, that movie theater was no more his home than Chateau Bow-Wow was Howie's or the animal shelter where the Monroes had found me as a puppy was mine. Chester, who as a kitten was given to Mr. Monroe as a birthday present, has no memory of where he came from. But it doesn't really matter. When you're a pet, your home is with your people and your people are your family.

The reason Bunnicula missed his mother, I think, was that he never felt entirely at home here—not as long as Chester was threatening his very existence. But that's all changed.

"So you're no longer worried that Bunnicula is a vampire, eh, Chester?" I said one evening after dinner. Howie, Chester, and I were sprawled out on the front porch enjoying the warm spring breezes.

"Nonsense, Harold," Chester replied snappishly. "Of course he's a vampire."

"Then why are you no longer trying to do him in?"

Chester yawned elaborately, letting me know that the topic of conversation was barely worth the bother. "Really, Harold," he said, "it's so obvious.

Vampires are indestructible. Don't you see? When Bunnicula wasn't killed in that pile of rubble at the movie theater, I suddenly came to understand that he had powers beyond defeat. How would I ever overcome such powers and save an unsuspecting world?"

"How, indeed?" I asked, bemused.

"No, no, I figured it was best to return Bunnicula to where he rightfully belongs. Who knows him like I do, Harold? Who better to use that knowledge in a different way than I have used it in the past to keep a close eye on him and make sure he does no harm?"

"So you've become his guardian, is that it, Chester? His protector?"

"In a way. Though I think of myself more as protecting him from himself."

I smiled and said nothing. I think I understood then that Chester had never really meant to destroy Bunnicula. He may have wanted to destroy the evil he thought Bunnicula represented, but Bunnicula himself? He was just a bunny. More than that, he was one of the family.

Now Chester has taken to napping next to Bunnicula's cage. The two of them sometimes sleep so that their backs touch and, although I would never embarrass him by pointing it out, I've noticed that Chester purrs loudest at those times. And Bunnicula? The sparkle is back in his eyes and the bounce is back in his step.

If there was any doubt that a new relationship had been forged between Chester and his Moriarty, however, it was answered one morning when I crept downstairs to sing Bunnicula to sleep. Imagine my surprise when I heard a familiar voice singing those familiar words in my stead. I stopped and listened. It was surprising enough that Chester knew the lullaby, but my astonishment was even greater when at the song's end, I heard hard-hearted old Chester utter the words: "Sweet dreams, Bunnicula, old pal."

As for Chester and me, we're back to being the best of friends. Chester understood that I was only trying to do what I thought was best for Bunnicula. And I understood that Chester was just being himself.

Howie, having lived through his own scary adventure, no longer reads FleshCrawlers. He says they're not realistic enough for him. But they did inspire him to begin writing stories of his own. He asked me to look at them, which I did, and I've told him he's pretty good—for a puppy. He still has a lot to learn, of course.

"Will you teach me, Uncle Harold?" he asked me the last time I read one of his stories. I told him I would. Who knows? Maybe he'll write books one day just as I have. Anything is possible.